John C. Hardin
2-22-97
Duluth, GA.

# GUADALAJARA

Also by the author:
*Cozumel*
*The Berlin Ending*
*The Hargrave Deception*
*The Gaza Intercept*
*Undercover: Memoirs of an American Secret Agent*
*Give Us This Day*
*The Kremlin Conspiracy*

# GUADALAJARA

## E. HOWARD HUNT

Scarborough House/Publishers

Scarborough House/*Publishers*
Chelsea, Michigan 48118

FIRST PUBLISHED IN 1990

**Library of Congress Cataloging-in-Publication Data**

Hunt, E. Howard (Everette Howard), 1918-
   Guadalajara / E. Howard Hunt.
      p.    cm.
   ISBN 0-8128-3077-6 : $17.95
   I. Title.
  PS3515.U5425G8   1990
813'.54—dc20                                    90-8160
                                                   CIP

To Frank Rollins
For a lifetime of friendship

# CARTAGENA

ON THE LAST day of his life, the man who called himself Lorenzo Soriano sat with his back against the sun-heated wall of a waterfront café and watched the boats and ships in Cartagena harbor. Caribbean sun scorched the cobbles of the old city; coral walls absorbed its rays as a sponge takes water. Offshore, tankers suckled Colombian crude piped from the Magdalena basin. Onshore, refinery storage tanks glinted blindingly. Smoke from cracking towers soared upward, dirtying the cloudless sky.

Yesterday the ocean yacht *Bal Musette* had arrived; home port of record, Port au Prince. Aboard, according to Soriano's informant, were Faustino Perez and Pedro Alonso, from Miami, and Ramón Calixto from San Juan. The *Bal Musette* was registered in his name, probably, Soriano thought, because Calixto was the only one without a federal conviction.

Today, a Mexican delegation was expected to go aboard for a conference that, the DEA agent assumed, would include Colombian officials who provided protection for the *narcotraficantes*. Soriano wanted their names even though, he reflected, it was unlikely that any of them would ever be prosecuted for trafficking or corruption. As government officials they were out of reach, and prosecutors daring enough to challenge them would be either bribed or killed.

He removed his woven palm hat and wiped his forehead and face. Sunglasses filtered the glare, but nothing could isolate him from the midday heat.

To replace lost fluids he ordered another beer and drank without pleasure. For a few moments the beer cooled him internally, but presently he was perspiring again. In Panama, this time of year, you could depend on heavy afternoon rains to lower the temperature for an hour or so, but Cartagena was something else. Next to Dakar it had to be the asshole of the world.

Squinting at the bay, he saw a whaleboat putting out from the yacht. Earlier it had taken out a load of market-fresh fruit and vegetables, liquors, and meats for the traffickers and their whores: a blonde Dane, two casaba-breasted Colombian Indians, and a Panamanian *mulata.*

While he was watching the whaleboat, a long, white Mercedes limousine rolled smoothly onto the pier and stopped. Behind it came a jeepload of soldiers. They got out and formed two uneven files beside the Mercedes—short, bandy-legged *indios* in ill-fitting sweat-stained uniforms. Each soldier held an automatic weapon.

From the limousine stepped two brown-skinned men. One wore the uniform of a Mexican military officer. The other had on a light blue suit and a white panama hat. Chatting cordially, they passed between the soldiers and went down waterside steps to the whaleboat.

After the arrivals were seated, the boat turned and sped toward the yacht, trailing a plume of spray. Limousine and jeep drove onto the quay and disappeared. Soriano found himself wishing he'd had the *cojones* to photograph the two arrivals, but as his chief once said in Bogotá, a bold agent was likely to become a dead agent. So he would rely on his informant, Raúl, to identify the two officials.

Soriano paid for his beers and left the waterfront café. One o'clock. He walked through narrow, winding alleys to the old hotel where he had a room.

Twice a day he sent out for food from the cantina around the corner. He was sick of its fish and meat fried in olive oil, the fizzy bottled water. The bread, though, was excellent. A man could live on it; an army would fight for it.

He eased back on the thin mattress that smelled of mildew and sweat, some of it his own. The hotel rented rooms to whores by the hour, so for what he was getting he was paying an incredibly high price. After he moved in, the first thing he had done was to string a fine-wire antenna from the window. His miniature shortwave transmitter was concealed behind a closet board. After Raúl reported, he would radio Bogotá headquarters and hope that the information transmitted would be worth the risk and effort of acquiring it.

After the *Bal Musette* left harbor, he mused, he should take a few days off. Maybe go fishing on the Cristal River, or off the Guajira peninsula. He could see himself, rod in hand, watching the old planes come in empty and light, then lumber off, loaded and barely making flying speed. The waters and jungle around the airstrip were an aircraft graveyard. His brother's body had never been recovered. Too heavy a load for the old DC-4, he'd heard, a reasonable explanation, considering Roberto's craziness for easy money. How easy is it now, *hermano?* he asked silently. Was it worth your life?

No, he would stay away from the Guajira.

TOWARD MIDNIGHT HE left the hotel and wandered over to a café set back from the waterfront. He went into Los Tres Grillos and ordered a *cafecito* of oily Colombian coffee. To it the bartender added a shot of colorless *grappa* and wished him good health.

As he drank, Soriano watched the bar mirror for arrivals. After a while, coffee finished, he left for the men's room. He urinated in a trough of running water, rinsed his hands, and unlocked a small side door.

It opened into a small storage room. A single light bulb lighted a table on which lay a deck of cards. Soriano shuffled the deck and began playing solitaire. Under his *guayabera* shirt, the cloth gun holster was soaked with sweat.

He played for an hour before his informant arrived.

"*Saludos,*" Raúl said as he sat down. He pulled over another chair and set his heels on it. He was a thin young man with a pencil mustache.

"You're late."

"I'm tired, my feet hurt. The chief steward works me like a dog."

"But the money's good, eh? You like the money, you and Rosalita. Well, my butt's tired from sitting here waiting for you. What's happening on the boat?"

"Big meeting."

"We know that. Who's the Mex general? The *criollo* in the expensive white hat?"

"Well, you know, they don't use names much. The *criollo* is from Bogotá, a sub-*secretario* of Interior."

"Name?"

"Cipriano."

"Cipriano *what?*"

Raúl shrugged expressively. Soriano stared at him. "Listen to me, *pendejo*, don't make me fuckin' drag it out of you. Who's the *pachuco?*"

"General Pedraza. Air Force."

"That's better. You get me Cipriano's full name, understand?"

Raúl nodded.

11

Actually, Soriano thought, with that much to go on the Embassy could identify the Colombian official, but he wanted Raúl to work for his dough. "What are they doing now?"

Elaborately, Raúl looked at his gold wristwatch. "Snorting coke, smoking Guajira grass, and fucking."

"How'd you get off the boat?"

"Said my wife was sick."

"That excuse is getting thin, better try something else."

"Tell me about my brother."

"Why?"

"I got more information for you."

"Motherfucker," Soriano exhaled. "Herminio's doin' fine. The new job I got him, he might get to love Atlanta."

"What kind of job?"

"Better than any you had at Raiford. Clerking for the day lieutenant. No more dirty hands in the machine shop. Depending on your cooperation, Herminio could get along just fine for the next seven years."

Raúl swallowed. "I do this for him."

"Sure, any way you want. He's lucky we're pals. If you hadn't up and volunteered, they'd have bored him a new asshole by now."

White spots appeared on Raúl's cheeks. "He's no *maricón.*"

"Of course not. You go into Atlanta straight, they *make* you a *maricón.* But I don't have to remind *you, pendejo.* What's the other info?"

"Big man coming tomorrow."

"How big? From where? Union City? Miami?"

Raúl shook his head. *"Criollo.* Omar Parra."

"Ahhh," Soriano said with satisfaction. "The kid brother. I'd heard he took over the operation after Luis got wasted in Miami. So he's big league now. Congratulations. What else?"

Raúl spread his hands. "That's it, *jefe.*"

"It's not enough. I need to hear about keys and bales. Where it's going, how much and when. That's what will keep Herminio at a desk and out of the latrines."

Raúl swallowed. "When us waiters are around they stop talking."

"So, you'll have to bug the dining salon."

"Jesus, if I was caught, they'd kill me."

"Don't get caught." He handed the informant a microtransmitter of black plastic. It was the size of a silver dollar and twice as thick. "Stick this on the chandelier over their table."

Raúl stared at it as though it were a viper. "No," he whispered.

"*Sí, amigo. Sí, sí, sí.* You go *all* the way with me. No backing down."
Slowly, Raúl put it in his pocket. "I better go," he said.
"All right. Plant the bug tonight."
Raúl wiped perspiration from his face. He glanced bleakly at Soriano and left the storeroom.
After the door closed, Soriano dealt four cards and smiled slightly. This was going to work out.

In Bogotá, Manny Montijo had told him how an ex-agent named Novak had terminated Luis Parra. DEA felt good about it. If he was able to bury brother Omar, the agency would feel even better. But it wouldn't be easy. The Parra plantation was like an army base.

With a sigh he gathered the cards together and turned out the light. After leaving the room he followed Cinco de Octubre back to his hotel.

In his room he transmitted a brief report to Bogotá, stashed the transmitter, and fell into a light sleep.

Toward dawn he heard footsteps in the hall and sat up. The footsteps stopped at his door. He reached for his .44. A knock, then, "Soriano?"

"Who's there?" he called in Spanish.

"Raúl," the voice said huskily. "We have to talk."

Silently he left the bed and moved into the dark zone beside the window. Raúl knew better than to come to his room. "I've got a woman," he called. "Come back tomorrow."

A kick splintered wood around the lock; the door burst inward. The hall's dim light showed four men. Three were alive, guns in their hands. Between them hung Raúl, tongue sliced, throat cut, eyes gouged out.

Dropping to his knees, Soriano fired and saw muzzle flashes, heard bullets slam the wall above him, smash window glass. One man holding Raúl staggered back, and the dead informant's body dropped. The other men waded into the room firing their MAC-10s. Soriano fired back. A red-hot lance pierced his stomach, another broke his thigh. No way he could run, no way to survive. They would torture and mutilate him as they had Raúl. One bullet left.

Soriano turned the revolver muzzle into his mouth, pulled the trigger, and blew out his brains.

# I

# ONE

**M**ONTIJO FOUND ME in Miami.

Walked up to the front door of the Kendall duplex and rang the bell. Inside, he pumped my hand and gave me a big Hispanic grin. I said, "Drink?"

"Why not?"

Manny was one of the few guys in DEA I liked to remember. Smooth olive skin and handsome features. White choppers like Pedro Armendáriz. As I poured Añejo over ice, I said, "How come you don't look *chicano?*"

"Probably because my mother was Spanish. I was born there, went to Jesuit school in Seville, Southern Cal here."

Our glasses touched. *"Salud,"* I said. "Still with the Houston office?"

"Yes and no." He smiled. "Right now I'm here."

"So I see."

He looked around the living room, squinted at the dinette. "Nice place, Jack."

"Yes, it's Melody's."

"Is she around?"

"Traveling." I sipped Añejo and sat down. First drink of the morning. My mood welcomed it.

"Last time I saw the two of you, on Cozumel, marriage was in the air."

"It's in the wind now," I told him. "We might make it to the altar one day, but at the moment the prospect seems remote." I drank more of the dark rum. "She's either studying at the university, practicing diving,

17

or off at diving meets. Yesterday she left for Paris, Madrid, Berlin, and Rome. Took me the regulation four years to get out of the Naval Academy, but with all of Melody's shore leave it'll take ten for her degree."

"Well, hell, you couldn't expect her just to put away her Olympic silver, Jack. Not if she's going for gold next time."

"I suppose," I said, and saw him look around the room. At my packed suitcase. "Heading for Cozumel?" he asked.

"It's where I make what money I make."

"Still flying that amphib plane?"

"The Seabee gets around. Forty years old and lifts off like a gull."

"Glad to hear it." He sipped thoughtfully. "Open to a proposition?"

"Maybe. What's going on?"

"Bad news. You finished off Luis Parra, to everyone's satisfaction, but brother Omar has taken his place." He looked moodily at his glass. "So we learned in a message from Cartagena before our man was killed."

"Anyone I know?"

"Doubt it. He worked Panama and West Africa when you were with the agency. Cover name Soriano. True name Ed Diaz. His brother once piloted for Luis. Anyway, Ed hooked onto something in Cartagena, but apparently his informant got careless and both of them got killed." He drank deeply from his glass.

"What do you want from me?"

"Few weeks' work around Guadalajara. You'd bring your plane to Lake Chapala, about an hour's drive from the city."

"And?"

"Go in as a singleton, pick up what you can."

"What's the pay?"

He hesitated. "Thousand a week?"

"You'd slip that to a street informant. If I'm flying, it'll be double." My charter boat needed a new engine and bottom work. Ramón, my captain, had a shipyard estimate of eight thousand U.S. "Besides," I said, "I hear Guadalajara and the whole state of Jalisco has been classified Red Zone."

He blinked. "Who told you?"

"Just from what I read it seems Jalisco has become a separate country, ruled by *narcotraficantes.*"

He sighed. "True, but it won't be said officially."

I added more rum to our glasses. "Does that creep Corliss know you're talking to me?"

"You crazy? Phil hates your guts even more than he did before you nailed Parra. The Miami office doesn't even know I'm here."

"That's a break," I said. "How do you fit in?"

"I'll be in the Guadalajara consulate."

"Replacing . . . ?"

"Yeah, the guy they butchered. His mistake was to think he could trust the Mexican police. I won't make the same mistake." He stared moodily at his glass. "The corruption is unbelievable—from Mexico City all the way down to customs inspectors." He paused. "Like that Captain Jaramillo you blew away."

"Correction—drowned in the pool he bought with drug money."

"Whatever. Point is, where our work's concerned we now have to consider Mexico a denied area, work alone like CIA does in Moscow."

"Charming," I said, "with a two-thousand-mile open border. Manny, you're not paying me just to eavesdrop in cantinas. What's the operation?"

He grimaced. "Colombian white stuff is being flown to Guadalajara. The principal protector is thought to be an air force general named Pedraza. Gilberto Pedraza. Gil to his friends."

"Have many?"

"As many as money can buy."

"And the snowman is Omar Parra?"

"So we believe. One of his well-placed protectors is in the Interior Ministry—Cipriano Gonzalez. Bogotá's looking for some way to deal with him. Through diplomatic channels, of course."

"Yeah. Tell them to try brothers Colt, Smith, and Wesson." My wife, Pamela, had died of an overdose, and all I did was beat up her supplier when I should have killed him. "The diplomatic waltz goes nowhere, but the music goes on and on. What else?"

"Pedraza built himself a palace outside Guadalajara that's guarded like a fortress. One of his current diversions is bankrolling a movie co-production with some Hollywood characters. Last I heard, they were shooting around Puerto Vallarta."

"Or shooting up," I remarked. "So, you'll be Mr. Inside and I'll be Mr. Outside. Can't fly on empty tanks, so I'll take a week's pay now—for avgas."

He'd come prepared. Laid out twenty hundred-dollar bills and a receipt. I signed it and slid the money in my wallet. "Expenses extra," I said.

"Naturally. I suggest you take a room at the Fiesta Americana. It's central, modern, and the bartender is a contact. His name is José."

I smiled. "All Mexican bartenders are named José."

"So it seems." He got up. "How soon can you get to Guadalajara?"

"Couple of days. Wind up a few things in Cozumel and fly to Chapala. Meet at the hotel?"

He nodded, and we shook hands. I saw him to his rental compact and went back to the duplex.

Inside, I set the air-conditioning low to suppress mildew, transferred refrigerator food to the freezer, and checked the bedroom to make sure I'd taken all my clothes. The round bed was my idea; the ceiling mirrors, Melody's erotic fancy. We'd shared a lot, too much to leave easily, but our divided romance was under strain.

As I walked downstairs I wondered if we'd ever share the circular bed again.

Carrying suitcase and garment bag, I went out and locked the front door. I glanced back once, and got into my rental car. Drove to the airport.

That's how it began.

# TWO

**T**HE MEXICANA FLIGHT paused at Mérida to unload a dozen tourists eager to visit Mayan ruins, then crossed the Yucatán peninsula without gaining much altitude. Off Cancún I looked down and saw the dark outline of Luis Parra's yacht. *Solimar* had been a floating drug factory until I sank it in deep water.

Closing my eyes, I recalled how the big boat had looked going down by the stern that night. The huge explosions when drums of ether and acetone let go. One of the most spectacular—and pleasing—sights I'd ever seen. And when the chopper came after me, Melody had shot it down as easily as a clay pigeon. A night to remember.

We came in low over the beaches, Cozumel Island's one town, San Miguel, off to port. Customs and Immigration whisked me through, as they'd been doing ever since the death of Captain Jaramillo. I'd never been charged with anything, but word must have filtered around because I was shown respect in a lot of quarters. I liked that, and it made life easier in a foreign land.

The taxi let me off in front of my gate. It was set into tall chain-link fencing, and by the time I'd unlocked it my Dobes, César and Sheba, were bounding out to meet me. It was a pretty messy homecoming with all the licking and wet nuzzling. Sheba's dugs were heavy for she was still nursing her first litter—four small brown-and-black crawlers. The way my dogs carried on you'd have thought I'd been away longer than four days, and I wondered whether Ramón's wife, María, had looked after them.

But their water bowls were full, and the food pans showed traces of recent feeding. So the dogs were glad to see me, and I was glad they were.

Without Melody's occasional weekend visits the place was going to be lonely. My living room walls still showed where repair plaster had shrunk into shrapnel holes. Holes made on the night Jaramillo fired his grenade through the window—killing not me but Chela. An hour later he was at the bottom of his pool with waterlogged lungs. Reprisal didn't bring Chela back to life, but if I hadn't terminated the Capitán he'd have tried again.

I took a Veracruz cigar from the humidor and lighted it. Dark, strong leaf. I tempered the taste with a shot of Añejo and checked the rest of the house.

Fresh fish in the refrigerator, nicely filleted and ready for the patio grill. María had quartered limes and bagged them. I took out a section and bit in. Tart and delicious.

In my closet hung starched *guayaberas.* Clean laundry filled my drawers. I was ready to resume life on Cozumel.

While the fish grilled I made myself a planter's punch with fresh fruit and played with the puppies. Sheba moved nervously around us, maternally apprehensive but too polite to interrupt our play.

I ate my fish with slices of buttery *aguacate*—avocado—looking along the pier at my old Seabee as it tugged its snubbing lines. The old girl seemed to be asking for action, and it occurred to me that a few days on Lake Chapala's fresh water would clear the hull of sea-growth and barnacles.

Reminding me of *Corsair*'s problems.

I fed the dogs and drove over to Ramón's place. María was roasting a big chunk of alligator tail and invited me to stay for dinner, but I explained I'd dined early. So she wrapped a couple of pounds of the raw flesh for me. The meat was white and tasted like good tuna. Lunch, tomorrow.

Ramón went with me to the boatyard where *Corsair* was hauled up on the ways. Despite copper paint, toredo worms had started work on the bottom. Sheathing was recommended, he told me, and what about a new engine? I counted out Montijo's two thousand and told him to see how far it would go. "Every day I don't go out costs money," he reminded me, "and the fishermen are starting to come."

"I've been thinking," I told him, "about increasing business. The big cruise ships come in around dawn, and we should have kids on the pier distributing ads for half-day fishing trips. You'd have *Corsair* waiting nearby, ready with rods and bait, cold drinks and lunches. What do you think?"

*"Bueno,"* he said, "but first we have to get this boat in the water, *jefe."*

"Meanwhile, get a couple thousand handbills printed up. Offer to take out a morning party of six for, say seventy-five apiece, another party in the afternoon."

"Lotta work, *jefe."*

"It's how people get rich. Depending on how large the party is, hire a mate or two. Then all you do is run the boat. *Estámos?"*

I slapped his back. "Instead of waiting for business to come to us, we'll go where the business is."

DRIVING HIM BACK to his home, I said, "This is a port of many temptations, Ramón. When I hired you to captain my boat we had a little talk, remember?"

*"Sí, jefe."*

"What did we talk about?"

"It was"—he swallowed—"about the white powder. *Nieve. Cocaina."*

I nodded. "I have this thing about narcotics. It cost me my wife and altered my life. As long as you work for me, stay clean. If I ever find a trace of white powder, a leaf of grass, or a stain of hash on or around my boat, I won't just fire you. I'll make you wish you'd never been born. And no free-lancing. When men with thin mustaches, sunglasses, and heavy gold necklaces invite you over for a drink, your future depends on saying no. You can say it politely or with a finger, but the answer is no. *Entiendes?"*

*Sí, jefe, sí. Comprendo."*

"Enjoy your dinner."

I drove on to San Miguel and had a Tecate on the porch at Morgan's, watching well-dressed tourists come and go. Evening crowds were gathering in the town square for a band concert. Kids scrounged paper cones of flavored ices and played hide-and-seek among their elders, as kids do everywhere in the world.

A pleasant scene, I reflected, with peace and goodwill.

I wondered what Guadalajara would bring.

After the concert was noisily under way, I left Morgan's and drove home. For a while I listened to music from Radio Mérida, but found myself wondering about the late Ed Diaz; what he looked like. Had I ever met him? What we had in common was the Parra family, and brother Omar had established a connection in sunny Mexico.

Bad news for any *gringo* in law enforcement and especially bad for

Manuel Montijo. DEA's Guadalajara operation sounded loose as a dead snake, and Manny was supposed to get it together.

He hadn't said so, but he wouldn't be paying me two large a week if things were tight in Jalisco.

The house was well stocked with weapons cached here and there. I got out a 9mm Beretta and a MAC-10 machine pistol, beloved of cocaine cowboys. Why not meet them on equal terms?

I slept, as always, with a 12-gauge Remington beside my bed, and in the morning I drove toward the deepwater pier and parked beside a warehouse. The sign said *Abasto Náutico*. It was a small chandlering firm I'd bought into at a time when Rogelio Caborca needed additional capital and I was in funds.

Inside, the *abacería* was busy. Fork lifts loaded cases of canned goods and liquors onto trucks for shipside delivery. Business looked good, but when I went into Rogelio's office he had a different story.

"Look, *socio,* at the exchange rate we barely make overhead. The *peso* drops daily, and the dollar soars like an eagle. We pay in dollars, get paid in *pesos,* it's that simple." He dropped a pile of papers on the desk.

*"Curioso,"* I said, "that before I bought in you were making good money. I invest, and suddenly the money's gone."

He shrugged and stared at the desk top.

"Not good enough," I told him. "I'll be away for a while, and when I get back the books had better show a good profit. Otherwise . . . " I let the thought hang in the air.

In a surly voice he said, "Maybe you should buy me out."

"We'll talk about it when I get back. Meanwhile, I recommend you do your best to invigorate business."

I went back to the jeep and drove home. I packed the machine pistol in my suitcase and wore the Beretta in a nylon shoulder holster. After feeding the dogs I walked down the pier and inspected the old Seabee carefully. *Capitán* Jaramillo had once booby-trapped the plane, but I'd been lucky to find the explosive charge, so a little extra caution topside was better than eternity on the ocean floor.

At low altitude I flew to the boatyard and gassed up, noticing Ramón haggling with the foreman. I paid him for the gas as Ramón said, "He'll do the bottom work, but wants another two thousand before ordering the engine."

"I've got news for you," I told the foreman. "A thousand will get the engine here from Veracruz." I scratched off a check on Banamex and gave it to him. "When I get back here, you'll get the rest."

He looked doubtfully at the check, but we'd done business before. Reluctantly he stuffed it in his pocket.

"Besides," I said, "you have the boat until I pay."

The logic appealed to him. *"Sí, Juan,"* he said agreeably. *"A sus órdenes."*

With Ramón I walked over to where I'd snubbed the plane. "I don't know how long I'll be gone, but I'll phone from time to time."

He nodded. "María will care for your house and dogs."

We shook hands and I got into the cockpit. I started the Lycoming engine and let the pusher prop idle while Ramón untied the lines. He shoved out the bow and I throttled into the wind.

The route took me two hundred and twenty miles across the Yucatán peninsula, checkpoint the coastal village of Celestun. I gained altitude over the shallows of the Bay of Campeche and saw a cluster of offshore drilling platforms to port. On a course of 290° I settled back for the long cross-bay flight to Tampico, hoping the engine would hold all the way and the old fabric wouldn't tear off the airfoils. If I had to ditch in the bay, it would be a long paddle back to land.

Tailwind helped me reach Tampico with about a pint of gas left in the auxiliary tank. After refueling, I set course for Lake Chapala by Guadalajara's radio signal and climbed to eight thousand feet to cross the mountain ranges. Updrafts bounced me around, but I stayed on the tower signal and after three hours saw the long east-west mirror of Mexico's largest lake begin to glimmer off the nose.

As I flew above it I could see speedboats and water-skiers chalking the water below. Spiraling down to lose altitude, I spotted mooring buoys off the resort town, then touched down smoothly on the glassy surface and taxied to the nearest buoy.

FROM THE NARROW beach a *chamaco* was rowing his ancient boat through a broad fringe of water hyacinth to reach me. I tossed him the nose line and he secured into the buoy ring, took my suitcase, and steadied the boat while I got in.

On the beach I tipped the boy, got directions, and in the hot afternoon sun lugged my suitcase three blocks to the sunstruck bench near an old Franciscan church where the bus to Guadalajara stopped.

The Mexican sense of time is notoriously elastic, but finally, after an hour in the baking heat, I saw the bus rumble up and stop. Forty minutes late, not bad for a hot afternoon.

I hadn't expected the bus air-conditioning to work and wasn't disappointed. Even with open windows the heat was oppressive. The cargo was a mix of children, trussed hens and fighting cocks, hampers of vegetables and long-stemmed flowers, bulging suitcases, and the usual scattering of potbellied farmers puffing long, black, handmade *puros.*

Ahead of me were two *gringo* tourists on the economy plan, rucksacks on their laps as the bus swayed and bumped along.

I'd noticed them briefly as I'd walked aft looking for a seat. The male was in his mid-twenties, bearded, with thick unkempt hair. The girl looked more recently bathed. At the hairline her long hair was bleached nearly white. She wore a black coral necklace that made her smooth tan seem even darker. She'd glanced at me under long lashes, and I'd noticed a snub nose and a troubled mouth. Now that I thought of it, her appearance was Danish or North German; her shaggy boyfriend could have come from anyplace, and probably had.

Road dust hung suspended in the heated air. The bus putted along the lakeside road for a while, turned inland and blatted through Ajijic's cobbled streets, which resembled rough creekbeds in texture and appearance. Chickens fled the smoking juggernaut, and children scampered to safety on high curbstones that bordered the narrow course.

Ajijic was a pleasant little town that reminded me of Taxco with its small, neat houses. In them lived artists and writers who hadn't done spectacularly in the States, but in Ajijic found comfort in numbers. There the alienated could toast Trotsky and badmouth the imperialistic USA without fancied reprisal.

The bus came to a jarring stop by a construction site, and I decided I'd suffered enough. On the other side of the street stood a battered-looking taxi. It couldn't be worse than the bus and promised a faster trip.

I got out of my seat, stretched cramped muscles, and pulled my suitcase from the rack. As I lugged it up the aisle, the bearded youth touched my arm. "What's here?" he asked.

"Opportunity," I told him, and moved on. I crossed the street and looked into the taxi. Empty. A barefoot kid gestured at the corner cantina. I went in and looked around.

Asleep in a table chair was the driver, identifiable by his punched-out cap. On his table was a row of "XX" beer bottles, and a plate blanketed with flies. I started over, but a waiter stepped in front of me. "It's the *taxista's* siesta. He gave orders not to be disturbed."

"For how long?"

He shrugged. "One hour, maybe two. *Quién sabe?*"

"Who knows, indeed," I said, and went out.

26

At the curb I stopped to let my bus groan past; waited a few moments longer for the black exhaust smoke to disperse. Then I crossed the street, noticing the *gringo* couple standing on the sidewalk with their rucksacks. The girl was pointing at the taxi, but the man shook his head. I walked up Calle 16 de Septiembre and eased into the Posada Ajijic.

Almost at once it was cooler. The walls were thick, and overhead fans slowly moved the air. The girl at the desk gave me a room that opened onto a well-tended garden filled with flowers, trees, and tropical birds. After the bus it was a glimpse of Paradise.

I took a long, cooling shower, pulled on swimming trunks, and walked toward an inviting-looking pool surrounded by coco palms. The rim was decorated with mosaic tiling that I sat on to dangle tired feet in the water.

At the far end of the garden was an open-air bar. The economy travelers were seated at a table under a white umbrella. They seemed to be arguing. I dived into the pool, did two lengths underwater, and surfaced considerably refreshed. The couple looked at me in surprise. The man came over to the pool edge. "Staying here?"

"For a while."

"You speak Spanish?"

"I do."

"Maybe you know how often buses run to Guadalajara."

"The schedule says every twenty minutes. But like the airlines say, 'certain limitations apply.'"

"Yeah? Like what?"

"Heavy snow in Acapulco."

"That figures," he grunted. The girl came over, removed one dusty sandal, and dipped her toes in the water. "Ummm," she exclaimed, "that feels good, Gerry. We ought to take a swim, cool off."

She was wearing a blue denim shirt and bluejeans, both faded. The color, I noticed, was a close match to her pale blue eyes. The jeans showed that she was a well-formed young female, and her tight shirt was under heavy strain. I wondered why she was traveling with a creep like Gerry. Even six feet away I could smell him.

"I'll have another beer," he muttered and wandered back to the table. The girl's glance met mine. She removed the other sandal, rolled up trouser cuffs, and soaked her feet.

I said, "If you've got a swimsuit, you can change in my room." I gestured at the open door.

"Thanks, but—well, it would just upset Gerry. I'll make do with this." She wiggled her toes. The water swirled and glistened.

27

Turtledoves burbled in the eaves. Overhead, a brilliant macaw fussed in the palm. A dragonfly darted at the pool, pricked the calm surface, and vanished toward the bougainvillea.

The girl said, "Are you staying here long?"

"Probably not."

"You were on the Guadalajara bus. I thought you were headed for Guadalajara."

"I could say the same about you."

"That's . . . true." She withdrew her feet, wiped them with her hands. "You don't like questions, do you?"

"Depends who asks them." Gerry was slouched in his umbrella chair, eyes closed. I nodded at him and said, "Your brother?"

"No—why?"

"Couldn't think of any other reason you'd be traveling with him."

She frowned, then smiled slowly. "After that I think I'd better go."

"Tomorrow's Sunday. If you're here, the inn has a nice brunch. People come down from Guadalajara to enjoy it."

"I'd like that," she said, "but not Gerry." Holding her sandals, she plodded through the springy grass toward their table.

I swam six lengths underwater, wishing I were sixty feet down on Palancar Reef, off Cozumel. The currents were strong there, but the coral heads were awesome.

Refreshed, I took a long siesta, and when I woke it was after dark and I was hungry. Posada guests were using the pool and bar, and as I dressed I reflected on how much more I would enjoy the setting if Melody were with me.

Walking around the garden's perimeter, I entered the inn and found my way to the dining room. The woman in charge said there'd be a short wait for a single table, so I found a seat at the bar and ordered Añejo on the rocks. A pianist playing standard background tunes and the candlelit tables made a pleasant relaxing scene. I sipped my drink and began thinking about dinner.

Then loud voices erupted toward the end of the bar. I glanced down and saw Gerry arguing with the bartender. From what I could hear, Gerry claimed he was being overcharged; the bartender denied it and tried showing him the bill. Gerry slammed *pesos* on the bar and lurched away, jarring a dining table as he went. The hostess didn't try to stop him from leaving, which, I thought, was a prudent decision. Another ugly *gringo* with too much beer under his belt.

Presently his blonde companion left the bar and came toward me. Her

28

face showed shame and resignation. Pausing long enough to say, "He gets that way," she trailed after him.

A mismatch if I ever saw one, I thought, and finished my drink. Their problems were not mine.

For dinner I had soup and barbecued chicken with vegetables, flan for dessert. Took coffee and brandy at the outside bar, which, I noticed, was named La Jaula. Around the pool there was some good-humored shoving and splashing and, for a Saturday night in Mexico, not over-much tipsiness. I was glad I'd stopped at the posada to recuperate and wondered if Manny Montijo had reported in at the Guadalajara consulate. If he hadn't, my only work contact was a bartender named José.

Manny was a reluctant beneficiary of the agency's minority promotion policy; reluctant, because the inside office job had kept him off the street for more than two years. It would take him a while to become accustomed to the undercurrents of the drug world, talk and think like a *narcotraficante*. Until Manny could re-identify with the *ambiente* I was to work the street.

I left the garden's merriment and asked the desk to book me a taxi for morning departure. That accomplished, I went back to my room and turned in, feeling a lot better than when I'd arrived.

It was dark and the garden was silent when my door opened inward. I slid my Beretta from its holster and pointed as the door closed behind a shadowy figure.

*"Alto!"* I called. "You're covered."

And switched on the light.

# THREE

EYES WIDE WITH fear she stared at me. Her face was dusty and tear-streaked, blonde hair askew. Her shirt and jeans were dirtied and there were dark bloodstains across her shirt. She was trembling on the edge of shock. "Please—don't shoot," she said in a voice that corkscrewed upward in a reedy wail.

"No intention of it," I said as matter-of-factly as I could. "Lock the door and have a chair." I reholstered the pistol and got out of bed. I pulled on trousers quickly, on the chance she was going to yell rape. But she locked the door and sat down, her face white between patches of road dirt.

I got out my auxiliary first-aid bottle and poured a glass of Añejo. "Drink it down," I told her. "No argument."

As she took the glass I felt the back of her hand. Clammy cold. Obediently she gulped the rum, shivered, and stopped halfway through the drink. "You haven't asked why I'm here."

"You know how I feel about questions. When you feel like it, you can tell me."

Her trembling subsided. "Drink up," I said, and poured a shot for myself. The time, I noticed, was three-fourteen. The room was small, so I sat on the edge of the bed as she drank. When the glass was empty, she put it on the table and licked lips that were showing more color. I said, "Gerry know you're here?"

She shook her head. I said, "Look, I have no designs on you, but I think you'd feel better with a shower."

No reaction. I said, "Got a room for the night?"

She shook her head. "No money, no room."

"Sorry," I said. I hadn't thought about that, but I wasn't surprised. I unpacked a *guayabera* and handed it to her. "For after the shower," I told her and tugged her from the chair. Like an automaton she moved to the bathroom and closed the door. When I heard water running, I opened the garden door and looked out. No light, no people, no Gerry lurking outside. Nothing. Except for the rucksack she'd dropped beside the entrance. I brought it inside and relocked the door. Temptation was strong to go through her possessions, but I resisted.

I was wide awake, but by the time she emerged from the bathroom I was half-asleep again. The too-large *guayabera* ended above her knees and showed legs that were as shapely as they were clean. Her face had a well-scrubbed glow and her hair was damp from washing. She said, "Thank you. I feel a lot better now. I took so long because I was washing my clothes. You don't mind?"

"In for tuppence, in for a pound," I said. "There's only one bed, but we can work it out. One of us sleeps topside, the other between the sheets. Deal?"

She smiled. "Very kind of you. I get the impression you're used to unexpected arrivals—no big thing."

"It's like this," I told her. "I put in half my time rescuing damsels in distress from the dragon."

"And the other half?"

"I'm the dragon."

"At least you warned me." She sat delicately on the edge of the bed.

"I'm Jack Novak. Down here I go by Juan. Or occasionally Juanito." We shook hands formally. "Before turning off the light you might tell me why you're here. What happened to Gerry?"

"I . . . " Her lips began trembling again. "I think he may be dead."

I swallowed. This could be a heavy trip. "You think?"

Her face was calm again. "His blood on my shirt. You saw it."

I didn't want to ask if she'd killed him. In fact I didn't want to know any more about it. "Let it go until morning," I suggested. "Over breakfast it'll be easier."

"No, I won't sleep until I tell you. It—you see, it was partly my fault."

"Are you *sure* you want to tell me?"

Solemnly she nodded. "After he got kicked out of the bar here he went to another bar, a rough place where no one spoke English."

"Plenty of them in Mexico. Even in Ajijic."

"Uh-huh. I wanted to use the rest of our money for a room, but Gerry was in one of his moods—he hasn't had it together for a long time—

32

and kept on drinking. Then when the bartender wanted money, Gerry tried ripping him off." She swallowed. "He's . . . Gerry's not very physical—into meditation—and you know . . . these two gorillas socked him and kicked him out. I picked him up, but he was hurt and crazy and started running away. I yelled for him to stop, wait for me, and I must have got through to him because he did stop." She hesitated and the lips trembled again. "A car came around the corner and knocked him down. It . . . kept on going." She began to sob. I poured us a shot of Añejo, drank mine, and forced her to swallow. When she was feeling better she said, "Someone in the bar called an ambulance, I wanted to go with him to the clinic, but they said I'd have to pay for him if I did. So . . . " Her eyes watered again. "I was so tired, you wouldn't believe how tired I was. I don't know anybody here. I don't speak much Spanish, just what I picked up in Colombia, and all I could think of was finding you."

"Glad you did," I told her. "'Mind telling me why?"

"Because when we talked today I got the feeling you had it all together."

"That's debatable—but a nice compliment. Sheltering a fellow American is no big deal, leave it at that."

"Uh-uh," she said with the beginnings of a smile, "that would be false pretenses. I'm Canadian."

"A fellow North American, okay?"

"Okay. Will you help me find Gerry tomorrow?"

"Sure. Probably only one clinic in town."

A thought hung heavily between us: *What then?* Maybe a good night's sleep would do for Gerry. Needing mine, I turned off the light. "You get under the covers, I'll flake out topside."

Wordlessly she wriggled between the sheets. I got a pillow under my head and lay back. She said, "Sometimes you talk funny. Like 'flake' and 'topside.' Why?"

"U.S. Navy," I told her. "Old habits die hard."

Her voice was tired. "You married?"

"Widower. No more questions, go to sleep."

TOWARD DAWN I got up and went into the bathroom. Her shirt, jeans, and panties were hanging in the shower, damp but clean. Gerry had bled a lot, but drunks often survived trauma lethal to others.

My bedmate hadn't volunteered her name, so I unzipped her rucksack and went through it. A rising odor of marijuana came from a scatter of seeds and stems, some adhering to dark brown smears that were hash

33

resins. No surprise—she'd mentioned Colombia. There was a plastic box with four 'ludes and a couple of badly made joints. A small purse held a few coins, Mexican and Colombian. A handkerchief, panties, and a Canadian passport three years old. The photo showed a younger, softer face. She was twenty-three years old, five-five, and one twenty pounds. Her name was Inge Langer, born in Toronto.

I wondered where she'd hooked onto Gerry, or vice versa, and replaced her possessions. Inge Langer. North European heritage. As I glanced at her sleeping face she looked about fifteen. How long had she been on the road? I wondered. Did her parents care?

I got back on the bed, reflecting that she was, after all, part of the human flotsam whose compass was the availability of low-cost drugs. Itinerants who existed by scrounging, begging, theft, drug sales, prostitution, smuggling, and occasional unskilled labor.

There had been no track marks on her arms, hands, or legs, so she wasn't yet hooked on the hard stuff. But that didn't mean she was clean of herpes or AIDS, diseases that had become hazards of the road.

SOUNDS OF MOVEMENT woke me, and I saw daylight through the curtains. The girl was in her street clothing, and she was pulling my billfold from my trouser pocket. "Leaving?" I asked.

With a shocked, guilty glance, she jammed the billfold back where it had been. I said, "You don't need to be grabby. I was going to give you money without being asked."

"I . . . I'm sorry."

"For being caught? Or succumbing to temptation?"

"Both I guess." She swallowed. "Thanks for your charity. I'll go now."

"Without breakfast?" I swung off the bed and reached for my trousers. "Just a precaution," I said, "while I shave."

WE HAD BREAKFAST at one of the open-air tables at the foot of the garden. A man was skimming the pool, another scrubbed the colored tile border. Birds skittered back and forth in the eucalyptus trees while we shared a gut-filling Mexican omelet with bacon. The omelet was great, the bacon could have been cut from sun-dried hide. Inge didn't complain, and her appetite was ravenous. She drank three cups of black coffee sweetened with tan sugar crystals, and we finished off with thick slices of toast and orange jam.

Toward the end of the meal she told me her name and began talking about herself in an almost pleading-for-understanding way. Her parents, she said, were affluent, raised her in suburban Toronto comfort. When she was twelve her father died of cancer, and two years later her mother remarried. Her stepfather soon began making passes at her, succeeding one afternoon while her mother was away. She was fifteen at the time and too traumatized to tell her mother. The stepfather continued using her until she left for McGill University at eighteen. In her second year, psychologically disoriented, she fell under the spell of an Indian swami who promised peace of mind to his devotees. What peace she found came from pills and hashish supplied by the swami. In exchange, she begged for him in public places.

At a rock concert she met Gerry Fein who advised her to leave the swami, get her act together, and travel with him to sunny lands. They'd been companions ever since.

"Whatever else Gerry may have done," she said, "he got me away from the swami."

"That's a blessing," I said, "but mixed. Your life with him couldn't have been all that great."

She nodded. "Ever hear of crack?"

"Evil, mind-bending stuff, worse than Angel Dust."

"Well, Gerry got into crack and it changed him. God, how it changed him. He used to be sweet and loving and caring, but not any more. Then we went down to Colombia to make a buy. Gerry said we'd make so much we could do whatever we wanted, live where we chose."

"Coke?"

"Yes."

"Gerry financed the buy?"

"Well . . . not exactly. We met this Mexican in El Paso. He told us who to see in Medellín, bought our plane tickets, and gave Gerry twenty thousand U.S. in cash. We had to make the buy and deliver the stuff in Guadalajara." She sighed. "Only Gerry got ripped-off."

"In Colombia?"

"Before we'd even left. Two gunmen came to our room and took the coke."

"Sent by the man who sold it to you," I told her. "Typical drug scam. The alternate version lets you get as far as Colombian Customs where they're waiting for you. The coke disappears and you go to jail. Let me tell you, Colombian jails are worse than Mexican, if that's possible. Count yourself lucky, Inge. And Mexican Customs doesn't like imported coke competing with the local brand."

She eyed me quizzically. "You know a lot about it."

"Sort of a hobby—ever since my wife OD'd."

Her expression was stricken. "I'm sorry, Jack."

"So am I. You and Gerry are on your way to the Guadalajara contact?"

"That's right—to explain what happened down the line."

"Unwise," I said. "He won't be minimally understanding, and I'd suggest a change of plans—assuming Gerry can travel."

"But, we can't be blamed for the rip-off."

"Why take a chance with your lives? Twenty thousand to a dealer is like a *centavo* to you or me, but principle's involved. The presumption is you bought the coke with his money and sold it, claiming you'd been robbed. He has neither his money nor the coke, so he's obliged to take reprisals. There's no more dangerous business, Inge, and nowhere more so than in Mexico."

She shivered, gulped the last of her coffee. "I have to tell Gerry."

"Yeah. Let's hope he grasps the inner meaning."


MY HIRED TAXI took us to the Cruz Verde clinic where a young Mexican doctor told me the *gringo* patient had a skull concussion and internal injuries but no broken bones. For Inge I put the diagnosis in English, and she gave a muffled cry. "Will he live?"

The doctor said, *"Quién sabe?"*

"Can we see him?"

He gestured at a door, and we entered a room with a dozen metal cots. There were five patients, Gerry one of them.

His head was turbaned with gauze. His eyes were closed, and what I could see of his face was abnormally pale.

A bottle of clear fluid was being dripped into an arm vein, and as I watched I felt sorry for him, and for the numberless youths like him. So much wasted humanity, I thought; broken lives, distraught familes. For a chemical rush, a thrill, a high.

Inge went to him and called his name. Slowly his eyes opened. Kneeling, she began to cry. I left them and went back to the waiting room where the doctor was reading an entertainment magazine. I brushed aside the magazine and said, "Is the *gringo* going to die?"

He shrugged. "Without an operation . . . damaged spleen and liver."

"What's the delay?"

He looked around. "Does this look like an operating room?"

"No, *pachuco,* it doesn't."

He started to get up, measured me with his eyes, and sat down. I said, "Let's not keep it a secret. Where's the operating room?"

"Guadalajara. But he might not survive an ambulance trip."

"You've already said he's not going to survive here."

His eyes narrowed. "What's your interest?"

"Since you ask, I'm one of those insensitive *yanquis* you Mexicans complain about." I laid ten thousand *pesos* on top of his magazine. "I know it's Sunday morning when nobody works, but see if you can get your ambulance *chofer* to drive the young *norteamericano* to the Guadalajara hospital."

His skilled fingers withdrew the bills. "Is this a *mordida?*"

"An expediter."

He reached for the phone. I went back into the recovery ward. The patient stared at me without expression. To Inge I said, "The doctor thinks he should be taken to Guadalajara right away. He's to be operated on."

Her gaze searched my face. "We have no money."

"Fortunately," I said, "there's socialized medicine. You can ride in the ambulance, or with me."

"I . . . I think I ought to be with Gerry."

"So do I." I folded twenty thousand *pesos* into her hand. "Food and shelter for a couple of days. I'll be at the Fiesta Americana. Let me know how things turn out. "

Impulsively she kissed me, hugging me with arms whose strength I hadn't realized. The doctor came in with two stretcher-bearers. *"Vámonos,"* he said crisply, and they began lifting Gerry onto the stretcher while the doctor steadied the plasma bottle.

As Inge followed them from the room I murmured, "Good luck to you both," but I doubt that they heard me.

I waited until I heard the ambulance engine start, and presently the doctor returned. "Satisfied?" he asked.

"I will be," I said, "when you've phoned the hospital and alerted the OR. In time of crisis details can get overlooked."

Sitting, he grabbed the telephone and began dialing. I waited until he'd relayed the diagnosis, then I thanked him for his cooperation.

He leaned back in his chair until the springs groaned. He scratched stubble on his chin. "What if I hadn't cooperated?"

I opened the left side of my jacket so that he could see the pistol butt. "Never crossed my mind," I told him, and left the clinic.

THE MORNING WAS still young enough for mist to cling to the hilltops. We drove at a leisurely pace past somnolent *chacras* and churches where the faithful trooped in their worship finery. Breeze stirred banana fronds and green fields of *maiz* glistened with overnight dew. Along level stretches I saw *chayote,* and avocado and mango trees under cultivation. But generations of tilling and abuse had depleted the land, making each succeeding crop less fruitful, driving *campesinos* to the cities where they could earn a better living shining shoes, washing dishes. An occasional bus blatted toward us, filled with families heading for a day's enjoyment at the hot springs of San Juan Cosalá.

As we neared the Sierra Madre's steep beginnings, Route 15 wound upward alongside pastures with rangy-looking cattle to a misbegotten *pueblo.* The main road through town was so bad as to suggest its purpose was to impede traffic for the benefit of sidewalk *serape*-vendors. My driver sensibly shifted to low gear to get over the skull-sized cobblestones forming the roadbed. Then we were out of the town and winding among *lomas* until the broad expanse of Guadalajara was in view.

We drove past the botanical gardens' topiary display of dinosaurs, deer, elephants, and rhinos, even a castle, all sculptured from thick shrubs. The hotel was a tall, ultramodern building constructed of glass-faced walls and buff-colored stone. In front of it stood a heroic statue of the goddess Minerva, glistening from fountain spray.

I checked into a room on the tenth floor and looked out over the City of Roses. The air was clear, unlike Mexico City's choking brown smog, a prime reason I avoided the crowded capital.

The room was large and expensively furnished. King-size bed and walk-in closets, but the place lacked allure. It looked as hard and sterile as a dental drill. Still, I wouldn't be there long.

After changing into a *guayabera*, I locked my Beretta in the suitcase with my machine pistol. Then I went down to a pay phone and called the consulate general. No, Mr. Montijo hadn't arrived yet, but was expected later in the day.

At the bar I joined a midday crowd and ordered Añejo on the rocks. A strolling musical trio in *charro* costumes played guitars and sang traditional Mexican songs. As bartenders moved back and forth, I spotted one whose nametag read José. He was a solid-looking man with coal black hair and gleaming teeth in a blunt Huichol face. Mid-thirties, I guessed, but the smooth, Indian skin could be deceptive.

For a while I nibbled snacks, then paid for my drink and shifted down to José's section.

*"Para servirle, señor,"* he said courteously, hands on the bar.

"I might try a little Añejo," I mused. "Recommended by a friend named Montijo. Manuel Montijo."

His voice lowered. "You are . . . ?"

"Juan Novak."

He turned and spurted Añejo into a short glass. *"Hielo?"*

"By all means."

He added crushed ice and set the glass before me. "With that *guayabera* I thought you were *tapatío* like me."

"It's why I wore it. *Salud."* I sipped the cold drink. "How long are you working?"

"Until four. We can talk then—not safe here." He glanced around covertly. "Too many gold chains and Swiss watches. *Drogistas."*

I nodded. "Room ten forty-nine." He moved away to serve another customer, and I scanned the clientele.

Some were conservatively dressed business types, but there was a covey of foreign tourists in floral shirts, market hats, and sunglasses, camera straps around their necks. Harmless citizens all. Sitting at the best tables were the presumed *drogistas* in expensive leisure outfits, wearing impressive displays of gold jewelry. I spotted four of them, each with a minimum of two heavily made-up *putas.* The men needed the makeup more than the whores, for they were coarse-featured peasant types with shifty eyes and cruel lips. Waiters bowed and scraped attendance in anticipation of extravagant tips, while the *putas* regarded them with envious eyes.

As I watched the four I wondered if one of them was Gerry's backer. Blowing away Gerry and Inge would be a casual matter for any one of them—like swatting an annoying bug. For a mule, Inge had shown a dangerous innocence concerning penalties for non-performance, so I hoped that she and Gerry would take my advice and pass through Guadalajara without reporting in.

After lunch I phoned the consulate again, but Manny wasn't there. I opted for a siesta and turned in.

When the door buzzer woke me I assumed it was José, but the time was only three. Maybe he was on break, I thought, as I opened the door.

Instead, Inge stood there, hands clenched, eyes filled with tears.

# FOUR

**H**E'S GONE," SHE sobbed, and lurched toward me. "Died in the operation."

I closed the door and guided her to a chair. "I'm sorry," I said, "truly sorry." I poured her a drink from my first-aid bottle and pulled on some clothes. "What now?"

"I suppose I . . . should . . . bury him." More tears. Her shoulders shook.

"You could notify his family."

"Hasn't . . . hadn't any. Told me he was an orphan."

"Then I suppose he was. The hospital will handle things."

Her eyes closed. "Some potter's field."

I said nothing.

She said, "Would you give me money for a grave marker?"

"No," I told her, "but I'll lend it to you." An idea had been forming ever since breakfast at the inn.

"You know I can't repay you."

I pointed at the phone. "Call your mother."

She shook her head violently. "Never. Not ever. She loves my stepfather, not me."

"Then I have a proposition, Inge. Work for me."

"Doing what?"

Before answering, I thought for a few moments. "Being my companion, appearing in public with me."

Her sun-bleached eyebrows drew together. "Why?"

"Because of the business I'm in. I need a female companion. For appearance's sake we'd go out together, travel around, appear to be a couple."

"What business is that?" She dried her eyes on her shirt cuff.

41

"Cultivating people, getting to know them."

"You some kind of salesman?"

I shrugged. "Two hundred a week, plus clothing and keep."

Her eyebrows lifted. "Two hundred . . . *dollars?*"

"Yes or no?"

Her gaze settled briefly on the bed. "And I'd have to sleep with you?"

"No."

She took in a deep breath that lifted what were probably marvelous breasts. "I don't have much choice."

"All right." I looked at my watch. "Wash your face and go down to the beauty salon. Your hair needs work and so do your hands and nails. Bill the room. After that, we'll go shopping."

"For what?"

"Dresses, gowns, resort wear."

Her eyelids drew together. "Whatever you may think, Jack, I've never been a whore. I'm not about to start now." She stood up, pink spots on her cheeks.

"I'm not a pimp," I told her. "Bathroom's over there."

Slowly she went to it. The door closed, and I heard water running. She came out looking considerably better. I said, "Tell them to take their time, do everything a rich man's mistress might want."

"Who's the rich man?"

"Me."

"But it's all pretend?"

"Like a hashish dream," I told her as I opened the door.

After a while the salon manager called to confirm billing. He recommended a jacuzzi and massage finale, and I said go ahead. Manny might question my expense sheet, but in Guadalajara I was going to need the kind of camouflage that a good-looking young woman could supply. I didn't think of it as real money, anyway. It was paper confiscated from *narcotraficantes,* not a drain on the U.S. Treasury.

I added Añejo to Inge's glass and sipped while I waited for José. My only scruple about using Inge was the possibility of exposing her to danger. Still, she'd been living dangerously, and I'd probably saved her life by detouring her away from Gerry's expectant backer. And anyone trying to get at her would have to go through me. The risk was assumable.

About a quarter after four my buzzer sounded, and I let José in. He was wearing street clothes and a worried look. I sat him down and said, "Give me a contact phone number."

He did and I memorized it. Then I said, "What are you picking up?"

42

"I hear talk about a Colombiano named Parra. Mean anything?"

"Omar Parra? What about him?"

"I get the feeling he's expected in Mexico. He won't come in openly—some other way."

"He's got his own air fleet," I said. "What's the airport situation?"

"After the killings it tightened for a while, but the new gang of *oficiales* became corrupt. So now things are loose again. *Muy flojo.*"

"What about Puerto Vallarta?"

"Some of the big boys have palaces there. I think some of the *cocaina* arrives there by ship. It's picked up and flown here."

"General Pedraza is in the motion picture business, I hear."

He nodded. "Many movie people come here from PV. They move back and forth." He paused. "I don't think the movie is going very well."

"Why not?"

"If it were, they wouldn't be coming here so often. You saw those whores in the barroom? The ones with the big spenders? They're in the movie—little parts their *drogistas* got them through Pedraza. So they call themselves *artistas. Putas artísticas* I call them."

"But not to their face."

"No. The men are Oscar Alarcón, Fructo Cejas, Humberto Padilla, and Lucho San Juan. Dirt. They pay Pedraza for protection. Because they're *bien enchufados* no one can touch them."

"In PV where does the movie company stay?"

"The big people have suites at the Castillo Real. The others are in cottages and rooming houses."

"How many *gringos* involved?"

"Maybe six."

"Who's the head *gringo?*"

"The co-director, Chandler Bates." He pronounced it *Bah-tays* and it took me a moment to figure out the spelling. I remembered the name from years ago. As far as I knew, Bates hadn't had an American release in twenty years. I said, "Working tonight?"

"At eight."

"You may see me with a blonde companion, a *rúbia notable.* Anyone asks about us, I'm from Houston and looking for a connection. Be careful who you say it to."

He nodded again. "What about the *rúbia?*"

"She's part of my cover."

"Otherwise you'd have whores around like flies." He looked at his watch. "When do you want to see me again?"

43

"I'll let you know."

We shook hands and I let him out. José didn't waste words. Unlike a lot of informants he didn't come up with a lot of crap to make himself sound important. He passed on what he knew and that was that. We were going to get along.

I took a shower, shaved, and got into clean clothing. The phone hadn't rung, so I went down to the beauty salon.

They'd finished with Inge except for the manicure, and what they'd done was astonishing. Her hair was clipped and styled so that feathers of golden hair framed her face in a swept-forward way. Her eyebrows were accented, and with curled lashes and eye shadow her face looked like a cover-girl's. Seeing me, she blushed. "What do you think?"

"Resurrection. What do *you* think?"

"I never thought I could look like this."

"Probably never tried. Self-image is everything," I told her. "If you don't like yourself you can't expect others to be impressed. In short, people take you at your own evaluation. Ah . . . that's my ten-*peso* analysis."

The manicurist turned a blow-drier on her short, lacquered nails, and Inge studied them. "Now I have reason to let them grow."

The manicurist turned off the drier. *"Eso es, señor. Satisfecho?"*

*"Bastante,"* I said, and tipped her a bundle. She removed the sheetlike covering from Inge as I signed the bill. By Mexican standards it was enormous, but trivial compared to Stateside costs. As I led my Galatea from the salon she said, "What now, *señor?"*

"You'll see." We walked to one of the hotel shops and I went in. To the saleslady I said, "The *señorita's* luggage was lost in a car accident. She needs everything. Evening gowns, cocktail dresses, underthings, hose, shoes for street and evening wear." To Inge I said, "Play tennis?"

"Some."

"Sportswear," I told the saleslady, "and swimsuits suitable for Puerto Vallarta. Head-turners, if you know what I mean."

She smiled. "I do."

Inge said, "You must have a lot of money, Jack."

"It's a pretend world," I reminded her, "so let's enjoy it while we can."

"I am. Believe me, I *am.*" She went off with the saleslady, and I took the opportunity to phone the consulate again. The Marine guard said the consulate was closed and Mr. Montijo had left for the day.

I had no alternate contact number for Manny; besides, he was to contact me at the hotel. I was running low on cash and needed resupply from his office safe. *Pesos* would be fine.

44

I went back to the boutique and settled down in a comfortable chair. From time to time Inge emerged with her saleslady to ask my opinion of their selections, and with each new costume the girl was looking better and better. After a while the saleslady brought out Inge's road clothing and said, "Shall I discard this?"

"If you have designer jeans."

"We do."

Finally, shopping was complete, and I helped Inge with boxes and bundles. We stopped at a nearby shop long enough to pick up an assortment of costume jewelry, and then we went up to my room.

Once inside she began hanging up her new possessions. Abruptly she started to cry. I put my arm around her shoulder and said, "Everything's going to be all right. Don't worry."

"But I feel so guilty, having so much pleasure in all this—when Gerry's lying dead in the hospital."

"Nothing you can do for him," I told her, "and God knows, you were loyal to the end. From now on you have to think about yourself."

"But you've done so much for me—a stranger until yesterday."

"Well, friendships bloom on the road. Ever take a cruise?"

"No."

"Or see 'Love Boat'?"

She dried her eyes, smearing makeup. "Yes."

"Then you know how much can happen in an hour." I said, "I've a few purchases to make, and by the time I get back I want you dressed for cocktails and dinner. Okay?"

"Okay."

I went down to the men's shop and bought lightweight leisure slacks and an electric-blue *guayabera* heavily embroidered in gold, blue, and red. I figured it was the kind that would appeal to a sleaze-ball just in from Houston. The shirt was made in Seoul, anyway, and what did Koreans know?

At the desk I got a strongbox and slipped off my gold Academy class ring. I'd worked like a dog for it at Annapolis and didn't want it ripped off. I gave the clerk the box and pocketed the key. Wearing my new finery, I went into the bar and sat at José's section. He nodded and came over.

"Same," I said.

"Where's the *rúbia?*"

"Preparing herself."

"Mind if I say something? Don't mix business with pleasure."

"I coined the phrase."

There wasn't much traffic at the bar. People were either dining or dressing for dinner. José brought my Añejo and said, "Those four *chingados* usually come here after dinner. They drink until they throw up or pass out."

"Charming," I remarked and sipped my drink. *"Salud."*

*"Bienestar,"* he replied and moved over to an arriving patron. I noticed a petite brunette come in. Her waist was small and she moved sensuously as Latin women naturally do. Her hair was long and Indian-dark, and for a moment I was strongly reminded of Melody. The pang passed. A garishly dressed *puta* slid onto the seat beside me. She plunked her bag on the bar and lit a cigarette, watching me carefully. As she exhaled she said, "Allo, Americano. I name Julia. You wanna make jig-jig wi' me?"

"No," I told her, "but how about your kid brother?"

*"Maricón,"* she spat and moved two stools away.

José covered his mouth to choke back laughter. I finished my drink and looked at my watch. By now Inge should be ready to shine. I went up to the room, knocked on the door, and went in.

She was seated composedly in a chair. Her evening choice was a white ankle-length gown, gathered at the waist with a cord of braided silk. She looked stunning, and I told her so. "Frankly," she said, "I've probably never looked better."

"You'll knock 'em dead. *Vámonos.* Let's go."

On the way down in the elevator she said, "I've finally decided what you really do."

My mouth went dry.

She whispered, "Counterfeiter."

"You got it," I said, relaxing, "though I don't personally engrave the queer. I just pass it around."

Her face was troubled. "No, if you did, you wouldn't admit it so easily. Bad guess."

We left the elevator and took a table in the bar. José noticed us and signaled a "ten." From the waiter I ordered champagne cocktails, saying, "French champagne."

*Sí, señor."*

Inge said, "I haven't had champagne since I left home."

"But you like it?"

"Love it."

I glanced around and saw a couple of single males eyeing my date. "How does it feel," I asked, "to be the focus of all eyes?"

"I'm not accustomed to it."

"You will be," I said as the waiter arrived. He showed me the French labels of two chilled splits and uncorked them. The lotus glasses were frosty, and each sugar cube was stained with the regulation three drops of bitters. I said, "Fire away."

*"Señor?"*

"Mix," I told him and watched him pour, then stir the dissolving sugar. I used the plastic stirrer to get out the bubbles before we drank. "Ummmmm," she exclaimed. "That is *good.*"

We drank, and over the glass rim I noticed that a man had joined the hooker at the bar. As they talked, he kept looking around nervously. He had long black hair and he wore a jacket a size or so too small. It fitted him so tightly that I could see the outline of a handgun in his belt. That wasn't unusual in a country where pistol-carrying is as common as spurs on a *vaquero's* boots. But not every male was so obvious about it.

Suddenly I wished I'd worn my Beretta under my new *guayabera,* but in an upscale hotel I hadn't thought I'd need it.

Inge was saying " . . . tell me what to do, you know."

"Do what?"

"How to act with people. I've lost contact with the real world. Forgotten what to do."

"Act natural," I told her. "Let your face, body, and dress speak for you."

We finished our cocktails and went into a large and impressive dining room. When we were seated I said, "The choice here is Mexican or French cuisine."

"I'm awfully tired of *tacos* and *tortillas.*"

"French it'll be." I asked the waiter for Guaymas oysters, rack of lamb *garni,* and a bottle of Eschenauer red.

We were about thirty feet from a large, noisy table. I saw the four *narcotraficantes* who earlier had been in the bar, and nine overdressed *artistas.* Thirteen. The drug world is so superstitious that I was surprised the hosts hadn't altered the number.

The oysters arrived, large and succulent, and I prayed they were not bearers of a dread disease. I was forking the first one when the man who had been talking with the hooker came in, brushed aside the maître d', and came toward my table.

I would have ducked under it, except for the fact that he wasn't looking at me. His gaze was fixed on the festive table. Abruptly he halted, flipped up his jacket, and jerked out a shiny .45.

Waiters froze. A hush filled the dining room, except for the laughter of the thirteen diners who hadn't noticed the arrival. Inge uttered a small scream. I put my hand on her neck and pushed her down as the man thrust out the pistol in a two-handed grip, sighted, and fired.

I lunged at him.

# FIVE

**M**Y CROSS-BLOCK BUCKLED his knees, and he pitched forward, firing into the floor. While he was figuring out what to do, I kicked his wrist and knocked loose the big pistol. I scooped it up and toed him in the chest. "On your feet," I snarled in Spanish, and when he was standing I shoved the pistol into his gut and hissed, "Get out fast. I'll cover you."

Eyes blinking in astonishment, he bolted past me and disappeared through the doorway as three of the *drogistas* ran up to me, pistols in hand. I turned to them. "Excitement's over," I said in English. "Enjoy your dinner."

*"Demónios,"* one of them croaked, "you let him get away."

"What did you expect me to do? Shoot an unarmed man? Not my quarrel, gentlemen."

The maître d' was at my side, bursting with apologies. I handed him the shiny pistol and went back to my seat. Inge was staring at me, wide-eyed. Slowly the three *pistoleros* put away their handguns. The one who had complained came to me and said, "You were right, *señor,* and we owe you our thanks. He could have killed us all. My name is Fructo Cejas, *a sus órdenes."* He bowed slightly.

"I'm Jack, this is Inge."

He shook hands with both of us and waved the other two over, introducing them as Humberto Padilla and Oscar Alarcón. More hand-shaking and Spanish courtesies that I pretended not to understand. The fourth man, their partner, was standing at the table, swearing loudly as a waiter tightened a napkin tourniquet around his upper arm. The beige

49

fabric was wet with blood, so the shooter hadn't missed entirely. Too bad the bullet hadn't smashed his heart, I thought.

Cejas said, "It appears our friend Lucho is wounded, *Señor* Jack, otherwise I would insist you join our party. But, permit me to buy your dinner."

"Not necessary," I said, "perhaps another time."

He was staring at Inge, and I could imagine with what thoughts. Taking her hand, he kissed it briefly and turned to me. "Anything I can do for you . . . Fructo Cejas is my name. You are a brave man, *señor. Muchísimas gracias.*"

"Anyone would have done the same."

"Perhaps in America." With a parting bow he rejoined his table. Two waiters assisted Lucho San Juan to the exit door. So much for that.

Leaning toward me, Inge said, "Why did you get involved?"

"Opportunity," I told her and swallowed an oyster.

"Opportunity? For what?"

"To save the lives of some prominent Mexicans."

"So you can do business with *them?*"

"Try the oysters, they're great."

Resentfully, she said, "I'm not sure I want to keep working for you."

"Were you injured?"

"I was half-scared out of my pants. I'm not accustomed to violence." Slowly she pronged an oyster. "Basically I'm a nonviolent person."

"That's tough to be in a violent world." I noticed that she was gazing uncomfortably at the big table where good times had resumed. Quietly she said, "I'm glad he didn't notice me."

"Who?"

"The man who was wounded—Lucho. He's the one who financed our trip to Colombia."

"Close-up, is he likely to spot you?"

"I . . . I can't be sure. There wasn't much light in the room, and we didn't stay long." Then she smiled. "I was forgetting how much I've changed since then. I look entirely different now."

"That you do," I agreed, thinking her mother wouldn't recognize her. "So let's put it behind us and enjoy the rest of the evening." Contact had been made.

That night we shared the bed. It was wide enough that we could sleep comfortably without body contact. Inge was up first and off to the hospital where Gerry's body was stored.

While she was gone I had breakfast in the room. About nine o'clock the phone rang. Manny was in the lobby.

Over coffee I told him what had happened to me since leaving Cozumel. Then he asked, "Who was the guy who shot Lucho San Juan?"

"Who knows? Some aggrieved citizen. I imagine there are plenty like him."

"Was Lucho his target?"

"I wasn't looking through his gunsight—but one's as bad as another."

"The big four owe you one."

"And I plan to collect," I told him. "First, I need considerable expense money and a flash roll. After all, I'm posing as a big *Tejano* looking to make a buy."

"Going to stay here awhile?"

"Maybe another day. Then down to Puerto Vallarta."

"Why?"

"Pedraza's movie company. And the Gang of Four is likely to be around. By the way, got a photo of Omar Parra?"

"Sure. He was arrested once in Miami, booked, printed, and photographed. Then, of course, he jumped bond. Half a million it was, but we'd have rather had Omar in the tank."

I grunted. "Some asshole judge would have found technical defects in the arrest and released him to sin again."

"True—only DEA can't say so." He finished his coffee and stood up. "Until I find an apartment for my wife and kids I'll be at the Sheraton. Later today I'll leave a package for you at the desk. Money and photo." He smiled. "José says you're okay."

"I like him. A non-bullshit guy."

"His kid sister was hooked on drugs. They turned her into a street whore and he never saw her again. Probably dead. "

"If lucky. I think I'll fly the Seabee to Vallarta. Maybe someone will make a proposition."

"You don't need my advice on how to handle things. Just be careful—and don't rely too much on Inge." He hesitated. "What's the nature of your relationship?"

"I'm her social worker."

Before he left I looked up and down the corridor to make sure there was no surveillance. Soon he'd be identified and tailed by *traficantes,* and he'd have to contact agents by phone. Meanwhile we could meet discreetly.

51

By the time Inge returned I'd showered, shaved, and dressed. Dealing with the morgue people had depressed her, but she seemed relieved that Gerry would have a marker on his grave. I wondered how many other young people were in potter's fields and still sought by their families who were waiting for the prayed-for phone call: "Mom, help me, I want to come home." The call that never came.

In the lobby we hired a sight-seeing cab for a city tour. It began in the old section, dominated by the gold-tiled towers of the cathedral that faced a sizable plaza of fountains and well-tended ornamental trees. Behind the cathedral extended Liberation Plaza with more fountains, trees, and banked flowers. It ended at the neo-Grecian façade of the Degollado Theater, which, according to our driver-guide, was the center of the city's cultural activities.

From there to the government palace and three huge murals Orozco had painted on walls and ceiling. Inge commented on the strong faces and bold colors, and I said it was all a little grotesque for me, not being a partisan of political art.

"Still," she said, "we can agree on the beauty of the flowers and fountains?"

"Completely."

From there we drove into the northern residential sections: Providencia, Country Club, Lomas del Valle, and Colinas de San Javier. What impressed Inge the most was the tranquility of the well-kept neighborhoods. Most of the homes were hidden by ten-foot walls, but occasional grillwork gates afforded glimpses of substantial dwellings where law-abiding *tapatíos* lived in comfort and seclusion.

Inge said, "It's been a long time since I've seen anything of family life."

"Me, too."

At an intersection the driver said, "And now, there is something special to show you. Castles of our billionaires."

"Okay," I told him. "How do they make their money?"

His glance was sly. "Who knows, *señor?*"

So we crossed south through the city and took the airport road. Off to the left, nestled against a gentle slope, stood a huge, four-story mansion that looked newly built. An unusually high, wire-topped wall surrounded thirty or forty acres of land, and the wall had guard posts at intervals, manned by soldiers. The driver said proudly, "They say it has twenty bedrooms and a ballroom big enough to hold an entire village. Everywhere are swimming pools and beautiful art."

"I'm impressed. Who's the owner?"

He winked at me. "General Gilberto Pedraza."

"Lucky man," I remarked. "What pay does a Mexican general get?"

"In dollars, about a thousand each month."

"Then he's invested a lifetime's salary."

"And more. Much more." In his voice, pride clashed with envy. "Also a fleet of German automobiles."

"Better and better," I said as we drove away.

Another mansion was under construction nearby. The owner was Oscar Alarcón, according to the driver. The compound was slightly smaller than Pedraza's Alhambra, but the mansion no less ostentatious. The driver pointed out other showplaces that, he said, belonged to *Los Intocables.* He couldn't translate the word in English, but I could. "The Untouchables," I whispered to Inge. "Meaning they're beyond the law."

"I think that's awful," she bristled.

"Well, I thought you should see how drug kings live, the life-styles you and Gerry were contributing to."

Inge said, "So much wealth is unimaginable—and all from drug profits?"

"Every *centavo.*"

Over his shoulder the driver said, "Even the President of Mexico cannot afford such a grand home."

"But he will," I said. "As soon as he leaves office, he will."

*"Sí, señor,"* the driver nodded. "Most assuredly. He will build expensively and live like a king the rest of his days."

The driver took us back to the hotel. I paid him and asked for the room key at the desk. The clerk gave it to me along with a gift-wrapped box that had my name on a card.

While Inge was in the bathroom I opened the box and found a manila envelope. It contained a stack of ten-thousand *peso* notes and a black-and-white photograph.

Omar Parra had long, bushy hair and a wild look in his eyes. There was a thin mustache on his upper lip, and a spade goatee on his chin. I stared at his face long enough to fix it in my mind, thinking that he looked even crazier than his late brother, Luís. Then I tore the photo into small pieces and, when it was my turn in the bathroom, I flushed them down the toilet.

Inge was wearing a red-mesh bikini with matching peekaboo halter, and a striped jacket. I had on conventional swim trunks and a towel. We went down to the pool, swam for a while in the clear blue water, and had drinks and lunch at pool-side.

As she stretched out in the sun Inge murmured, "I could get to love this kind of living. Is this your usual style?"

"Not exactly," I confessed. "Actually, I lead a rather simple life, close to nature."

"Why?"

"For longevity. People like the Untouchables tend to live in showy bursts like Fourth of July rockets. Everyone oohs and aahs at the display before it disintegrates into nothingness. That kind of trajectory was never for me."

She was applying tanning cream to her front, then she turned over and I coated her back and legs. As I applied it I saw Fructo Cejas and his group arrive. Lucho San Juan's left arm was in a sling. I didn't see a cast, so it must have been only a flesh wound. Too bad. Today there were only four females, all wearing floppy sun hats and minimal bikinis. They stayed in the shade while the males arrayed themselves on pads and ordered drinks.

I saw Cejas looking around the pool, and when he saw me, he got up and came over. "I hope you are enjoying yourselves," he said, as Inge sat up. "Very much," she said.

"Then I hope you will linger in Guadalajara."

"Afraid not," I told him. "We're going to Puerto Vallarta tomorrow."

"Excelente," he said, "a delightful place," and turned to Inge. "Señorita, you are so charming and beautiful I must ask if you are in moving pictures."

"Not yet, Mr. Cejas."

"Then you should be." He sat down beside her, gold chains glittering as he moved. "It occurs that I have friends making a picture there at the very moment. I can arrange that you be part of it."

"That would be nice," I said, "if it's not an imposition."

"How? After you risked your life last night? Please allow me to do a little something for you."

"If it's no trouble."

He shrugged. "I will make a letter for you to take there. My friends are at the Castillo Real."

"That's where we're staying."

"Then it is convenient, no?"

"Very convenient. But if nothing happens, we won't be disappointed."

"Oh, she can definitely be in the picture." He turned to me. "What are your interests, Señor Jack?"

"Beautiful women, having a good time."

54

He nodded understandingly. "What kind of business do you have?"

"Buying and selling."

"My business, too. Is that why you are in Mexico?"

"I had contacts around Monterrey, but not any more."

"What happened?"

"They were arrested in California. But this is no time for business." I glanced at Inge.

"I understand. Well, perhaps I'll see you in the bar—for a drink."

"I look forward to it," I said. He bowed to Inge and returned to his party. His female gave us a ferocious look.

Inge said, "Is that true about your contacts in Monterrey? They were arrested?"

"True." I'd arranged for their arrests, but that was not for her to know.

"And you want to do business with Cejas?"

"Desperately."

"Even if it's . . . illegal?"

"In Mexico illegal means you get caught. Are you looking forward to acting in the picture?"

"*If* it happens it would be . . . interesting. The short time I was at the university I did some one-act plays—small parts."

"Ample background." I gestured at the four *putas* on the shady side of the pool. "They're in the flick, too. How much acting experience do they have?"

Her mouth made an unpleasant noise. "X-Rated, I imagine. When did you decide on Puerto Vallarta?"

"Yesterday."

"You didn't tell me."

"It was a busy day. Getting you re-conditioned, fending off the dining room gunman."

"Well, that's so, and I won't ask more questions. I should just go along with whatever you say? That it?"

"That's it."

We had a long swim then, and Inge seemed to be rediscovering forgotten skills. She was a good companion and useful in a support role. How resourceful she was would be determined in PV.


AFTER SIESTA I left Inge sleeping and took a taxi to the *rastro,* the local flea market. There I hunted down an ornate belt buckle inlaid with gold and silver and encrusted with fake gems. Across the center of the star

55

the word *Texas* was engraved. After some spirited bargaining, the owner agreed on four thousand pesos, with a braided leather belt thrown in.

I wore it because the buckle was tacky enough to enhance my contrived persona as a buck-heavy *Tejano* on the prowl.

Back at the hotel bar I found José getting ready to go off duty. After pouring me a generous shot of Añejo, he said, "Glad you came. About an hour ago Fructo Cejas tipped me five thousand pesos and asked about you, said he'd noticed us talking. I told him you were a Texan who laid money around, and I thought you were looking to make a drug buy. He seemed satisfied with that and went away."

"That saves me introducing the subject."

"Last night you kept a man from killing the four *cabrones*."

"As a way of getting their confidence."

"I understand. But the man you knocked down talks of killing you."

"Why? I saved his life."

"He doesn't care about his life. He wants to kill drug dealers. Like my sister, his wife got hooked on *heroina,* and they shipped her to Mexico City as a whore. I used to know him when we were kids in the same *barrio.* Javier Madero."

"If there's a next time, tell Javier I won't interfere, but if I find the *pendejo* pointing a gun in my direction, I'll blow him away. This is serious business, no space for *locos.*"

He shrugged. "Drugs make everyone crazy."

"Tomorrow we're leaving for Puerto Vallarta. Castillo Real. Cejas wants my lady to act in Pedraza's picture. Bit part."

"You've made fast progress."

"What's the picture about?"

"I don't think they know. The script has been rewritten a dozen times. The story has to do with some Mexican heroine who killed a lot of Maximilian's soldiers when they came through her village. The star is Sarita Rojas. Very big in Mexican films and very attractive. Pedraza wants her, if he doesn't already have her."

"Tell me about Sarita."

"Born in Sonora and raised in Nogales. She learned English there. Border English."

"A *pachuca,* then." I stirred my drink.

He nodded. "Don't say it to her face. They say she has a violent temper."

"Never fear. What's a good restaurant away from the hotel?"

"I hear La Diane recommended by customers, but stay away from La Langosta and Ciro's disco. Their clientele is rather . . . special."

"I'll remember."

José continued washing glasses and polishing his section of the bar. Before his replacement arrived I paid for the drink and left.

In a luggage shop off the lobby I bought a three-piece matched set of simulated Vuitton baggage for Inge's clothing, a three-suiter for myself.

Then I sent Inge down to the beauty salon for touch-up work and told her to meet me in the bar. I chose a table where my trashy buckle would show to advantage, ordered a drink, and waited.

After a while Fructo Cejas came in, looked around, and came to my table.

# SIX

**W**E SHOOK HANDS and I invited Cejas to join me. "Pleasure," he said and snapped his fingers. At once a waiter materialized. Cejas said, "Dom Perignon, *bien fría, dos vasos.*"

The waiter scurried away, and Cejas turned to me. "You are waiting for the *señorita?*"

"Eventually. You know how it is with women."

He chuckled appreciatively. "That one, she is worth waiting for, no?"

"She's indispensable," I said, "and I hope you weren't kidding about the movie part. She's counting on it."

"You will see." From his pocket he drew out an envelope addressed to *Sr.* Chandler Bates, Hotel Castillo Real. "I never kid."

Looking at his coarse features I could believe it. I said, "This will mean a lot to her—and me. We're obliged for the favor."

He waved a hand. "Nothing."

The champagne arrived. The waiter uncorked and poured with hands that trembled noticeably. Cejas touched his glass to mine and said, "Success."

"Success." We drank together, and Cejas smacked his lips. "You come here on business, no?"

"Pleasure and business."

"Those contacts of yours in Monterrey—suppose I could talk to them. What would they say?"

I smiled. "They would say, 'Be very careful who you do business with.'"

"Good advice. Always good advice."

I drank again. The champagne was icy and delicious. At about a

59

hundred dollars a bottle it should be. "In California they dealt with unknown persons, and now they have time to regret it."

"The Monterrey men—who were they?"

"Let's see . . . " I wrinkled my face and forehead. "One called himself El Jaguar, one said his name was 'Emilio,' and the other was called El Cochino."

"El Cochino, the fat one?"

"No," I said. "He was skinny but he ate like a pig."

He slapped my shoulder good-humoredly. "Exactly. I am being careful, you see."

"So you knew them."

"Knew *of* them. Very small-time. I am big-time." He clinked his gold-link bracelets.

"You mean . . . ?"

"Perhaps I can satisfy your needs."

"That's interesting," I remarked, "since I haven't said what they are."

"Come, *Señor* Jack, in Guadalajara the only business worth discussing is the white powder, no?"

"I'll have to think about that. After all, you could be working for the authorities."

He laughed boisterously, wiped tears from his eyes. "A great joke, *señor*. In truth, the authorities work for *me*."

"If so," I said, "that certainly lowers the risk."

"And here in Jalisco you are under my protection." His arm made a broad sector sweep. "How much you wanna buy?"

"Maybe a hundred, two hundred thousand dollars now. More later, if everything works out."

He frowned slightly. "Hardly worth my trouble, *señor*. Normally I sell only a minimum of one million dollars, but you did us a fine favor, so I will accommodate you one time." He refilled our glasses. "For your trip to Puerto Vallarta, let me send you in one of my planes."

"Thanks, but I have my own."

His eyebrows lifted. "You are a pilot?"

"How else would I get stuff across the border?"

He nodded thoughtfully. "This vacation of yours might become more profitable than you imagine."

"Always interested," I told him, "but only where there's no risk."

"Well, then, we'll talk more—in Puerto Vallarta. Okay?"

"Okay."

We shook hands, and his grip was powerful. He laid two hundred-dollar bills on the table and walked away. The waiter gaped at them until I said, "Take them, they're yours."

He snatched up the money, stuffed it in his jacket, and refilled my glass. I saw Inge come in and watched her walking to the table. To the waiter I said, "A fresh glass for the lady," and helped her into the chair.

Pool-side sunning had deepened her tan and lightened her blonde hair even more. It seemed to be overlaid with a sheen of platinum. "How do I look?" she asked.

"Better than ever." I showed her the envelope addressed to Chandler Bates. "This could be your ticket to fame and fortune—unless it's a Four-X movie."

"I wouldn't want that," she said with an expression of distaste. "I've refused offers before."

The waiter brought a glass and filled it with Dom Perignon. I said, "Courtesy of Fructo Cejas."

Before drinking she said, "He and his friends give me the creeps."

"Rightly so. In addition to being drug kings they're extortionists, killers, whoremongers, and pimps. And always on the lookout for fresh talent. In Puerto Vallarta I won't always be at your side, so use discretion about situations that could get threatening."

Her voice was thin. "Now you tell me."

"You took greater chances with your life every time you popped a pill. If you want to back off now, okay, no hard feelings. But I need to know."

She shrugged. "I'll stay—I think you need me."

IN THE MORNING I hired an air-conditioned limousine to drive us to Lake Chapala. The trip was a lot more comfortable than the bus ride. I was glad to see my Seabee snubbed to the buoy where I'd left it. An Indian paddled over in a *chalupa*—log canoe—and took me out with two pieces of the baggage. While I checked the panel and interior for pilferage and possible damage, he went back for Inge. I tested the controls. Fine. The *chalupa* bumped the hull. I moved scuba gear out of the way and helped Inge into the cabin. The Indian passed in the other two bags, and I paid him a thousand *pesos* for his trouble.

After the engine started, the Indian untied the bow line and I taxied away from shore. Inge buckled into her seat and said, "This is a thrill. I've never been in a small plane before."

"Don't panic." I gave it some throttle and lowered flaps. On the in-flight I'd noticed a marina farther down the lake. After takeoff I headed there and filled the tanks with 100-octane gas that I hoped was well

61

filtered. Before taking off again, I tooled around over the calm surface, listening carefully to the Lycoming engine. If there was dirt in the gas this was the time to find out. But the revs stayed high, so I richened the mix, found a slight breeze, and turned into it.

Puerto Vallarta lay almost due west, beyond the Sierra Madre range, so I climbed to nine thousand feet and made for the coast. Inge was enjoying the flight, gasping at some of the tall, spiked ridges, and pointing out various features of the rugged landscape. Then we were over the mountain spine, and the Pacific Ocean lay beyond.

The Bahía de Banderas—Bay of Flags—was a smoothly curving crescent twenty-five miles long. The shoreline lay below steep cliffs, and beaches were scalloped into coves between rocky outcrops that looked as raw as if they had been ripped out by some gigantic claw. Ranging up and down uneven hillsides were hotels and bungalows. I could see winding terraces where cottages perched, and here and there a trickling waterfall. Divided by a river, the tile-roofed town of Puerto Vallarta looked old and abandoned in the morning sun.

Our hotel curved away from the strand of golden beach. In front of it grew well-spaced coco palms bordered by ranks of conical, thatched chickee shelters. I buzzed low over the waterfront, turned back, and throttled down. The Seabee met the water nicely, Inge sighed in relief, and I taxied toward the beach.

When the hull nudged sand, Inge got out and waded barefoot through a few inches of foam. A small crowd welcomed her, and a waiter from the open-air bar carried our luggage ashore. Two bathers shoved the plane into deeper water, and I taxied over to a rocky cove, anchoring away from where most swimmers were likely to be.

A speedboat came by, picked me up, and dropped me off in front of the hotel. As I walked to it, I overheard chatter about the handsome couple that had arrived on the funny-looking old plane.

Inge was waiting in the lobby when I came in. I picked up our reservations at the desk, and we went up to the suite on the ninth floor. It had a large bayside balcony, a jacuzzi in the bath, and stained rafters that arched over the thick, beige carpeting. Inge dived onto the giant-size bed. "Heavenly," she exclaimed. "Just heavenly!"

"Good things come to nice people," I said sententiously, and began hanging my small wardrobe in the paneled closet.

She wandered around the suite, touching the drapes and finally going out on the balcony. Wind tugged at her hair and ruffled her blouse, and I thought that she had never looked more lovely. Like a butterfly she'd emerged from shabby chrysalis and was learning to spread glorious wings. I rang for room service and ordered Añejo for myself, margaritas for Inge. Before the waiter left I gave him Cejas's letter and told him to leave it at the desk for *Sr.* Chandler Bates.

Inge showered first and slipped into the jacuzzi while I took a shower. Then I stepped into the foaming water and let the submerged jets massage back muscles strained from hunching over flight controls.

The waiter brought our drinks to the jacuzzi, and while we were enjoying them the telephone began to ring.

The caller's voice sounded old and bored and affectedly British. "Is . . . ah . . . Miss Inge theah?"

"Bates?"

"Yes. Chandler Bates heah." The voice warmed slightly.

"She'll be out of the shower in a moment—or I could take a message."

"Please do. Ah . . . if you've no conflicting plans, do join us for a bite of lunch. Several of the cast will be heah, and this will be a splendid chawnce to become acquainted."

"I'll accept for us both."

"Splendid. Penthouse B, then, around noon."

"Look forward to it." I replaced the phone and gazed at Inge. "I think your movie career has just begun."

PART OF THE penthouse was roofed, the rest open to sun and sky. There was a wet bar near a good-sized pool in which several topless Mexican girls were frolicking with a float shaped like a burro. The buffet table was set under eaves that shaded it from the overhead sun. The centerpiece was a yard-tall seahorse sculptured from ice. Around it sat pods of iced shrimp, *ceviche,* crab claws, and oysters. There were bowls of salad, and a six-rib standing roast carved by an aproned chef. And that was only part of the spread.

Chandler Bates stood nearby, talking with Inge. He was a tall, thin man in a short-sleeved linen shirt and paisley ascot. He wore beltless cream-colored slacks and openwork *huaraches.* His gray hair was thinning on top, and his face was as tired as his telephone voice. Patches of tiny veins marked his nose and cheeks, and eye pouches hung like dewlaps on a beagle. His thin lips were vaguely pink, and when they parted they showed unattractive teeth. It occurred to me that, with directors half his age bringing out Hollywood's major films, time had passed by for Chandler Bates.

I saw that, for him, Inge was a pleasant surprise after some of the

63

hookers he'd been forced to employ. The girls in the pool were big-breasted Indian kids with sturdy waists and large behinds. I didn't know if they were in the movie or there for decoration. Their long, black hair and streaming, coppery skins made me think of green rain forests and jaguars and Aztec idols.

A woman in a wide-brimmed straw hat strolled toward me. She wore fantasy sunglasses, an embroidered shirt drawn around her waist by a tasseled cord, tight-ankled slacks, spike heels, and a bored expression. She held a topped coconut in one hand and sipped the contents through a colored straw. "Carla Santiago," she said, "Enjoying yourself?"

"Well, I haven't really gotten into things, but I see possibilities."

She looked at the pool girls with distaste. "What appeals to most males is the general air of lechery." She sucked noisily at the dregs of her beverage.

"I'm Jack Novak," I told her, "just a bystander."

"And the blonde is your protégée, I hear."

"We're at least friends," I said. "Fellow pilgrims traversing life's byways."

"How poetic. You must also be a friend of Gil's."

"Don't know him."

"Astonishing. General Gilberto Pedraza. His money is paying for all this—everything." Her arm swept spatially. *"And* the disaster our Chandler calls a motion picture." Her tone was bitter.

"You're part of it, then?"

"Unfortunately." She tossed the empty coconut into the pool, almost conking one of the *indias.* "I have the highly questionable privilege of playing Sarita's mother. *Mother,*" she spat. "For God's sake I'm not *that* old!"

But she was. The veins on the back of her pale hands, and the sagging mouth told the story. Now I noticed the fine scarring at her earlines, the skin too tightly drawn across the bridge of her nose.

"I was in films with Pedro Infante, great films that made millions of *pesos*—when *pesos* were worth something. Now I'm associating with this *basura.*" She looked around, contempt in her eyes. "Whores, *cocaineros,* and incompetents. If you're fond of your girl, don't let her get involved."

"She's a free agent," I said. "I don't ask Inge for advice, and she doesn't consult me."

"Poor kid, they'll swallow her like *ceviche.* But don't worry about Chandler, he's impotent." Her mouth twisted. "I lived with him three years. You can't snort coke that long and still get it up—I know." Tears

64

welled in her eyes. She scooped another *coco loco* from a passing waiter and drew on the straw. I wasn't particularly interested in her revelations, but in that *ambiente* a *confidante* could be useful."

"So, when does the general make his appearance?" I asked.

"Not today. He usually comes when they're shooting Sarita. His pals come all the time—with the dirty sluts they shoved into the film." Her face tensed. "I forgot, you're a friend of Cejas. Do forgive me."

"No offense. He's a barroom acquaintance, not a friend."

"If you want some advice, keep it that way."

There was a stir by the buffet, and I saw Sarita Rojas come in. I recognized her from films I'd seen on Cozumel, and she was even more beautiful than on the screen. Indian blood gave her dark eyes and coal-black hair, high cheekbones and olive skin. But nose, mouth, and figure showed Spanish ancestry, and the girls in the pool stopped playing long enough to stare at her with envy.

*Mariachis* struck up a welcoming tune—the theme from one of Sarita's most successful films—and she bowed unsmilingly. Guests clustered around her, and I noticed two burly bodyguards separating her from the momentary crush.

Chandler Bates hurried over to greet his star, and managed to get his arms around her. But her head snapped aside, and she spat something that made him back away. Beside me, Carla Santiago trilled with pure pleasure. I smiled.

She was a faded veteran of one-night stands who'd danced too late too many times and was left without pretensions. I said, "Sarita doesn't care for Chandler?"

Her laugh was more of a bray. *"Like* him? What a precious thought. The old fool fancies himself in love with the little tart—and Sarita is not amused." She bussed my cheek. "You are a dear young man, Jack Novak, and if I were Sarita's age, I would carry you off to my room." She stepped back. "From that appalling buckle I gather you are Texan."

"Yes, ma'am," I said humbly. "Houston. No offense."

This time her laugh was genuine. "Aren't you the artful lady-pleaser, with your sly dissembling. All calculated to charm the unwary."

Hard as it was, I kept a straight face. "Is that what I'm up to, Miz Carla?"

She laughed merrily. "Massa Rhett Butlah, ah'll thank you to keep a civil tongue in yo' head, suh."

"Us Houston folks," I said, "know how to cultivate ouah bettahs."

"Indeed you do—*if* you're from Houston. My goodness, but you've put me in an unusual mood. Texan? My flaming arse." Grasping my hand she dragged me toward Sarita Rojas, shoved tribute-payers aside, and glared at a bodyguard. "Dahling, it's my considerable pleasure to introduce Jack Novak. Jack, the divine Sarita."

Uncertainly, the actress gave me her hand. "How do you do," she murmured, and our eyes met. Hers were deep and liquid, and filled, to my surprise, with a curious innocence. I said, "I'm an admirer of your films, *señorita.* It's a privilege to meet you."

"Thank you," she said, letting her hand linger in mine. "Do you suppose I might have a drink?"

"Of course." She took my arm, and we parted the circle to move toward the bar. With her free hand she motioned the bodyguards away. The bartender stared at her open-mouthed, fever in his eyes. "Your pleasure, *señorita?* he gabbled.

"Cuauhtemoc," she said in a silken voice, and turned to me. "Yours?"

"The same, please."

The bartender opened iced bottles with shaking hands, filled two chilled glasses, and wiped his forehead. *"Servidos,"* he said.

After sipping, she said, "As a child I drank beer, and so far as I can tell it never harmed me."

"On the contrary. I notice you ate your spinach, too."

She smiled. "If that's a compliment, it's unusual, and I accept it . . . Jack." She sipped and glanced around. "Did Carla bring you?"

"I came with the blonde in the halter top, as her escort of the moment. Her name is Inge Langer, and she's been invited to join the company."

"Endless," she said and shook her lovely head. "Just endless the way people are added to the cast. Not that I object to your Inge, understand, but things have been, well, difficult."

"We met a few days ago," I told her, "and in Guadalajara she apparently impressed some gentlemen connected to this picture."

Laconically she said, "Gentlemen? I don't believe I know any *caballeros* involved with this film." Her eyes narrowed. "Now I remember. The two of you arrived in that little plane! Would you take me up in it?"

"Gladly," I said. "Then I can tell friends in Houston that you flew with me."

"In Houston your friends wouldn't know my name."

"In the *barrio* they do."

"That's true. And nice of you to say so." She glanced at my Texas buckle. "Not every *Tejano* is so courteous."

"Nor every Mexican young woman as lovely as Sarita Rojas." Our glasses touched. She said, "Are you staying long?"

"If it will give me an opportunity to see you perform."

Turning, she smiled broadly at the crowd. "See—I'm acting now. If it weren't for you I'd have left. I *hate* this scene. Hate it, hate it!" Her lips trembled and she drank quickly. "Despite appearances, I'm a prisoner. I do what I'm told, travel here, there, act, sleep, get up, groom myself . . . less freedom than a monkey in a zoo."

"Appearances to the contrary, beauty bears its chains," I said, not being able to think of anything more comforting.

"Now *that's* worth remembering." She repeated my just-coined epigram and nodded approvingly. Then her features set. "If you do cocaine, here's opportunity."

Indeed it was. A waiter was passing a silver tray among the guests. It held a mound of white powder, a razor blade, lines of coke, and disposable straws. People snorted the lines, sighed, and glowed as the rush hit. Carla Santiago snorted, as did Chandler Bates. The Indian girls climbed out of the pool, clamoring for shares, and were rewarded while men from the movie company palmed and nuzzled their conical breasts.

I said, "Looks like great fun, but I'm a health nut. I take natural substances by mouth—fruits and vegetables."

She laughed lightly. "Me, too," she said, then sighed. "I really should leave now. An hour's make-up and costuming before shooting the next scene." She shook her head. "So much effort, so much wasted money— for a film that will probably end up in the refuse can."

"With you in the film? Impossible."

"You'll see. We'll talk again."

Leaving the bar she went to Inge, interrupted a conversation, and introduced herself. For a few moments they chatted pleasantly, and then Sarita surrendered to her watchdogs and was no more to be seen.

Inge came over to me looking dazed. "What a lovely person. I just can't believe she's the star."

"Believe it. And beloved of millions around the hemisphere. Right now she's on a bad wicket, but once this film's done, she'll recover and go on to better things."

"Jack, she actually welcomed me to the company. Now that's really something. I thought she'd be resentful and spiteful to a beginner. But she was just the opposite. What a figure . . . and that voice . . . like a quiet brook."

I nodded. "My impression, too. What has Bates lined up for you? Speaking part?"

"A few words in Spanish. I'm to be one of the village girls the bad soldiers . . . rape."

The last word hung on her tongue. I put one arm around her shoulders. "Make believe, Inge. It's all pretend."

As I spoke, the thought came to me that Sarita Rojas could have been primed to meet me, and only pretended to find me *simpático*. She was, after all, Pedraza's girlfriend, and that was something I couldn't afford to forget.

We ate from the lavish buffet, and now that people had noticed Sarita's acceptance of Inge, they came around to introduce themselves and compliment her clothing, sandals, complexion, hair style, and so on. There were four darkly tanned good-looking men and several gorgeous fellows who clustered by themselves. As I downed another iced shrimp Chandler Bates moved beside me. "I do believe your lady friend has what it takes."

"Whatever that is."

"Hmmm. For her scenes she'll have to wear a black wig—unfortunately —but in her next picture Inge should be seen in her natural blonde beauty."

I munched another shrimp. "What picture is that?"

He squinted at the bay. "One I've held close to my heart for many years. A young girl, innocent, lovelorn, takes to the road and encounters many adventures—and adventurers—maintaining her virtue throughout . . ."

"Sort of a modern-day *Pamela*," I suggested. "A vehicle once suitable for Toby Wing."

"Quite—without Richardson's tedious moralizing. Such a role would be ideal for Miss Inge. Under my inspired, personal direction her career would head . . . to the moon."

He was halfway there himself, I thought, thanks to the white stuff in his noodle. A working title for his inspiration might be *Sleazy Rider,* but I didn't tell him so.

Inge said, "Would there be frontal nudity?"

"No, no, nothing crude or suggestive. A shower scene, perhaps, a topless frame or so—obligatory in today's physically exploitive, anti-intellectual climate. But the entire thrust would be character development through surmounting obstacles."

"Sounds good," I said. "We won't sign elsewhere until we've seen a script."

Inge gave me a puzzled glance, but Bates had drifted away. He thought in frames, in scenes, and this one was completed for the day. She said, "I can't believe all this is happening."

"Feet on the ground," I advised. "Maintain close contact with *terra firma.*"

"Of course I will. But, it's . . . exhilarating."

"Heady stuff," I agreed, "so it's best to count on nothing. If something materializes from Bates' snowstorm, we'll both be pleasantly surprised."

The waiter with the silver tray had vanished, the ration had given out. There was a lot of yawning among the partakers. Even the girls in the pool were drifting and dreaming. Their skyward-pointing breasts looked firm as rubber. The toy burro bobbed away, forgotten.

We ate our fill, had a *coco loco* each, and then we thanked our host for his hospitality. Carla was clinging to his arm as Bates said, dreamily, "So glad you came. We'll do great things together, all of us." He patted Carla's shoulder. "Am I not right, m'dear?"

"Absolutely," she slurred. "Don't have too big a night, Inge. The location van leaves at seven."

"I'll be there," she promised, and we went down to our suite.

From the balcony I could see my plane in the cove at the north end of the beach. A speedboat roared past, pulling a parasailer at low altitude, the chute's bright stripes glistening in the sun.

Farther out, water-skiers slashed swaths of white in the green expanse, sent rooster-tails high in the air. My eyes were tired from too much sun. I pulled off shoes and *guayabera,* lay down on the wide bed, and closed my eyes. After a while Inge came out of the bathroom, and presently I felt her move onto the bed. I was half-asleep when her hand curled into mine.

Inge was physically attractive, and there was nothing wrong with my virility. But in her I'd sensed a quality of bewildered innocence that I'd found in my wife, Pam, before drugs took her from me. In memory I still prized that innocence of hers, and it was one of the few things I wanted to remember. So I couldn't violate it by coming on to Inge. I couldn't exploit her dependence on me, and besides, I didn't like men who took advantage of the helpless.

So I lay beside my ward, and went to sleep.

While we slept, a light tropical shower drifted across the bay. I heard a soft spattering on the balcony deck, and when I woke, the air was washed of its sea-scent, fresh and clean.

THAT NIGHT FRUCTO Cejas and his *cofrades* checked in.

# SEVEN

INGE AND I were down on the hotel beach, enjoying the huge buffet set under the palms. There were colored lights and flaming torches, a dance platform, and lively music. Watching the younger crowd writhe, bob, and thrash to the rhythm reminded me of Melody doing the *hunca-munca* from her native Brazil. I noticed the Mexican pool-girls had added minibras to their negligible costumes and were dancing uninhibitedly with three beach boys. The big chickee-bar was doing heavy business, and one way or another guests and the movie crowd were enjoying themselves.

When Inge nudged me I saw the four drug lords and five female companions taking a large reserved table not far from the buffet. As usual the men were expensively dressed and showing extravagant amounts of gold. Their women were in abbreviated playsuits, and without dark glasses their faces looked sharp and rapacious.

I looked around for Sarita Rojas, but she was nowhere to be seen, nor were Chandler and Carla Santiago. Well, the night was young, and in that hedonistic setting unexpected things could happen.

Lucho San Juan's arm, I was glad to see, was still sling-bound, and his face was sullen. Inge said, "He still frightens me, Jack. I'm so afraid he might recognize me."

"Unlikely, having seen you only briefly, as a road tramp, he wouldn't expect to see you here. Hell, he's probably forgotten the deal. Since then he's financed a dozen smurfs to make the trip."

Her face sobered. "That's all we were—Gerry and me—just smurfs, as you call it."

71

"Smurfs, mules. Expendables. You're out of that scene, so don't think about it."

A supporting player named Raúl came over and asked Inge to dance. I nodded agreement, and they crossed the sand to the dance floor. By now, there were several ice buckets of champagne at Cejas' table. Spotting me, Cejas came over with a bottle and two glasses. Uninvited he sat down and poured. After I'd sipped he said, "That your plane over there off the beach?"

"Right."

"I thought you meant a plane that can carry a real payload."

"I can lift off with a thousand pounds of cargo," I told him. "Cover better than six hundred miles without refueling."

He drank thirstily. "A thousand pounds are . . . four fifty keys. Where would you land it?"

"I fly in low, under radar, land on country roads or farm ponds. So far I've never been noticed."

"Always a first time, eh?"

"So my Monterrey friends learned. What price are we talking?"

"We're not talking price. My friends"—he gestured at his table—"they don't like to do business with *gringos.*"

"That's where dollars come from. *Gringo*-land. You do everything your pals tell you?"

He leaned forward. "For that insult I would kill you, but you saved our lives so I don't take offense."

"I'm grateful for that," I said, "but I was only asking a question."

"I do what I want to do. I don't ask nobody nothing." He glanced around. "Where's Inge?"

"Dancing. She starts movie work in the morning."

"You going out to watch?"

"Too early for me," I said. "I'll let her tell me about it later. Most of it's waiting around, I hear."

"Maybe we talk more tomorrow."

"Sure. Think about a price per key."

Shrugging, he got up and walked away, leaving the Dom Perignon on my table. With Cejas I had to strike a balance between overeagerness to make a deal and selecting the right deal, one I could afford. I had that kind of latitude because I wasn't working for an office confiscation quota. Manny might be but that wasn't our agreement. Whatever Cejas offered I could take, or walk away. I had to move our relationship into his line

72

of business, but there was no hurry, and I hadn't yet come across General Pedraza.

I sipped champagne, and after a while Raúl brought Inge back. "Hungry?" I asked.

"Not as hungry as Raúl. He wanted me to go to his room and make out. And we'd only been dancing a couple of minutes."

"Only normal," I remarked. "In his way Raúl was complimenting you. He figured not to make the offer would have been a sort of insult."

"How so?"

"You'd have thought he didn't find you attractive enough to want to go to bed with." I filled my glass and handed it to her. "Under the circumstances I should be the one taking offense. You're seen as my property—and using one's property without permission is a social infraction."

"Good God. You going to do anything about it?"

I shook my head. "As a *gringo* I'm supposed to be insensitive to such things, ignorant. So let's overlook it and repair to the buffet."

While we were filling our plates, Chandler Bates and Carla appeared. They surveyed the crowd, sniffed, and joined the buffet line. Carla waved at us and I waved back, but not enough to encourage them to join us. As we returned to our table Inge said, "So far, no one's bothered to tell me the movie's title."

"They may be trying to keep it a secret. *La Heroina Rebelde* translates two ways: The Rebel Heroine, or Rebellious Heroin. An in-joke, I guess, since drug money is bankrolling the flick."

"Do you think Chandler was really serious about a movie career for me?"

"At the moment he said so he was. But it was all a flight of fancy."

"From cocaine?"

"You noticed." As I helped her get seated, a slightly built youth strolled past. He was wearing black coral wristlets, a blush of rouge, and a kinkajou around his neck. The furry, long-tailed animal's eyes were closed. The youth's glinted damply in torchlight. His lips trembled and his expression was distraught. Doubtless someone had been unkind to him.

Watching him drift away, Inge said, "This is really a weird scene, Jack."

"Well, it's entertainment and drugs, and never the twain shall part." I cut into my stuffed lobster and concentrated on consuming it.

The rock combo gave way to the *mariachis* who had serenaded at Bates' penthouse luncheon. The three water-babies responded by plunging into the nearby pool where they began pulling off each other's skimpy bras.

73

Pool-side loungers got into the sporting spirit, and soon the water fun was at a crescendo of hilarity, with people being tossed in shrieking, and intimate garments floating around.

A muscular-looking man with a heavy, black mustache was standing beside Bates' table, yelling and thrusting a thick finger under the director's nose. Carla Santiago got up and came over to us. "God, it never ends," she said distractedly. "Don't know how much more I can take." She drank from Inge's glass and set it down. "I needed that."

"Is our boy being threatened?"

"What else? The gorilla is Fernando Aguila, the co-director—which means he interprets Chandler's directing into Spanish for this cast of mental cripples." She looked around disdainfully. "Playing grab-ass in the pool is their idea of sophistication."

"I take it there are artistic differences between Chandler and Aguila?"

"The word 'artistic' is lost on Ferdy. He wants gore and tits and heavy emoting. And he wants world release for the abortion." She gazed at Inge. "Getting an idea of what the movie business is like, behind the scenes?"

"Uh-huh," Inge said composedly.

"Then on location nothing should surprise you."

Aguila had gone away, leaving Chandler white-faced and shaken. Carla said, "I should comfort him now. Times like this he needs me." Heavily she got up and made her way back to the table.

I said, "I think they've played this scene before."

"Yes. I feel sorry for them both. Old, cast aside, nowhere to go."

"A glimpse of the future," I told her. "Plan yours accordingly."

She sipped champagne slowly. "I've messed up my life so far. From here on I'll be trying to get it together."

Aguila had joined the Cejas table. He seemed comfortable with the female on his lap who was feeding him nose candy from a tiny spoon. Elsewhere, some of the younger, less extravagant crowd were passing joints around; the oily scent of high-grade grass clung to the humid air. This could be a yuppie gathering on Russian Hill, I told myself. Except for the moon.

Most *norteños* never see the moon naked of city smog. Our moon hung over the horizon like a silver orb. Its brilliance lay a shimmering path all the way to the beach, and I could understand why aborigines had worshiped it. Toltec pyramids consecrated to the moon rivaled temples to the sun in grandeur.

Inge said, "Are you coming on location tomorrow?"

"You'll do fine without me. Besides, any action that could interest me

74

will be here, not in some dusty *barranca.* By the way, take insect repellent. Maximilian's cavalry is bound to draw plenty of flies."

WE FINISHED CEJAS' bottle, and when his pals began shooting at lights in the palm trees I decided it was time to leave. Their marksmanship was poor, but that could be because of liquor or coke. I was glad my plane was tethered out of range of their .45s. They might sink it just for chuckles.

Inge and I took turns in the shower and jacuzzi, and when we were lying in bed she murmured, "You don't find me attractive?"

"Of course I do."

"But you treat me as a sister, or a niece."

"That's how I've come to think of you. Besides, I'm your employer."

"I know," she said, "and I'm grateful for all you've done for me." She sighed. "Every girl dreams of the man she hopes will be her lover, her husband. I always visualized someone older than me, who was strong and intelligent. You're all those things, and handsome, too. I've come to depend on you, Jack, I don't need to tell you that."

"You're getting stabilized," I told her, "and you'll be able to handle things better than in the recent past. But you have to start believing in your own abilities. When you do, I think you'll be amazed at how much you can do with your life."

"I believe it because you say so. And if you want to make love with me, I just want you to know I wouldn't object."

"I'll remember," I said, and held her hand as I kissed her forehead. Still holding her hand I fell asleep.

BEFORE LEAVING IN the early morning, Inge closed the balcony blinds so that I could sleep on. About nine I got up and had breakfast on the balcony: fresh papaya with slices of pineapple and limes, *huevos rancheros,* rolls and coffee.

Offshore, beach boys were surf-sailing, water-skiers zipped across the bay, and on the beach a game of burro-polo was underway. Another day at a fashionable resort, I reflected, and began putting together an expense sheet for eventual submission to Manny Montijo.

Toward eleven the phone rang and Fructo Cejas said, "You want to talk business?"

"If you're ready."

"We'll have lunch at my house. Meet me in the lobby at noon."

I got my suitcase from the closet, unlocked it, and took out my MAC-10. Too bulky for wearing under my *guayabera.* I replaced it and weighed

75

the Beretta in my hand. The temptation was strong to go armed into the lion's den, but one of Cejas' guards might pat me down, and I was short of explanations. Regretfully I put back the Beretta and locked the suitcase. I set it in the closet and trapped each clasp with a hair. Inge's dresses hung nearby, and I wondered how her first day on location was going.

While shaving I remembered her bedtime overture and was glad I hadn't responded. Things were going well without sex, and emotional involvement might detour my judgment.

Considering the men I was dealing with, that could be fatal.

CEJAS' LIMOUSINE WAS an extended white Mercedes with privacy windows behind driver and guard, and a built-in bar. As the limo climbed past rocky outcroppings, I could glimpse the bay ringed with luxury hotels and cottages. Cejas' pleasure palace stood high on a precipice between PV and the airport. The surrounding wall was about twelve feet high, topped with rolled razor wire and glass shards set into cement. There was an electronic alarm system, and video-scanners covered grounds and building. The heavy, iron-grill gate was guarded outside by two soldiers, inside by a pair of gorillas who checked with Cejas before letting the driver turn up a broad, cobbled drive in front of the mansion.

A jacketed Indian opened the car door for Cejas, and bowed respectfully. Instead of going up the steps, Cejas beckoned to me, and I followed him down the slanting drive to a garage. He pressed a sequential lock, and the door rolled up and out of the way.

We went in.

There was a smell in the air that made my scalp prickle. Cejas switched on a light and said, "This is how we deal with enemies."

My gaze followed his to a ceiling girder. Hanging from it by chained wrists was what remained of Javier Madero.

# II

# EIGHT

**B**EFORE CLOTTING, BLOOD had drenched his shirt and pants from twenty or thirty stab wounds. His feet had been blowtorched, the stench of the blackened crusts had hit my nostrils moments before. Where his eyes had been gouged out, dark-red sockets remained, and bluish entrails bulged out of a long belly slash.

I hoped Madero had been unconscious long before the *coup de grace* that severed his throat. But I doubted it.

Nausea revolved my stomach, but I kept breakfast down.

Staring at the corpse with satisfaction, Cejas said, "Recognize him?"

"No," I lied.

"You interrupted his assassination attempt."

"Ah," I said, and turned away. "For that you killed him?"

"He was caught last night coming over the wall. With a gun."

"And the torture?"

"To find out if he was acting alone. In Jalisco we have a monopoly." He gestured at the corpse. "That is how we keep it."

I'd seen bodies more bestially tortured by the VC, but compared to this spectacle, Oriental torture was refined. "I get the point," I said, and stepped out of the garage past one of the gate guards who carried a Uzi across his back. Fresh air cleansed my nostrils, filled my lungs. Behind me, Cejas gave the guard orders in Spanish. "Pedrito, dismember the body with a chain saw. Weight each part separately, and drop them at least a mile offshore. Use the chain saw on the face. Understand?"

*"Sí, padrón."*

It would have been far better for Javier Madero, I thought, if I'd let

79

him be cut down in the hotel dining room, but I hadn't thought this far ahead. Who could have? I owed him a corpse or two.

Cejas came out and said, "Because we will do business together I wanted you to see how safe it is."

"I see. But I'm not sure I can handle lunch right now."

As we walked up the incline, he said, "He was a crazy man. In time he would have tried to kill you for protecting us. Think of it like that, *señor*."

We ascended marble steps and entered a large foyer, part of which was one end of a free-form pool that extended through a huge two-storied room and ended at a sunny patio. A patinaed fountain of a voluptuous, naked Diana tossed into the air water that glittered like countless diamonds before spattering into the crystal pool.

The thickly carpeted room was festooned with long, low sofas and antimacassars. A life-size painting hung across the far wall. In ultra-vivid colors it represented a naked female bullfighter facing a black bull whose pointed horn was dangerously near her unprotected crotch.

Below the painting stood a large, tiled bar, behind which a topless *artista* was mixing drinks for the luncheon group. I knew the men's names, but I let Cejas reintroduce me to Oscar Alarcón and Humberto Padilla. Lucho San Juan thrust out his free hand, "I got to t'ank you for w'at you done, *señor. Estoy muy agradecido.*"

Cejas said, "He says he's grateful."

"My pleasure," I lied. "Can I get a drink around here?"

"But of course." He snapped his fingers, and a naked *artista* materialized. "Añejo," I said, and watched her saunter to the bar, spike heels driving the long muscles in her legs. Cejas indicated a place for me to sit. It gave me a view of the patio where two nude *artistas* were sunning, while one floated at the sun-struck end of the pool.

Without their pancake makeup, the women looked less whorish and years younger. My drink arrived, and the *artista* retired to the far wall, out of earshot. I drank a jolt of the dark rum, hoping it would erase the vision of Madero's violated body that hung in my mind. Cejas said, "You want to make small buy? My *socios* and me, we agree to help you."

"What's the kilo price?"

"Twenty thousand U.S."

"Maybe on the far side of the border," I said, "but not in Mexico. Ten's my limit."

He shook his head. "I return your brave favor by asking only eighteen thousand a kilo."

80

"Twelve."

"How many you want?"

"This is a test run," I reminded him, "so I didn't bring much money."

"How much you bring?"

I smiled. "A hundred thousand—in *pesos.*"

"*Pesos?*" He frowned.

"Flying snow is risky enough. If I'm caught taking more than five grand out of the U.S., that's jail time, too. They haven't gotten around to barring the export of *pesos.*"

"Okay, I take your *pesos*, and you get the snow for fifteen. Six keys, ninety thousand dollars."

"Add another key for ten."

"Okay. Seven keys for five million *pesos.*" We shook hands on it, and I hoped Manny had that much in his office safe.

"Or," Cejas said, "I got a better proposition. Fly a full cargo across the border and keep seven keys for yourself."

"How far would I have to fly?"

"South of Bisbee."

"Arizona," I said musingly. "That's fifteen hundred miles over some very bad mountains. Three refueling stops."

"Same to Houston."

"I didn't say I was flying to Houston."

"Well, what do you say?"

"I'll sleep on it."

"Good. No more business today." He clapped loudly and the *artista* more or less came to attention. His partners got up and filed around the pool to a shaded portion of the patio where a chef and a helper presided over a buffet table no less lavish than yesterday's. Like trained dogs the females followed us along the buffet, Alarcón amusing himself by pinching bottoms and tweaking nipples until the victims squealed.

There was an almost tangible air of carnality and cruelty, and I wondered if the playmates knew about the brutalized corpse in the garage. I thought I could hear Pedrito working the chain saw, but it could have been my imagination.

We sat at a large round table, the ten of us, and my partner told me her name was Lupita. "I you gorl for now."

I had hoped to avoid close encounters, but as she ate with one hand she started working on my fly with the other. Cupping my hand, I whispered, *"Señorita* Lupita, do you have herpes?"

"'Erpees? How 'erpees? I no got 'erpees," she said indignantly.

"Too bad—I have," I said and shrugged helplessly.

Her active hand jerked away and she shrank from me. "Sorry," I said. "We could have made beautiful music."

"Not wit' me, *señor*. You try anudder gorl."

Sighing, I cracked a crab claw, dipped it into mustard sauce.

The girls took turns eating and serving us French wine, and between courses I looked over the balcony at the steep hillside below. Steps followed its contours down to a crescent beach. From it a pier extended into deepening water, and two boats were tied at the far end of the pier. One was a fifty-foot Bertram rigged for fishing, the other a formula Cigarette racer, designed to go eighty knots in a moderate sea and worth at least a quarter of a million dollars. With twelve-hundred horse it could outrun anything the U.S. Coast Guard had in the water. Only a chopper or a plane like my Seabee could surveil its thunderous run.

"Nice boats," I said to Cejas.

"You like fishing? We go fishing sometime."

"Fishing's not my bag," I told him. "The other boat's my style."

"You fly to Bisbee, you buy one like it."

"That's a thought," I said and let Lupita fill my wineglass.

I finessed dessert, settling for a cup of dark coffee boiled from toasted Mexican beans. It cleared my head and let me think about my obligations. I wasn't in PV for French cuisine and fine wines. The four *chingados* were my target, plus General Pedraza, if he ever appeared. That made me think of Sarita and wonder if she were toiling in the hot afternoon sun as the Rebel Heroine. And I wondered whether Inge was liking her first day's work before the cameras.

I saw movement below on the hillside, and made out Pedrito and the other inside guard lugging green plastic bags down the long staircase. I didn't want to think what the bags contained.

Lunch over, the men began stripping for fun in the pool. The girls went in first, and soon there was a good deal of laughing and splashing and phony shrieking. Before Cejas joined them he said, "Come in. Have a swim, Jack."

"Thanks, but I've got a bad head from all the wine. Can your driver take me back?"

"Okay. See you tomorrow." He slid into the pool and lunged for the nearest girl.

I glanced over the balcony and saw the two guards on the Cigarette. There was a hatch open and they were dropping the plastic bags inside. I wondered if both were going out on the funeral run.

Miguel, the limo driver, was hosing blood from the garage floor. He was whistling at his work, and didn't hear me when I went up to him. "Hotel," I said, and saw him jump. *"Señor* Fructo says you take me, okay?"

"Okay." He turned off the hose, dried his hands, and opened the limo door for me. As we headed down the drive I saw that the guards had left the Cigarette and were climbing back up the stairs. The foliage was thick, suggesting to me that the butchered Javier might have made his approach from the bay.

At the hotel desk there was a message with my key. Inge, I thought, until I read the typed words: *Call Penthouse D.*

From a house phone in the lobby I dialed and heard the sleepy voice of Sarita Roja. *"Qué?"*

"Jack Novak. Just got your message."

"I've been waiting so long I decided to take *siesta.* Where have you been?"

"Out to lunch," I said. "Aren't you working today?"

"I was, but the heat was frightful, so I left."

"Don't blame you. Also, the horseflies."

She laughed. "So you know about them. Yesterday you said you'd take me flying in your plane. I'm free, if you are."

"Let's do it." I didn't much feel like flying, but anything was better than thinking about Madero's bloody corpse.

SHE CAME DOWN in a little while, wearing dark glasses and a large sun hat, sapphire beach shorts, and Italian sandals. A large beach bag hung from one shoulder. There weren't many people in the lobby, but those around stared at her and murmured recognition..

We followed the shady fringe of the beach to the cove, where a boy with mask and fins was spearfishing from a *chalupa.* Sarita got him to take us out to the plane. I unlocked the cabin door and helped her in. Then I tipped the fisher-boy and got behind the controls. After I'd started the engine I ran slack in the anchor line and retrieved the hook from the sand bottom. Beside me, Sarita watched interestedly as I waggled the controls, let down flaps, and nosed into the breeze.

Before revving the engine, I said, "Any special place you want to go?"

"About thirty miles north, toward Mazatlán, there's a small island where we can swim."

Over the bay I gained altitude and took a heading at Mita Point.

We followed the rugged coastline for a quarter of an hour, and then she tugged my arm and pointed ahead. There, off the nose, was a tiny tear-shaped island, thick with palms and surrounded by white beach. Cupping her hands, she called, *"Isla Paraíso.* Paradise Island."

"That's its name?"

"It's the name I gave it. Once I made a movie there. I was supposed to be a Polynesian princess." She shook her head. "Always I'm filmed as something I'm not."

"That's an actor's trade. You made only one movie there?"

"The director saw some snakes. He was deathly afraid of them and said he'd never come back."

"What kind of snakes?"

*"Víboras, coralillos."* She shrugged. "Maybe others."

Vipers and coral snakes. I hated them, too.

I flew over and around the island looking for a place to come in where reefs wouldn't rip the hull. I found a good, wide channel, lowered flaps, and touched water a hundred yards offshore. As I taxied toward the beach she said, delightedly, "That was exciting. You fly as if you're part of the plane."

"When I'm flying," I told her, "I am." Then I gunned the engine and nosed onto soft sand.

She was first out, into calf-deep water, splashing onto the beach where she dropped her beach bag and sailed her broad-brimmed hat into the wind. The tide line was fringed with seaweed, dried kelp, and a scattering of driftwood. I carried the anchor ashore and sank it in the sand.

When I looked around, the child-woman was rolling over and over on the sand, flinging her arms coltishly, drumming her heels, and tossing handfuls of sand into the air. Abruptly she stopped and called, "God, but it's good to feel free. You don't know *how* wonderful it feels." On hands and knees she crawled back to her beach bag, opened it, and spread a colorful towel. Then she took out a pint bottle and tossed it to me. Tequila.

While I was opening it she ran up to the tree line and disappeared in the foliage. After a few moments she reappeared and flung something at me the size of a baseball. A lime, the largest I'd ever seen.

Pulling off jacket and shorts, she said, "Got a knife?"

"In the plane."

"Never mind. Let me have the lime." She cut around its circumference with her thumbnail and twisted the lime in half. I handed her the open bottle, she drank from it, and bit deeply into the lime. "No salt," she said, "but who cares?"

84

I swallowed warm liquor and sank my teeth into the tart lime.

"Feel better?" she asked. "I do."

I sat down beside her and pulled off my shoes and shirt. Her bikini looked like two pasties joined by thigh strings. Turning her back to me, she lifted her long hair and said, "Undo me."

I fumbled with the halter catch and finally freed it. The bra dropped across her thighs. She tossed it on her beach bag. Stretching back on the towel, she murmured, "I'm so glad we came, Jack. I was afraid I'd never come here again."

I had another swallow of tequila. It wasn't my favorite beverage, but the fresh lime juice helped a lot. I didn't want to stare at her breasts, but I couldn't help myself. They weren't rubbery-looking like the Indian girls'; rather, they looked full and soft, and infinitely inviting. Small, conical nipples showed she hadn't suckled a child, a presumption borne out by the flatness of her belly. Shading her eyes, she said, "Aren't you going to get some sun?"

"Well, I am," I said, and swallowed. I undid my nauseating buckle and dragged off my trousers, leaving only boxer shorts between me and nudity.

She laughed. "I believe you're bashful."

"I don't know you very well."

"You must be putting me on. C'mon." She grasped my hand, rose, and raced into the water. It seemed expected of me, so I followed. The tequila made blood pound inside my head, and when we were hip-deep in the water she plunged ahead and began stroking strongly. I dove shallowly and dolphined after her, wishing I'd worn a mask to better see the smooth coordination of her body.

Then, when the water was shoulder-deep, she stopped and lowered her legs to stand.

She screamed piercingly.

At first I thought a barracuda had slashed her legs, but I ducked under and saw she'd stepped on a sea urchin. Poisonous spines had broken off in her flesh, and already the creature was drifting away with the current. I grabbed Sarita around the chin and hauled her into shallow water where I could gather her shivering body in my arms and carry her onto the beach. She was moaning and shaking, white-lipped with pain, as I lowered her face down on the sand. Bending back her leg, I saw three punctures in the arch of her foot, broken spines barely protruding above the skin. "Hold on," I said, "try not to move." Baring my teeth, I used them like tweezers to draw out the spines, pulling very carefully until each one was clear of her flesh. Then I sucked the punctures, and when blood began to ooze I spat it out and went to the blanket where we'd left the lime.

With the sole of her foot horizontal I squeezed a puddle of lime juice onto her skin, let it soak for a few moments, and began working it in. More lime juice, more gentle massage until, finally, she gasped, "That's better. God, that was awful pain. What happened? What did you do?"

Keeping her foot horizontal, I showed her the thin brown spines, and explained the medicinal value of lime juice against the toxins of sea urchins and jellyfish. Then I carried over the tequila bottle and told her to drink. It brought color to her face and lips, and I said, "You can turn over now."

As she did she said, "If you hadn't been with me, I think I would have died out there. The pain was worse than the worst cramp I've ever had."

"Well, we got out the spines and poison early, neutralized it with the juice. How do you feel?"

"Better. Much, much better. My foot tingles but almost all the pain is gone." She sat up, looked at me, and smiled impishly. Until then I hadn't realized my shorts had vanished in the water. Well, it was in a good cause.

She passed me the bottle, and as I drank she said, "I think I can make it to the towel—with your help."

So, with one arm over my shoulder, she hopped to the towel before lowering her injured foot. I said, "Meat tenderizer is an even better antidote. I keep a bottle in the plane, but I didn't want to waste time getting it."

Facing me she put her hands around my neck and drew me close. Her breasts cushioned my chest as she kissed me open-mouthed. I began to respond, and with one hand she freed the bikini and pressed against me. "You do everything just right, don't you, Jack?" she murmured.

"I try," I managed, dropped onto the towel and drew her down. Wordlessly we kissed and stroked and touched each other's bodies until she lay fully back and took me between her parted loins.

As passion overwhelmed me, I wanted to think that we were the first two humans ever to make love on Paradise Island's sands.


HEAT SLATHERED OUR bodies with perspiration. After a while we got up and walked toward the shade of a large ceiba tree. As she moved ahead of me, I thought that, like everything else about Sarita, her buns were spectacular. Firm and round. I tweaked one and she snapped, "Stop it!" Turning, she said, "Sorry, Jack, but Gil's always trying something like that." She rubbed her haunch. "I told him if he didn't keep his hands off me I'd cut off his balls."

"Sorry. It was an oafish way of expressing admiration."

Her glance softened. "One reason I've been so strongly attracted to you is that you're so totally unlike my . . . protector." Kneeling, she spread our towel on a gentle sandy slope and lay back. I joined her, feeling breeze on my body. The shade dropped the heat at least twenty degrees. While we were making love, understandably, I hadn't noticed the sun's direct rays.

Languidly, she said, "I know nothing about you, *querido*. Will you tell me about your life?"

Taking her hand, I said, "I was born poor, in Chicago. Joined the Navy, did a tour in Vietnam, and decided to look around for easier ways to get rich."

"And have you? Are you rich enough?"

"No one is," I said. "I can afford to indulge myself now and then, but money spent has to be replaced."

"Which is why you're involved with the Gang of Four."

"The Cejas group? Try not to think too badly of me." I kissed her warm cheek.

"Jack, they're dangerous men, deadly. If you have money, they'll kill you for it. If you haven't, they'll kill you anyway." She stroked the sensitive part under my arm until I shivered. "The General is said to be the deadliest of all, because he has soldiers do his killing for him." Her mouth twisted. "So far I've been able to keep him out of my bed, but I'm afraid of him, Jack. I want to be rid of him—God, how much I want my freedom— but if I left, he'd only drag me back, then *macho* as he likes to think he is, he'd rape me, perhaps kill me. You can't understand the kind of power he has."

"I've seen his palace, off the airport road."

"Then maybe you get an idea of what I mean." Turning, she moved her thighs against me. "No more talk of *El General.*"

"What about you?"

"Me?" Her gaze moved away. "I'm the bastard daughter of a woman who worked in a sweatshop and became a whore when she lost her job. For money she let men play with me, finger me, when I was only ten. The worst part is any of them could have been my father."

"But you're educated, and you speak perfect English."

"It wasn't always so perfect. Fortunately, I was a good student, and Mexican border schools are better than the hovels you find in the interior.

My playmates spoke English, and I learned fast. I learned . . . many things in Nogales."

"I admire you," I said. "Deeply. Believe me, I do."

"Ah, Jack, you said you were born poor, in a big city. I was born in a small village that had a priest and no doctor. In poverty you only read about these days. Like Africa, I guess."

"How did you get into motion pictures?"

She smiled. "If you really want to know, an American movie was being shot in Nogales—part of it. The casting director came to my school and asked for girls who could speak English. I was one of four he selected, and when we got on location I was given the better part." She shook her head. "From then on the story is trite. Two nights later I let him make love to me. He took me to Hollywood and cast me in a couple of cheapies, but I got screen credits, and when I'd saved enough money, I left and went to Churubusco Studios, near Mexico City. There, they made me what I am today." She stretched back. "Story of my life."

Bending over, I kissed her lips lightly. Her tongue emerged and traced mine until I got that melting feeling. We caressed, desire flooded us, and soon we were making love again.

TIDE WAS EBBING. The plane tugged its line. We were looking around for our clothes when Sarita said, "I hope we'll come here again."

"We will."

"It's all been . . . miraculous for me. Do you feel the same?"

"Wonderful," I said. "Perfect," and kissed the nape of her neck.

She murmured, "When it's safe, will you sleep with me?"

"Nothing I'd rather do."

We carried our shoes through the shallow water, and Sarita boarded the plane. I recovered the anchor, coiled the line, and shoved the hull into deeper water. Then I climbed into my seat and went through preflight check. Before I started the engine I heard her murmur, *"Adiós, mi isla."*

The breeze had shifted, and there were gentle swells off the island. I took advantage of them to lift onto the hull step and bounce into the air, noticing Sarita's eyes flash with enjoyment.

At four thousand I found a tailwind and turned south toward Puerto Vallarta. Sarita's face was tranquil, and I guessed that her foot pain was gone.

As we neared the port I saw a good-sized yacht coming into a slip. Sea-going size, it was more than a hundred feet long.

Sarita noticed it and said, "Reminds me, I have to go to a yacht party this evening. I'd like you to come, Jack. You and Inge, of course."

"Maybe later," I told her. "What yacht is that?"

"It belongs to a friend of Gil's. It's called the *Bal Musette.*"

# NINE

**W**HEN I WENT into my suite, Inge was asleep on the bed. I showered off body sand and relaxed in the jacuzzi. She was still sleeping. The sun was almost below the bay horizon, the hotel beach nearly deserted, and the air so still that I could hear parakeets bickering among the palms.

I still felt an inner glow from my hours with Sarita, but it diminished when I began to think about the *Bal Musette.* An agent named Ed Diaz had been killed investigating it, and the names of Ramón Calixto, Faustino Perez, and Pedro Alonso had long been familiar to me. I was eager to join the party and see the *chingados* in the flesh, but first there was another score to settle.

Kneeling beside my suitcase, I inspected the lock traps. Both hairs were undisturbed, so I got out the MAC-10 and found a plastic bag among Inge's things to wrap it in. I emptied a much larger shopping bag, laid the waterproofed machine pistol on the bottom, covering it with the swim fins and snorkel mask I'd brought from the plane. Over them I placed a towel and swim briefs, tucked in the submersible wrist compass, and was ready to go.

I left a note for Inge, telling her we were expected for a yacht party, and if she woke before eleven, to dress and wait for my call.

A taxi took me up the road to within a few hundred yards of Fructo Cejas' private beach, where I got out. After the taxi drove off, I made my way slowly and carefully down the rocky slope until I was on the dark beach.

I undressed and pulled on briefs, walked into the water, and got into my fins and mask. The bag containing my MAC-10 was held by a lanyard around my neck.

On the surface, I stroked around a point of land whose far side formed Cejas' cove. The end of his pier showed enough light that I could take a compass heading, and both the Bertram and the Cigarette were there.

I breaststroked toward them in an arc that kept me beyond the lighted radius, and then I dove deep and swam by compass toward the Cigarette's stern. My head almost bumped the rudder when I surfaced, and for a while I clung to the dive platform, listening.

It was possible that the bagged sections of Javier's body had been dumped while I was on Paradise Island, but that kind of work was usually accomplished after dark. I hoped Pedrito wasn't going to wait too long.

So I crawled up over the stern transom and stowed my fins under a pile of life-preserver cushions before I unlimbered my machine pistol. I dried my soles on shag carpet before easing forward into the forepeak stowage. The bow locker contained sailcloth fenders, flags, emergency gasoline, and an inflatable raft. I closed the locker door, made myself comfortable against the bundled raft, and cocked the MAC-10.

The boat's motion had a lulling effect, and I would have dozed off but for occasional bumping against the pier. Machine pistol across my thighs, I waited.

The night was silent except for the gentle lapping of water against the hull, as the tide returned.

Time passed.

At least an hour went by before I heard approaching voices, the scraping of shoes on the pier. I had counted on Pedrito being alone, but now it seemed there would be two.

Both men dropped heavily into the boat. In Spanish, Humberto Padilla's voice said, "I should be heading for the party, instead, I have to go with you on this shitty job. Next time I'll tell Fructo to clean up his own fucking mess. Lucho, too."

"Well, that's Fructo," Pedrito said, and started the blower system.

While the engine compartment was being ventilated of fumes, Padilla said, "I hope this isn't going to take long. How far out we have to go?"

"Fructo said at least a mile. Any less, and current brings the bags into the bay."

"*Mierda.* Is there a bottle aboard?"

"Not unless there's one down in that locker."

Before Padilla descended the short ladder, I had scrambled up the pile of gear, wedging as far into the narrow forepeak as I could. The locker door opened and I saw Padilla's hand groping around. "Nothing here," he called. "Got a flashlight?"

"Sorry. I must have forgot."

*"Carajo,"* Padilla snarled, and slammed the door shut.

I wiped wetness from my forehead and eased down to where I'd been. The engines started thunderously, then settled into a powerful burble as Pedrito backed from the pier. He swung the boat over into a sharp turn, hit the throttles, and the Cigarette leaped and reared like a bronco. The bow stood so high out of the water that gear began to shift and roll against my back. Air scoops forced fresh air into the locker as the high-powered boat hurtled into the night.

It didn't take long to clear the bay. I could feel rougher water pounding the keel, and soon Pedrito throttled back and pointed the bow into the current. Then he idled down and slid the clutches into neutral. "Far enough," I heard him say. "Let's get it over with."

I could hear them moving aft toward the closed hatch that Pedrito had filled at midday. Gripping the machine pistol, I opened the locker door and heard the hatch creak open.

I climbed onto the wide seat and shoved the MAC-10 over its back. Pedrito was kneeling and groping in the hatch while Padilla, in white Bermudas, bent over, ready to help unload.

Sighting on them, I called, *"Alto! Manos arriba!"*

Padilla whirled and yelled, "The *gringo!"* He wasn't armed, but Pedrito was, and while he was grabbing for his Uzi I squeezed off a burst of three. The bullets caught him on the chest, slamming him against the side of the hatch. Padilla tried to snatch up the Uzi, but two shots in the belly shoved him back and down. He doubled over, hands pressing and clawing his belly, cursing and yelling in pain as blood came through his fingers and spread over his white shorts. With prompt surgical attention both men might survive, but an ER was far distant, and I had the active gun.

I walked toward them and saw Pedrito still trying to unsling his submachine gun. He was sitting on the plastic bundles, staring at me. Hatred in his eyes, he grated, "Fuck you, *gringo.*"

"Fuck yourself," I said and blew off the top of his head.

Covering Padilla, I said, "I didn't know Javier Madero, but whatever he was, he was a better man than you."

"I didn't kill him," he groaned. "Lucho and Pedrito tortured him. Fructo cut his throat."

"I'll remember that," I said.

"Don't kill me," he begged. "I'll give you anything you want."

"I have everything I want," I told him and shot him through chest and throat. Breath whistled as he fell sideways.

I toed his body into the hatch atop Pedrito's and went forward.

From the locker I dragged out the emergency raft, then the can of gasoline. I unscrewed the top and sprinkled the bodies and bundles. Then I closed the heavy hatch top and opened the engine compartment. The twin V-8 engines idled smoothly as I lowered the open can onto a greasy ledge. A wave bounce should topple it. I closed the compartment, retrieved my swim fins, and rewrapped the MAC-10 in its plastic bag. Then I unrolled the two-man raft, laid it athwart the gunwale, and pulled out its drogue to slow the drifting.

After a final look around I went to the console, jammed the wheel with a seat cushion, and shoved the throttles forward. The response almost staggered me as the stern bit in with a *whoosh*. I jerked the toggle of the raft's air bottle and pulled the billowing raft overboard as I dropped over the side.

Mask on, I breathed through the snorkle and stroked to the inflated raft. Climbing over the smooth, cylindrical side, I could hear the Cigarette roaring toward open sea, but all I could make out was its phosphorescent rooster-tail wake.

I unclamped the two small oars and fitted them in the oarlocks before hoisting the nylon sail. Until breeze filled it, I bobbed around like Jim Hawkins in his coracle. Then came a steady onshore push, and I untied the drogue.

Over the town of Puerto Vallarta, passing clouds gave off a yellow glow. The bay's long crescent was a necklace of sparkling light. I felt tired from playing prosecutor, judge, and executioner all in one day, but perhaps Javier was happier in the Great Beyond.

Across the water a loud detonation reverberated, and I saw flames rocket into the western sky. So long, Humberto, I said half-aloud. *Adiós,* little Pedro. I settled back while wind, tide, and current bore my raft toward shore.

IT WAS ABOUT ten-thirty when I dragged into the room. The bed was empty, and at first I thought Inge had gone, then I saw her at the balcony table, dressed, coiffed, and ready to go. Turning to me, she said, "I've been watching the sea, Jack. So quiet and peaceful . . . I almost fell asleep again. But you—you look sort of wasted."

"That's a good description of how I feel." I carried mask and fins into the closet and locked up my MAC-10.

"Where have you been?" she called.

"Doing something foolish—swimming at night—alone."

"It does sound dangerous." Rising, she came toward me.

"How was your day?"

"Well . . . mixed. Like you said, a lot of standing around and waiting, *and* flies, *and* mosquitoes, *and* lizards—"

"Iguanas," I said, "which reminds me, *Night of the Iguana* was filmed around here—Mismaloya."

"Oh, the Richard Burton thing. My makeup kept melting, but I was in two scenes. And my wig was like a furnace. Things can only get better."

"Let's hope," I said, and took a quick shower.

WE TAXIED TO the port and walked down to the slip where the *Bal Musette* had tied up. The yacht was festooned with lights, and at the gangway, a couple of gorillas were checking names against the guest list. Because we were late arrivals they looked us over carefully before letting us on board.

There was loud music and too many people. Waiters with drink trays forced their way through the crush of moving bodies. It looked as though half of PV had been invited to join the merrymaking.

I grabbed two glasses of champagne from a stalled waiter and gave one to Inge. The music came from the fantail where a group of movers and shakers were bumping elbows and fannies in what looked more like a gang battle than a civilized dance. Taking Inge's arm, I drew her into the salon where an oval buffet table offered caviar and the usual PV assortment of fresh seafood and other delicacies, including Scotch grouse and Iceland salmon—specially flown in, I assumed. I was hungry from recent exertion, and Inge said she hadn't eaten since the outdoor picnic lunch. Plates in hand we began loading them, when Carla appeared and bussed us both. "My dears," she chortled, "so late, so naughty," and shook a finger in mock reproof. "Ah, were I young again, I'd gladly choose the tranquility of a romantic bedchamber over the hurly-burly of a chaise longue."

"Me, too," Inge said, and wrinkled her nose. "I guess."

"Ah," Carla sighed, "so much is wasted on the young. So much of life, of *living*. And how was your day on location, dear?"

"Hot," Inge replied, "and tiring."

"Nevertheless, Chandler reports you did well, conducted yourself with dignity and aplomb. Congratulations. He's convinced you have a great future as a blonde ingenue."

I said, "We went over that yesterday, but I figured it was only coke chatter."

Her face sagged into wattles. "Still, it's fun to dream," she murmured, then recovering the mood, she said airily, "Isn't this a splendid gathering? Jet-setters, local officials, and movie people. Just like old times." She leaned forward and whispered, "Sarita told us you were both coming. I must say she's taken to you young strangers. And for Inge, it's always helpful to have an influential friend in the business." She snatched a drink from a waiter's tray and knocked it back. This was an old campaigner, liquor a trusted friend. Peering around, she said, "Have you seen Humberto?"

Inge said, "Humberto?"

"Fructo's . . . partner. Humberto Padilla."

I shrugged. "Not since lunch. Why?"

"Fructo's concerned, said he left early to come here but hasn't arrived."

"Beats me," I said. "Maybe Bert got waylaid by a trim ankle and a twinkling eye."

She pushed me playfully. "Laid? Laid? You said *laid?*" she shrilled. "Massa Rhett, yo' sho'nuf *is* the one." Another shove almost spilled my plate.

Inge had managed to get down a couple of mouthfuls, and said, "Jack, can't we find a table? I'm dead on my feet."

"You poor child, I've been running on and on. But . . . you *have* met the guest of honor?" Carla asked.

"Who's that?"

"Why, Gil—General Pedraza. He's holding court with his prize possession." Blowing us kisses, she lurched off.

"That should be interesting," Inge remarked. "Let's go see the billionaire general."

"My stomach can't wait, the general can." I led her from the salon toward the foredeck, found a small table and chairs. As we sat down I noticed a couple in the shadows, chewing each other's faces like gouramis. Tonight, everyone was hungry. I attacked my food and felt better almost at once. There were few sensations I enjoyed more than a protein rush. Gnawing a king crab leg, Inge said, "Thanks to you I'm eating better than I have in years." She placed the empty shell on her plate and stared at me. "Who invited us, anyway?"

"Sarita Rojas thought you might enjoy the scene."

"That's better. I thought it was probably Cejas."

"Why?"

96

"He seems so fond of you. And you lunched with him, didn't you?"

"Oh, that. He wanted to show off Xanadu. And he's not 'fond' of me. It was a business lunch."

Fernando Aguila came up then and asked Inge to dance. She glanced at me. I nodded and took her half-empty plate. Not much could happen in that crowd, I thought. If you died dancing you couldn't fall down.

Something hurtled past the railing and plunged into the water. I glanced up and saw two of the Mexican water-babies in the rigging. They wore briefs and nothing else. One jumped outward, soared, and jacknifed into the water. A few observers clapped, and I thought that the kids worked hard for, apparently, very little. The third did a floating swan, striking the water like Mirador divers in Acapulco, but to much less applause.

After finishing my plate I decided coffee would help brighten my mind, and went back to the salon. Fructo Cejas spotted me and came over. *"Buenas tardes,"* he said. "You brought *Señorita* Inge?"

"Actually, she brought me. Her invitation." I took coffee and sipped it black. "Quite an affair."

He looked around. "Have you seen Padilla?"

"Not since lunch. Carla Santiago asked me earlier. Is he missing?"

He nodded. "He wanted a ride around the bay in my speedboat. Humberto hasn't returned."

"Did you notify the Coast Guard?"

"They don't like to go out after dark."

"In the morning I can take up my plane, look around."

"Good idea. Come and meet our general."

Docilely, I followed him to the deck below and along a companionway into what looked like a large library. Seated among a lot of floral displays was Sarita Rojas, dressed in a primly ruffled blouse and long, black skirt. Beside her sat a man in a tailored uniform that showed a lot of gold ornamentation and three rows of ribbons. Noncombat awards, since Mexico hadn't fought a war in more than a century. I bowed to Sarita, said, *"Señorita,"* and she gave me her hand for a moment, face impassive.

Cejas said, "And this is General Pedraza, military commander of our State of Jalisco. General, *Señor* Jack Novak." As we shook hands, Cejas murmured to me, "He speaks some English."

"General, pleasure to be here."

"Equal. Glad you come."

Sarita looked at me with distaste. Stepping back, I saw that Pedraza's eyes were dark, and his brown face, while not handsome, was strongly masculine.

Standing around the paneled room, drinks in hand, were others of the General's coterie. Alarcón and Lucho San Juan nodded at me, and I wondered if they were as worried about Padilla's nonappearance as Cejas was. The Gang of Four now totaled Three.

Three too many.

Cejas guided me over to the men standing beside his partners and introduced me to Ramón Calixto, Pedro Alonso, and Faustino Perez. All spoke English. Calixto said the yacht was his, and I congratulated him. Perez gestured at a plump man and said he was the deputy governor of Jalisco. The DG was talking with a uniformed man who, Perez said, was the state's police chief. "So, you see, we got important people on board."

"Plus a lot of interesting movie folks."

"Yeah."

Alonso said, "You here for pleasure?"

"Uh-huh. My business is pleasure."

He gave me a sly grin. "Me, too." His was the only question asked me, and I didn't ask them anything. Then, from behind, a man lurched against me, and I felt the hard outline of a weapon under his *guayabera*. He was short and muscular, and his face wore a heavy beard. He stared at me as though the bump was my fault, so I shrugged and said, "Sorry, *amigo*."

The man turned and said, in Spanish, "What's the *gringo* doing here? I don't like *yanquis*. I kill *yanquis*."

Cejas appeared at his side. "This is a business friend. He did us a big favor, so behave yourself, Enrique."

The *barbudo* glared at me. "Okay," he grunted, and staggered away, spilling liquor from his glass.

Cejas said, "Do you ever hear of Comandante Enrique?"

"No."

"He's Guatemalan. Was a student leader, now he leads guerrillas against the government."

"A real, live revolutionary."

"One who enjoys capitalist things." Lowering his voice, Cejas said, "Enrique controls mountain territory where poppies grow." He winked and I winked back. "Got it," I said.

"Guatemala is much closer to Mexico than Colombia, and anyone can cross the frontier without trouble. We send him guns for poppy juice. The more territory he controls, the more poppies."

"I get the idea," I told him. "Brilliant. Who'd have thought it?"

Cejas tapped his head. "Me."

A guard came up to him and whispered in his ear. Cejas frowned, said, "Bad news," and followed the guard from the room. I wanted to talk with Sarita, but she was speaking with Fernando Aguila. Where was Inge?

I walked back along the companionway and went up on the weather deck. I heard a woman cry out, so I walked quickly to where I had eaten dinner. Inge was struggling with Enrique, who was pawing her breasts and trying to drag her dress above her hips. She spat in his face, and he shoved her away, cursing.

"That's enough," I said, and the *barbudo* turned and squinted at me. He was drunk, but not too drunk to whip out his pistol and wave it at me.

Inge screamed.

# TEN

I DON'T LIKE *YANQUIS,*" he snarled. "I kill *yanquis.*"
I was moving toward him, staring at the gun. "Not this one," I said, and kicked his gun wrist. The pistol arced outward and fell into the water. Comandante Enrique blinked, lowered his head, and charged. I kneed his face, and when he snapped upright, holding his broken nose and howling, I kicked him in the crotch.

That doubled him over again, so I worked him to the rail, got behind his body, and set my knee at the base of his spine. His legs straightened, and I levered him over the railing, saw a big splash, the flare of his white *guayabera,* then bubbles.

From the yardarm, all three water-babies dropped into the water and went down for him like pearl divers. Leaving the *barbudo* to experienced hands, I took Inge's arm. "Time to go."

Her body was shaking. Her neckline was torn and the skirt seam split. She mopped at her eyes with a napkin. "God, I thought he was going to rape me. Then I thought he was going to kill you."

"Sober, he may be a charming fellow, but drunk he's just another pig." I guided her to the gangway, and we walked down the pier to a column of taxis.

"Castillo Real," I told the driver, and helped her in. As the engine started I patted her hand. "Thanks for coming. Early call tomorrow?"

"Yes." She was regaining composure. "I hope it's not so hot on location."

"Maybe it will rain."

DURING THE NIGHT it did. Thunder woke me from a shallow sleep, and when I couldn't drop back I went out to the balcony and let rain splash

101

on my face. Wet palm fronds glinted like rows of bayonets, reminding me of arms for Enrique.

An interesting connection, I mused. Raw opium for weapons. One way to finance a revolution, and the poor monkeys who tapped the poppies and did the fighting never knew the larger picture. Eventually, the Gang of Three would ponder the advantages of having more than the state of Jalisco at their disposal and start slavering over the prospect of controlling an entire nation—Guatemala. Land of the long-tailed *quetzal.*

South of the border, it seemed, almost anything was possible.

And there was something I'd left undone.

I pulled on pants and a *guayabera,* slipped into *huaraches,* and went down to the lobby. Past the boutiques there was a pay phone, and with tinkling coins I managed to rouse the *larga distancia* operator. She connected me to Montijo's room at the Guadalajara Sheraton, and by luck he was awake and attentive.

"I need five million p's in a hurry."

"Five . . . you *loco?*"

"It's buy money," I told him. "I may not have to pass it, but I need it to show. I'd have called earlier, but it's been a day so busy you wouldn't believe. Among other things, the Gang of Four is minus one."

"Yeah? Who?"

"Bert got revoked. Unexpectedly."

"You implicated?"

"Not likely. I've been asked to land four hundred keys near Bisbee. What's our coverage there?"

"Loose."

"Well?"

"You mean, should you? I'll have to make inquiries—if you know what I mean."

"All too well," I said, remembering prolonged delays when I needed fast decisions. "I need word *pronto.*"

"Do my best. At minimum I'll give you a local contact."

"Just do it soon." I left the phone hoping his wasn't tapped. Near the elevators I heard the clicking of heels and saw Sarita striding toward the desk. Her key was ready before she got there, she smiled thanks to the clerk, turned, and saw me. Her expression softened slightly, as did the rhythm of her walk. As any *caballero* would, I held the elevator door open until she entered. After it slid shut she said, "Jack, I've had a rotten evening, and I need to talk."

"What about Gil?"

"Too drunk to walk, so he's staying on the yacht." She pressed fingers to her lips, transferred the silent kiss to mine. "Penthouse D. I'll leave the door open."

She left the elevator and walked off in the provocative, sinuous sway Latin women affect when they want attention. She already had mine.

I rode down to the eighth floor, stepped out, and let the elevator go. I pressed the up button and waited. This car I rode back to the penthouse level and went quietly down the carpeted corridor. Her door was unlocked, the foyer dark. I went in and locked the door.

There was no light anywhere. Only a few stars winking over the bay that I could see beyond the open balcony door. I went through it and looked around. The first thing I saw was starlight reflecting from her eyes, then the light contour of her body in the pool. She was sitting on one of the steps, submerged to her shoulders. I said, "It's stopped raining, but you're all wet."

"I like it this way. Bar's over there. You might fetch us a Dom."

There were about ten bottles of champagne in the refrigerator. I selected the middle one and carried it poolside. Using both thumbs, I popped the cork and spilled some of the fizzle on her upturned face. She licked it from her lips.

I gave her the bottle while I undressed, and she said, "This is delicious. The last bottle we shared was tequila."

"How well I remember. How's the foot?"

"You have to kiss it to make it well." She lifted it above the water. I said, "Any other hurts?"

"Plenty."

I bent over, kissed the sole of her foot, and upended her. She bobbed up thrashing and laughing, grabbed my ankle and pulled me in. The water was air temperature, but her lips were fire. Her breasts rubbed against me, and I was ready. But she handed me the bottle. "Drink first, play later."

I drank. Cold and delicious. I quaffed again and set the bottle on the pool rim. Hands circling my neck, leaning back so that her head touched the water, she said, "I wish I'd seen you beat up Comandante Enrique."

"That? Prelims on Amateur Night."

Her thighs scissored my hips. "Is there no way you can accept a compliment gracefully? You're so self-confident I'd think you arrogant— if I didn't know you."

"It's a trait useful in my trade."

"Whatever it is. Oh, God, *Jack!*" she moaned as her loins made life's basic connection. I drew her torso upright and kissed her lips. Her arms tightened around my shoulders. "I'm ready," she whispered, "whenever you are."

So we made love in the water, slowly and easily, and the surface hardly rippled. Overhead, clouds had moved on and stars were bright pinholes in the indigo sky. We hugged and caressed and the champagne refreshed us, and after a while Sarita observed that life was supposed to come from water—the sea. I said, "Do you want children?"

"I'd love to, but"—her features set. "At eighteen I had an abortion . . . infection set in and, well, I can't ever conceive."

"I'm sorry," I said, and held her very close.

After a while she said, "You're a sensitive man, something I don't expect in a drug dealer."

"You're a sensitive woman, something one doesn't expect in a star of the Technicolor screen."

"I can't ever show it," she said. "If I did, I'd be lost."

Geckos chirped, and I saw the little lizards on the balcony railing. They scurried around, biting each other's tails, and making whirring noises. Not unlike my recent life, I thought, and kissed the beautiful woman in my arms. Presently we moved apart and Sarita said, "Why don't you bring a fresh bottle to the bedroom? She rose from the pool, water dripping from her slim, molded flanks, tossed me a huge towel, and wrapped another around herself. I plucked another bottle from the fridge, placed it in the bedroom, then joined her in the shower. We soaped each other's body, tickling and laughing and having fun, and afterward I toweled her hair reasonably dry and chased her onto the bed.

We made love again, and Sarita fell asleep beside me. I dozed for a while, but remembered that she had an early-morning wardrobe call. I didn't want to be around when her maid came in to wake her, so after kissing her I left and dressed beside the pool. I stacked the first empty bottle behind the bar and walked to the door.

Training and experience had taught me to open doors quietly and slowly. I glanced right and left along the corridor, and saw the elevator door open. From it came Oscar Alarcón and Fructo Cejas. Between them, half-walking, half-stumbling, was General Pedraza.

No way I could bolt without being seen—and more than Sarita's reputation was at stake. My life was in the balance.

I backed away fast, turned, and sped to the balcony. Looking over, I saw the ninth-floor balcony below. Only one way to go. I got over the railing, squatted on the ledge, and gripped the vertical bars.

With my back to the beach, I lowered myself until I was hanging in space. It was quiet there, so quiet I heard the hall door open. The three men came in, talking. Light flooded the suite. Time to go.

I began swinging in and out like a pendulum until I thought I had a fair chance of landing on the balcony below. I swung again for momentum, and let go.

My body slanted inward and barely cleared the lower railing. Knees bent, I hit on my heels and took the rest of the impact in a forward roll.

With a glance at the couple asleep in the bed, I got up fast and sprinted across the bedroom. I raked off the snub chain, opened the door, and found the corridor empty. I went quickly down to my own door, unlocked it, and slipped inside, heart pounding.

Inge slept soundly. I undressed and got under the sheets. Moonlight slanted through the balcony door, and I wondered what was going on upstairs. Pedraza had his own bedroom, but drunk as he was he might flounder into Sarita's. She could take care of herself, but if suddenly wakened, she might speak the wrong name.

For me, that would be a menacing mistake.

It took awhile for adrenalin to drain from my bloodstream, but finally I fell asleep.

SUNLIGHT FILLED THE room. The phone was ringing. I grabbed for it and noticed the table clock. Eleven-twelve. "Yes?"

"Porter's desk," a man's voice said. "Can I send up your bag?"

"My . . . bag?" I wasn't yet functioning.

"Yes, it's—"

"Okay, sure. Send it up."

I draped a towel around my middle, and when the buzzer sounded I opened the door as far as the snub chain allowed. A smiling bellhop stood there, holding a suitcase.

I opened the door, took the bag, and tipped him. Then I carried the suitcase to the nearest table. Both clasps were locked so I broke them with a knife and saw more Mexican currency than I'd ever seen. Good for Manny, I thought. Next time we met I'd sign a receipt. I transferred the money to one of Inge's empty bags, locked it, and called room service.

While I was showering, breakfast arrived. I ate slowly, reviewing yesterday's events. The phone rang, and I heard Sarita's voice. "Are you all right?"

"I'm perfect. Where are you?"

105

"Between scenes. In the make-up trailer where it's cool. I'm glad you got home . . . safely."

"Me, too. I had about ten seconds to manage it."

"You must tell me about it later. Frankly, I was scared to death."

"Don't be. If I went out there, would I be allowed on the set?"

"I'm sure there's no problem—Inge's here after all. And there's a rumor about one of your friends."

"Which one?"

"Padilla. Apparently he went out in Fructo's boat, and it blew up."

"That's why I prefer sailing. Stink-pots are dangerous."

She laughed. "That's what you call motor boats?"

"It's what blue-water sailors call them. And Padilla is nothing to me."

"Nor me. I'll be back about four—if you're interested."

"I just ate, but I'm hungry again."

"We'll see. Oh, have to go. Goodbye."

"Goodbye," I said, but the line was already dead.

She was something, I reflected. One of the most beautiful and intelligent females I'd ever had the good fortune to know. Comparing her and Melody wasn't fair. Sarita was thirty and sterile. Melody, nineteen and dangerously fertile. Melody was in Europe. Sarita was here—with me. But after the operation ended, I wondered if I'd ever see her again.

The telephone rang, and I heard Cejas' voice. He said, "You busy? I need to see you, talk."

"Where are you?"

"Penthouse."

"I'll come up shortly."

Again, I considered strapping on the Beretta, but I wasn't expecting trouble. So I finished dressing and went to Cejas' suite.

A guard opened the door, and when I went in he patted me down, then gestured at the sitting room. General Pedraza was in a chair drinking what looked like black coffee, and Cejas sat on a nearby sofa. He had a .45 in one hand. Looking up, he twirled it and sighted at me. "Come here," he ordered. "Where were you last night?"

# ELEVEN

"WHAT TIME?"

"After you left the yacht. After you almost killed the Comandante." He glanced at Pedraza, who guffawed.

"Put away the piece, and maybe I'll tell you."

"Just kidding."

"If you shot me, it wouldn't be accidental. I saw you blasting those beach lights the other night."

He nodded appreciatively and laid down the .45. "Well?"

"Not that it's any of your fucking business, I went into town."

"Where?"

I remembered overhearing some late party plans on the yacht. "Capricio's. A disco."

"I know. What other place?"

"Mogambo's."

"Dancing with Inge?"

"No. Your Comandante pal scared her badly. She went to bed, but I wanted a little action." I looked at Pedraza, then back at Cejas. "If you were my priest, I might confess. What's your problem, Fructo? Mad because I busted up Enrique? I do that any time some creep makes a move on my woman."

He shrugged. "I would do the same. His nose is broken and the jaw is wired together. He says he gonna kill you."

"Fuck him," I snapped. "He had a gun on me and couldn't. Just another piece of shit."

"He was to go back to Guatemala today."

107

"He can use the rest," I said. "He knows less about fighting than he does about screwing."

What Pedraza understood, he liked. He grinned broadly.

Cejas said, "Comandante Enrique is no use to us in Puerto Vallarta."

"Fly him where he wants to go, give him a parachute, and let him jump. Or don't give him a parachute."

Pedraza chuckled. He was becoming a one-man claque.

Cejas scowled. "Forget Enrique. Last night I called your room. No answer."

"Keeping track of me? What the hell *is* this?" I was swinging in the dark, and I couldn't even see the balls coming.

"I needed you for something."

"What?"

"Look for my boat—the one Humberto took out."

"Yeah, I heard he didn't show."

"Who told you?" he asked sharply.

"Carla Santiago. You mean you wanted me to fly around in the dark looking for a boat? Forget it. I don't know the coast that well."

"Will you go now?"

"If you want."

"The boat sunk, but some stuff is floating out there. I want to see it."

"Let's go."

CEJAS DIDN'T ENJOY flying in my small plane. He didn't admit it, but I saw his clenched teeth and white knuckles as the hull bounced over waves during takeoff. Once we were in the air, his face relaxed and he crossed himself.

The life raft I'd used last night was sunk offshore in about thirty feet of water. I saw its light outline on the sandy bottom because I knew where to look. Even if spotted, it couldn't be connected to me.

So I climbed to a thousand feet and circled out over the bay. Cejas stared down intently, and I guessed that he wasn't just looking for pieces of the Cigarette. He wanted to make sure none of those plastic bags drifted ashore. After a while he motioned down, and I saw a cluster of deck planking broken up like matchsticks. Nearby floated two white fenders. I skimmed over the flotsam, low enough to see that the fenders' cloth was scorched. "Explosion," Cejas muttered. *"Carajo!"*

Turning back, I widened the circle, coming gradually toward shore. Eventually he was satisfied the body bags hadn't survived and said I could go back.

While I was securing the plane, Cejas said, "Pedrito knew that boat—I don't know what could have happened."

"I've been thinking," I said. "That man you had in the garage . . . before you caught him, maybe he put a bomb on your boat."

His fist struck the other palm. *"Sabotaje!* Has to be. No other way. Jack, I like the way you think." He hit my bicep playfully, then glanced back at my anchored plane. "You sure you can fly to Bisbee—with five hundred keys?"

"Four hundred, and I haven't decided to go."

"Well, make up your mind. I'm doin' you a favor because I got other ways to deliver."

"Give me a few days," I said. "Inge's happy, and I'm enjoying PV."

"Maybe you should live here, get a house in Gringo Gulch."

"That's an attractive idea, but I like to stay loose, move around. Besides, I wouldn't feel comfortable in anything less than that showplace of yours."

He smiled. "Around here, anything is possible."

So we left it at that. I had his gratitude and much of his confidence, but I needed to milk him for information.

Then I was going to revoke his license to live.

LOCATION SCENES WERE being shot in and around a wide *barranca* a few miles from town. Cejas reciprocated for the search flight by sending me in his limousine, so the driver and I rode out in air-conditioned comfort.

Scattered up and down the ravine hillside were thatched-roof hovels where peasants had lived until being displaced for the movie. About forty horses were tethered in the shade, and costumed cavalrymen dozed nearby. Crowd scene extras found whatever shade they could, and cameramen on booms had umbrellas positioned over their heads. There were big shiny reflectors, directional mikes on counterweighted poles, and half a dozen trailers for wardrobe, make-up, and comfort. Catering trucks were leaving when I arrived, and I hoped that carelessness and heat hadn't spoiled the company's lunch.

I found Inge reclining on a grassy bank, her face so flushed she looked on the verge of heat stroke. "Wish I were through for the day," she said, wanly, "but they're setting up another scene. And if you think it's hot in the open, try staying in one of those huts for an hour." She struck at a hovering horsefly.

"Otherwise, how are things going?"

"Slowly. The directors argue, cameramen and sound men fight. People pass out from heat . . . No wonder this picture is taking so long to make.

Sarita wanted a script change before her next scene, so they're working that out in the trailer. Where it's cool," she said enviously. "If I'm ever offered another part, I'll hold out for the Ice Capades."

"Can you skate?"

"In Canada, everyone skates." She wiped her forehead carefully, to avoid removing makeup. Even her black wig looked wilted.

A loud buzzer sounded. Maximilian's cavalrymen stirred, got up, walked over to their nags. Extras moved toward the scene area, and from separate trailers, Sarita and Carla emerged.

"Time to go," Inge said tiredly, "see you later—if I'm alive." With a limp wave she strolled into the blinding sunlight.

Chandler Bates got out of his camp chair and greeted his two female stars. With hand and arm gestures, he told them how it was going to be done, while Fernando Aguila briefed the shit-kickers. Presently the riders turned back, out of camera range. Sarita and Carla hid behind a bush. The marker boy came and went, and through a bullhorn Bates shouted, "Camera, action."

Up the rocky defile rode the emperor's men, bristling with guidons and lances. Suddenly, knife glinting, Carla charged the leader, grabbing reins and hacking at his legs. The horse reared, a lance flashed, and Carla staggered back before dropping like a bunch of rags.

Sarita ran from concealment, jumped astride the horse, and, from behind, cut the throat of the trooper who had speared her "mother." The actor dropped across the pommel and, seizing the reins, Sarita galloped away while cameras followed.

"Cut," Bates bellowed. "Very good. *Excelente.* That's a wrap." Everyone relaxed.

Inge, I saw, had been one of the cowed villagers in a reaction shot. Sarita and the trooper returned, and she slid lithely down. Her revealing costume reminded me of Magnani's in *Bitter Rice:* plenty of thigh showing and neckline torn low.

The next sequence had the cavalry spurring after their lost leader while Carla, clawing at her chest, simulated the agonies of dying in the dust.

After that, the crew began moving equipment up the hillside toward one of the huts where Sarita was supposed to take refuge and begin rallying the countryside against the foreign emperor. Historically, Mexican resistance had been led by Benito Juarez, but his stolid Indian face wasn't as photogenic as Sarita's. Besides, after thirty semi-historical films, he wasn't box office—and Sarita was.

I saw her go to the dressing trailer and figured she was through for the day. The crew would probably set up for hillside exteriors before tearing down a hut wall for interior scenes.

Like herded cattle, extras and supporting players followed the crew up the hill—among them, Cejas' five *artistas*.

I went over to the trailers and knocked on Sarita's door. *"Quién es?"* she called irritably, and I said, "Novak. I have to congratulate you on that spirited scene."

"Thanks." She opened the door a crack and cool air rushed out. "What brings you here?"

"Well," I said, in case anyone was listening, "I wanted to see Inge at work, and thought I'd pay my respects to you before leaving."

"That's thoughtful. If you like, we might have a drink later."

"I like."

The door closed and I went back to Cejas' limo. "Hotel," I told the driver, and we drove out of the lingering dust raised by the cavalry.

Passing the port, I saw the *Bal Musette* still at the pier, and wondered if Comandante Enrique had arrived on it. After the tubes were removed from his nose and the wires from his jaws, a relaxed voyage down the coast to one of Guatemala's small Pacific ports might be just the thing to rehabilitate his fighting spirit. And the *Bal Musette* could carry a good many tons of arms in its holds.

I wasn't in the arms-control business, I reminded myself, but if Enrique's *bandoleros* were cultivating poppies, that made his operation worthy of notice.

I wanted to get back to Guadalajara and make a full report to Manny, but the action was in PV for the present, and when Inge and the movie crowd went there would be time enough.

A SHOWER COOLED me off, and the jacuzzi improved my disposition. I was lolling in it when the phone rang, and I heard Sarita's voice. "I'm home. Want to come up?"

"Ah . . . after last night's unexpected invasion I'm reluctant to be where I'm not supposed to be. Why don't you slip down? Discreetly."

"Shall I bring a Dom?"

"Two."

*"A sus apreciables órdenes,"* she said and hung up.

I tucked a towel around my hips, and soon she was at the door, beach bag in hand, wearing a turquoise robe—and nothing else. As I locked the door behind her she said, *"This* is discreet? What about your girlfriend, Inge?"

I took the heavy beach bag from her hand. "I keep telling you we're just friends. That's it. Nothing more."

Her eyes were disbelieving. I said, "Look, I know the Mexican horn-book has it that every male automatically jumps every female he's alone with—that's Hispanic legend and culture—but I'm an exception. Inge's had problems, and I'm trying to ease her back into life's main currents."

"So you're pilot, sailor, and . . . social worker."

"Right." I stuck one bottle in the fridge, opened the other. "Glass?"

"Wouldn't be the same." She swallowed, coughed over bubbles, and gave me the bottle. I downed a good slug and said, "So, what happened last night? Gilberto bother you?"

"No, but those three *cabrones* made enough noise to wake me. My first thought was they'd kill you, then I couldn't think where you might be hiding. God, I was scared."

"I was pretty scared myself."

"How did you get away?"

"Swung down from your balcony to the one below. Took off like a thief and slid home safe."

She smiled. "He who loves and runs away will live to love another day. This is another day, *querido.*"

"And not a moment too soon," I said as the robe slipped from her shoulders. I put down the bottle and carried her to the bed.

WE WERE SHARING the jacuzzi when Inge came in. She gaped at us, blurted, "Oh! Forgive me—I didn't know," and turned away. She looked hot and disheveled. "Do you mind terribly if I take a shower? I've absolutely *got* to cool off."

"We're all friends here," I said. "We won't peek if you don't."

She shed her clothing and scampered into the shower enclosure. Before turning on the spray she said, "Jack, I'm so damn naïve—I just never thought that you and Miss Rojas had something going."

"Well, we do, and I'll thank you to keep it to yourself. Lives depend upon it. Ours."

"Of course. Trust me." The water went on and I left the jacuzzi long enough to fetch the second bottle of champagne. As I slid back into the foaming water, Sarita glanced at the shower. "Finally, I believe you."

"You're a hard case," I said, "and where's it all going to end?"

Soberly, she said, "I wish I knew. What I do know is that if I don't get out of this situation with Gilberto my life isn't going to be worth living. And I'll never make a decent movie again."

"Sure you will. Bates has no hold on you."

"But Gil has." Tilting the bottle, she drank again. "Movies begin with a backer. Money controls everything. Gil has money to burn." She paused. "Would it surprise you to learn that he and Cejas and the other three *traficantes* own this hotel?"

"No, but it explains a lot."

"Yes, it does." Her dark eyebrows arched, and she went on. "He wanted me to do this proletarian drama, said expense was no object. I was ... between pictures, as they say, and willing to be persuaded. So I signed a contract. If I break it, the union will make sure I never make another film in Mexico. So, completing even a lousy picture like this is better than breaking my contract." She sighed. "The other part is, Gil would kill me."

"Easy now, doesn't he love you?"

"He says he does. He's also said if he can't have me, no other man can. In Mexico that means only one thing."

"So, you'll finish the picture, and do—what?"

"Go far away. Chile, perhaps, Argentina. Live underground for a year, until Gil finds someone else."

I said, "Maybe he won't last that long. He's involved in dirty business."

Her gaze came from under thick lashes. "Odd you should say that. You are, too."

"Well, we don't always have to like what we're forced to do. Our situations aren't dissimilar."

"But I don't buy and sell drugs."

"I'm glad," I said, and kissed her tenderly.

Inge chose that moment to exit hurriedly from the shower. She snatched a towel and disappeared. Then called, "If you want the bed, I can sleep on the floor—I'm used to it."

"Take the bed," I told her. "We're winding down."

"Are we?" Sarita murmured, and moved over onto my lap.

BEFORE SARITA LEFT, Inge was fast asleep. At the door, Sarita said, "You make my days worth living. I don't want this to end, but I can't let myself get too involved. I want to, but . . . " Her face tilted upward. "You understand?"

"Sure. And I won't always be in this business. For me, it's a quick in and out."

"So they all say." She opened the door and walked off.

I felt a strong impulse to call her back, break cover, and tell her why I was there and what my real business was. But I'd given my word to

Manny, and confiding the truth to Sarita could prove hazardous. Besides, she might despise me for deceiving her. So, as I turned from the door I told myself it was best to let things run their course. I had confidence in Sarita, but I wasn't ready to trust her with my life.

I WAS SHAVING and thinking about a room-service dinner when the phone rang and Cejas was inviting us for cocktails on the yacht.

# TWELVE

THE PRINCIPALS were all there: the Gang of Three, General Pedraza, Calixto, Alonso, and Perez. Plus the police chief and the deputy governor of the state. We were in the salon, and I was the only *gringo*. Cejas said, "The *Señorita* Inge?"

"Too tired to move." I took a glass of champagne from the waiter. "No other females?"

"Our *amigas,* too, are conquested by heat. But all will return soon to Guadalajara." He shrugged. "Myself, I prefer this place."

"PV has its charms," I remarked. "Anything more on your boat?"

He shook his head. "Your idea, *sabotaje,* has the best logic. Also, no one else had reason to do it."

I doubted that, said nothing, and sipped again. I was beginning to feel uncomfortable. I was among more and higher level narcotics kingpins than ever before in my life, so I wondered what was behind the special attention. Never liking prolonged mysteries, I said, "These are all associates of yours, Fructo, big men. I don't have big money or influence—so why am I here?"

He grunted. "They want to look you over, *amigo,* make an opinion of you."

"Yeah? Why?"

"I said you could be useful to us. Make big money, live like a king. You like the idea?"

"Depends on the hours."

He smiled. "How many hours a week you wanna work?"

"About two," I told him. "After that my mind wanders."

He laughed uproariously, turned, and interpreted what I'd said to the

115

others. They smiled politely, but none found it as hilarious as Cejas had. "You a funny guy," he said. "I tell you something more funny. Comandante Enrique offer me a big price for you. What you thinka that?"

"How big a price?"

"Hundred keys gum *ópio*."

"I'm flattered," I said. "What did you tell him?"

"I said I think it over." He looked at his *compadres*. "They tell me, take it, give Enrique the *gringo*. What do I do?"

"Tell him to take me himself—if he's big enough."

Cejas doubled over with mirth. Finally he wiped his eyes and sputtered, "Fine idea. *Espléndido*. I do that, I tell Enrique he should do his own dirty work. Me, I got nothing against *gringos*. They buy what I sell. Without *gringos*, I got no business, eh?"

"A river with no water."

"Okay, no more Comandante *Chingado*. You ready to buy seven keys—or fly four hundred to Arizona?"

"I better just buy the seven," I told him. "I don't think Inge could do without me."

"You let a woman decide? Not so *macho, amigo*."

"She's a good kid," I said. "Used to be a user. I don't want to mess up her mind again. When do you want the five million *pesos?*"

"When you want the keys?"

"I can wait," I told him. "Like I said, no hurry. I'm enjoying life in PV." My armpits were soaking from tension. One TV product claimed to prevent it; I needed the jumbo jar.

"Okay," he said abruptly, "all this talk was bullshit. Earlier I tell my *socios* about you. They said, 'Bring him for a drink so we can look him over.' I called you, you come. Okay?"

"So this was a job interview?"

"Yeah. Pedraza says you're smart. I *know* you're tough. We need smart, tough men. All we got to do is convince Calixto and his pals."

I shrugged. Something big was being shoved at me on a plate. How the hell could I refuse? Still, I couldn't appear eager—that was the mark of the inexperienced narc. So I said, "Well, I didn't ask for anything, Fructo, and I'm not looking for anything more than those seven keys. They'll keep me happy a long time. I'm not greedy, see? I've got a good life, and I've never seen the inside of a jail."

"Jail?" He looked around at his friends. "Are we in jail?"

"Just so we understand each other."

"Look—I show you." He pulled out his wallet and flipped to one of the cards. It bore his photo and an official Mexican seal. I said, "What's it say?"

"It says I am an officer in the Security Directorate of the Ministry of Interior." He put away the credential. "No one don't arrest me. You work with us, you get the same card, okay?"

"Sounds good," I said. "Well, you guys figure out what you want to do. It's the same to me either way." I put down my glass. *"Adiós."*

"Where you goin'?"

"Hotel. I need dinner."

"We feed you here."

I winked. "You're not Inge," I said, nodded at the nine conspirators, and left the yacht, wishing the *pendejo* would stop trotting out surprises. Things were moving faster than I wanted. Manny hadn't told me what to do, and I damn well wasn't going to fly a cargo of coke across the border without DEA's okay. Trouble was, these *cabrones* could come up with a proposal I couldn't refuse and continue living. And the offer for my head was a hundred keys of gum opium. In dollars, worth about ten million to the refiners.

Walking to a taxi, I blotted my wet face. *"Mierda,"* I said aloud. Losing Padilla hadn't slowed them; one less snout at the money trough. For them, he'd ceased to exist. A pebble dropped in a large pond. Pedrito, a much smaller pebble. Well, I was glad they weren't making a big thing of their loss.

I needed a sit-down with Manny, but that would have to wait until I had persuasive reason to visit Guadalajara. Having placed a proposition on the table, the men on the yacht could have me tailed. Novice agents got canceled when they ran to the first pay phone to report a pending deal.

My cover was so thin as to be transparent. Worse, I was working in my true name. Neither Manny nor I had thought I'd get this deeply involved with the Mexicans, but it was too late now to get alias documentation. I had to go with the legend I'd offhandedly contrived.

The *Bal Musette*'s arrival was another unwelcome surprise. Omar Parra was connected to it, and anyone who knew the history of his late brother, Luis, probably knew my name, as well. My fervent hope was that Omar would tend his illegal crops in Colombia and not show up in Mexico.

The *Bal Musette* was smaller than the big Parra yacht I'd sunk off Cancún. I'd seen no chemists and hadn't sniffed the telltale stink of acetone and ether, but the boat was plenty big enough to carry arms to Enrique and bring back poppy juice by the ton.

117

If opportunity arose, I thought I ought to take a look below decks. In the *Bal Musette*'s holds.

I went into the hotel and entered the nearest dining room. It was called La Ostra and, not surprisingly, featured seafood.

After ordering a chilled bottle of *Etiqueta Blanca,* I went to a lobby phone and dialed Sarita's penthouse. After five rings she answered and I said, "Guess who? Are you busy?"

"Just sleepy. I'd love to see you, but it wouldn't be safe here."

"I just came from the yacht. Your protector was there."

"Sober?"

"Afraid so. It was a business get-together. I have to say I don't think he's working overtime protecting the citizens of Jalisco."

"So what else is new? Where are you?"

"Just starting dinner—but I could finesse it entirely."

She sighed. "I just have a feeling that tonight is not to be. Do you mind terribly?"

"Terribly."

"I suppose Inge is in bed?"

"Yes, but she's a sound sleeper."

"I'd be nervous and apprehensive, couldn't give you the attention you deserve. *Querido,* intuition tells me not to risk being with you tonight. But tomorrow is another day."

"So it is. Meanwhile, don't forget, you're Miss Everything, the Woman of My Dreams."

"That's nice. I'll go to sleep remembering it. Enjoy your dinner. Good night."

"Good night, honey," I said, and went back to my table.

WITH THE WINE, I had chilled shrimp, clams steamed in garlic beer, and a broiled filet of snapper that dissolved on my tongue. I thought of phoning Manny and decided it was unwise. Maybe he'd contact me tomorrow. In any case, I needed guidance soon.

For dessert I had a bowl of sliced fruit, then an espresso. What I ought to do, I told myself, was go to bed early and get a full night's sleep. But I couldn't get the *Bal Musette* out of my mind. Its presence affronted my principles.

DEA could have it stopped at sea, boarded, and searched, but only if there was enough reason to suspect contraband aboard. I suspected that Ed Diaz had been killed trying to provide probable cause, and Calixto, Alonso, and Perez were responsible.

118

That Cejas could carry a credential from the *Directorio de Seguridad del Ministerio de Gobernación* shouldn't have surprised me. It was no secret that corruption extended all the way to the Cabinet, but journalists were afraid to write the truth, and newspapers to publish it. Supplies of newsprint could be cut off, and the journalists' union forced to expel offending writers. Some had been tortured and murdered by a previous federal police chief now living luxuriously in Spain with his mistresses and grafted millions. So, while the pervasiveness of official corruption was common knowledge in the street, it was seldom mentioned in the papers.

For half a century Mexico had been a one-party state, whose successive politicians outdid each other at plundering public funds. Political influence and family ties took precedence over law, making the country into a lawless state. Ruled by those with money and power.

Every time I saw a ragged, barefoot child, I thought about these things—and realized how invulnerable they were to change. So, in Mexico, I had no scruples about doing whatever satisfied my conscience.

I went up to the suite and drew a cover over Inge, as I often had for Melody when a room became too cool. Then I went to the closet and inspected the traps on my suitcase locks. They were undisturbed, so I got out my holstered Beretta and set it aside. I was getting edgy about the five million *pesos* in Inge's suitcase, but I couldn't think of a better place to secure them. They were too bulky for a hotel strongbox, and I didn't feel it wise to open a bank account in Puerto Vallarta.

I pulled off my *guayabera* and strapped on the shoulder holster. Then I lay down on the bed and set the digital alarm for two o'clock in the morning.

ITS RINGING DIDN'T waken Inge. She turned, though, and flung out one arm, nearly striking me as I got off the bed. For a few moments I couldn't remember why I'd wanted to get up at two. Then it came to me; I was going to check action down at the *Bal Musette.*

A taxi dropped me off at the head of the port. I walked partway up a slope to a grungy cantina and ordered coffee with a shot of Añejo. From the low balcony I could see boats, the harbor, and especially the *Bal Musette.* Its decorative lights were dark, and no cabin lighting showed. A plainclothes guard lounged at the top of the gangway. Under a pier light a group of sailors squatted around a blanket, shooting dice.

Through the night air came a variety of musical strains. There were plenty of cafés and nightclubs within easy distance, and PV was a go-

go town whose visitors were frantic to cram maximum pleasure into a four-day package tour.

I yawned and ordered a second cup of coffee, no rum.

I was sugaring it when I saw a truck come down the access road and turn onto the pier. It didn't interest me until I saw it pull up alongside the stern of the *Bal Musette*. Presently the crap game broke up, and the sailors walked the length of the yacht to where the truck had stopped. A loading port opened and a heavy gangway extended onto the pier.

An interesting development. As partner in a provisioning firm I knew something about shipside deliveries, and three A.M. was a highly unusual hour. It meant either an imminent departure—or taking on cargo not meant to be seen.

I was too far away to tell anything about the boxes and crates being transferred from truck to yacht by crewmen using a forklift. But I could see a man standing just inside the loading port, checking a clipboard as each item arrived. There was a bandage across his nose, and the beard was gone, probably shaved when his jaws were wired together. So the odds were high that the cargo checker was Comandante Enrique.

That escalated my interest in the surreptitiously loaded cargo. The crates *could* contain uniforms and food, but from what Cejas had told me, I didn't think they did. To arrange a high-seas boarding and search I would have to give Manny more than conjecture. Evidence was needed.

Two men hopped down from the truck's cab and went over to the pier edge. Both wore army uniforms. They urinated into the water, waved at the crewmen, and got back into the cab. The beardless man with the bandaged face came over the gangway and peered into the end of the truck, then returned into the loading port. The truck backed around and drove toward the foot of the pier while crewmen hauled the gangway into the yacht. Presently the loading port closed. The whole operation had taken no more than twenty minutes.

The waiter said they were going to close, and asked if I wanted anything else. More coffee, I told him, and when he brought it I gave him a large tip so I could stay at the table. He thanked me and went away.

I stirred my *cafecito* moodily. In Europe the sun was rising, and I wondered where Melody was. She wouldn't approve of what I was doing, so it was just as well she was away. Would we get back together again? I loved her, and I was half in love with Sarita Rojas—Something I couldn't expect Melody, or any woman, to understand. But that was how it was.

The *Bal Musette* looked darker than before. The quarterdeck gangway was drawn up, the guard gone. The yacht seemed secured for the night. All hands asleep, or was there a roving guard?

Only one way to find out.

I finished my coffee, felt the butt of my pistol, and started down the hillside.

# THIRTEEN

I WALKED ALONG A pier that was parallel to the one where the *Bal Musette* was berthed, so that I could scan the water side of the yacht. Abaft the beam there was a partly open port about a meter above the waterline. It was probably used to transfer trash and garbage to scavenging bumboats at other anchorages; whatever its purpose, it was not dogged shut as it should have been.

Continuing to the foot of the pier, I sat down on a mushroom bollard and looked around. From the crescent hillside floated the liquid notes of a marimba, but the harbor itself was quiet. Only the water moved.

Below my feet, tied to a pier ladder, was a wooden dinghy with two oars lying on the duckboard. The way it bobbed in the gentle current and tugged its line, it seemed to be asking for action.

I climbed down the ladder and stepped into the boat. After setting the oars in rag-wrapped oarlocks, I untied the snub line and began rowing out into the harbor.

Water splashed through the duckboards and wet my shoes and ankles, and for a few moments I was reminded of time spent sculling on the Severn while I pondered problems or worked off tension. The Academy had transformed me from a street-wise kid into a disciplined officer, and the change hadn't been easy. So when pressures got too great to handle in the confines of Batt Four, Bancroft Hall, I took to the river and tried to work things out. When another midshipman got crosswise with me, we went to the gym and put on ten-ounce gloves. Usually we left the ring friends.

Comandante Enrique had gotten himself crosswise with me, but no matter how hard or how often we fought, we were never going to be pals. He was a smart-ass *ladino* with an unrealistic idea of his own abilities. Take that away from him and he was just another *campesino* hacking sugarcane with a machete.

Rowing had put me out beyond the lighted zone. I rested oars and scanned the yacht's weather decks, looking for movement; a guard, a dog, anything.

But everything appeared to be secured for the night. So I began rowing toward the stern. It was harder against the ebbing tide, but I put my shoulders into it, and in a few minutes I was able to catch hold of a hull cleat and peer into the compartment.

Dark.

I tied the bow line to the cleat and eased onto the compartment deck. Once inside, I saw barrels of trash, empty liquor crates, and oil drums. The place looked like an invitation to spontaneous combustion. Aside from the reek of oil and the stink of trash there was a light stale smell in the air. No ether, no acetone.

I tied a handkerchief across my nose, bandit-style, got out my Beretta, and began looking around. Hanging from a stanchion was a good-sized emergency lantern. I flicked it on and found it working. Pistol in one hand, lamp in the other, I moved quietly toward the watertight door, assuming it would open into a passageway.

It did, though I didn't open it until I'd placed an ear against it and listened for a while. The passageway was covered with blue linoleum, and across it was a large compartment filled with dry stores. Its far bulkhead was part of a transverse passageway. I explored it and found two of the three watertight doors locked by padlocks. I studied them and found wires leading to a contact breaker. I could defeat the alarm system, but I had no way of opening the door. Somewhere, there had to be keys.

I went up a short ladder. At the top was a mahogany door with a pane of glass. Peering through it, I saw the cabin deck passageway, with four cabins on each side. Forward, stretching from beam to beam, was the master's stateroom.

The door to the master's stateroom opened without sound, and I went in. The glow of a night-light showed Calixto lying between two of the Indian mermaids. Head back, mouth open, he snored.

Clothing clumped on a sofa. Atop it, an automatic pistol with silencer. I went through his clothes feeling for a key ring, found none, and decided to take the pistol. So I transferred my Beretta to its holster and picked up the Steyr automatic. I left the stateroom, closing the door.

Facing it was a companionway that led up to the pilot house. I entered cautiously, and found a panel of keys hanging beside chart stowage. Two ringed keys looked as though they would fit the Schlarff padlocks on the watertight doors, so I took them and retraced my steps.

Below, I opened one door and found it was the liquor locker. There were about thirty cases of champagne and twenty of gin, vodka, Scotch, and assorted hard stuff. I relocked the door and opened the adjoining compartment.

Shining the lamp around, I saw that it contained the long crates and boxes that had been brought aboard an hour before. The crates were steel-banded, and as I stepped into the compartment I saw that each one bore the stenciled legend: *Fuerzas Armadas de la Republica Mexicana,* with the eagle-and-snake seal of Mexico.

Right out of the national armory, I thought, and rounded the end of the nearest crate. Stenciled letters identified the contents as .30-cal. semi-automatic rifles, twenty per crate. The square boxes held fragmentation grenades and ammunition. The largest crate contained antitank rocket-launchers. The lamp showed me a claw-end crowbar. I stuck the silenced Steyr into my belt and used the claw to bend, twist, and break one of the steel straps. Then I pried open the boards until I could see the .30-cals wrapped in heavy, grease-soaked paper.

*"Qué pasa? Quién es?"* The voice came from the opened door.

Without turning I said in Spanish, "Heard a noise, came to investigate."

"Hands up, turn around."

"Come here," I said, "take a look at this." With my left hand I pointed at the pried-up end, as with my right hand I drew the Steyr from my belt.

"Who are you? Turn around."

With a shrug I began turning left, hoping he wasn't holding a gun on me, and wishing I'd closed the damned door. But I hadn't and I'd been caught in the act.

I couldn't see his face, just his silhouette. He couldn't see my face because of the handkerchief mask, but it made him gasp in surprise. He was looking at it instead of my gun hand when I pulled the trigger twice. The *phffffts* were soft, even in the confined space. The intruder staggered back, hit the wall, and sat down. There was a revolver in his hand, so I kicked it away. Faustino Perez was dying. His mouth opened as though he wanted to say something, but only blood came out. My bullets had penetrated his lung and heart, and by the time I picked up his revolver he was lifeless.

Killed by curiosity. Self-revoked.

I dragged his body into the compartment and stashed it between the stacked crates. Before leaving it I took out his hip wallet and transferred the money to my pocket. I jerked off his gold necklaces, gold wristlets, and Tissot watch, and put them in my shirt pocket. I wiped my prints from his revolver and pressed it into his hand before moving it a few inches away.

I slid the padlock keys into his trouser pocket, and remembered Calixto's silenced automatic. After wiping off my prints I slid it across the deck toward a corner. The Steyr was a nice piece, but I didn't want to be found with it.

I left the compartment with my lantern, closed the door, and replaced the padlock. Then I went quickly to the refuse compartment and hung the lantern where I'd found it.

The little dinghy was still bobbing in the current. I got into it and closed the unloading port before casting off.

As current distanced me from the yacht, I scanned for lights and movement. Seeing none, I unshipped the oars and rowed to the far pier, dropping Perez' jewelry overboard on the way.

At the foot of the ladder I tied up the dinghy and holstered my Beretta. Then I climbed the ladder and gained the top of the pier. Most boat lights were out. The harbor was silent.

I walked to the head of the pier, followed the road, and found taxis outside a just-closing nightclub. The driver took me away from the port, and I paid him not far from the hotel.

While opening the door of my suite I began visualizing the compartment where Perez now lay. About ten crates of semiautomatic rifles, four boxes of ammunition, three of hand grenades, and one crate containing four rocket-launchers. A nice haul for Comandante Enrique, I reflected, if they ever reached his dirty hands.

But that was up to Manny Montijo.

Blowing up the *Bal Musette* would have been easy enough, but there were innocents aboard, and nearby boats could have been riddled by exploding grenades and ammunition. But I now had evidence enough to justify a high-seas boarding.

I closed the door and switched on the light.

Inge lay on the floor, bound and gagged, eyes terrified. From the closet stepped a man with a gun in his hand. *"Manos arriba,"* he said and came toward me.

"What's that?" I said. "I don't speak Spanish."

"Hands up, okay?"

"Sure." Slowly I raised them. "Hey, take anything we got, just don't hurt us, okay?" On the closet floor lay two opened suitcases, one with my machine pistol, the other with the five million *pesos* that he'd been stuffing into a plastic bag when I'd interrupted him.

"Where you been, *gringo?*"

"Getting some action," I said, and glanced at Inge. "All she wants is sleep." I didn't meet his eyes because I recognized him as the guard who had helped Pedrito carry Madero's remains down to the Cigarette. "Go on," I told him, "take the money, I can't stop you."

"Maybe I keel you, *gringo.*"

"That would be a mistake," I said, "because I'm under the protection of Señor Fructo Cejas. We have business together, and he wouldn't like that."

He was coming closer to me. Abruptly he jabbed the revolver in my belly. *"Aaagh,"* I grunted, grabbed for my belly, and caught his revolver with one hand, twisting it backward, levering it against his fingers until I felt the thumb snap. He yelled, and I kneed him in the crotch. Very hard.

The pain took the breath out of him. He doubled forward, and the revolver fired into the carpet. I chopped his neck with the edge of my hand, and he dropped with a wheezing sigh. I toed away the revolver and untied Inge's gag.

She whimpered with fear and relief. I undid the rope from her wrists and started working on her ankles. Huskily she said, "My God, he could have *killed* you."

"And you." I undid the last knot.

She was staring at the closet. "Where did all that money come from? It's yours?"

"Think of it as my nest egg. Then forget it." I helped her to her feet. Numbly she stood there, rubbing her wrists, staring at the man on the floor. He was starting to twitch and moan. I said, "Get into the jacuzzi, you'll feel better. Close the door."

"Why?"

"Just do as I say."

Swallowing, she walked unsteadily away.

When the bathroom door closed, I grabbed the guard's wrists and dragged him onto the balcony. He was holding his damaged crotch and mumbling unintelligibly. I bent him over the railing so he could look down at the beach nine stories below. In Spanish I said, "Did Fructo send you— or was the ripoff your idea?"

"Fructo," he gasped, and tried to back off the railing.

I grabbed his ankles and lifted his legs. Before he could grab the railing I cartwheeled his body into space. As I stepped back I heard him strike a concrete table on the patio below. His body must have just cleared a chained macaw because the bird screeched and flailed at its perch. I tossed his revolver outward onto the sand. Then I closed the balcony door and looked in on Inge.

Her head and shoulders were resting against the rim of the jacuzzi. Her eyes were closed, and her body was being massaged by the submerged jets. I poured Añejo into two glasses and carried them back to the jacuzzi. "Drink," I said, "you'll feel better."

Her eyes opened as she took the glass. "I . . . I don't know what to make of you. Taking that gun away . . . that was terrific." She drank deeply. "Did you call the police?"

"Why bother them?" I touched my glass to hers before I drank. "He's gone."

"You let him go?"

"Yes," I said, for it was the literal truth. "Try not to think about it, you have another active day ahead."

She sipped from her glass. Moodily she said, "I guess what woke me was when he broke the suitcase locks. Like an idiot I sat up and screamed." She looked at me. "If this is going to keep happening, I'll play dead next time."

"Good idea," I said, then undressed and got into the jacuzzi. The warm, foaming water felt great on my body.

She said, "I didn't know you'd put money in my suitcase—how did he know?"

"Someone must have told him."

"One more thing. Where were you?"

"I wasn't anywhere," I said, "and that's the way the story will be told. Nobody came in, you weren't tied up, nothing happened. It was an uneventful night, and we slept through it until morning."

She got out of the water then, covering herself with becoming modesty, and dried off beside the bed. After I got in she gripped my hand for a long time, and then I felt her fingers relax as she slipped into sleep.

I hadn't anticipated my room being searched. Cejas had probably sent the guard to find out more about me, and the guard was dipping into my money to make the mission worthwhile. He probably figured I wouldn't tell the police, and he was right.

I was going to tell Cejas.

AFTER ONLY ABOUT five hours' sleep, I could hardly find the ringing telephone. When I picked it up, I recognized the voice of Manny Montijo. He was at the PV airport, and he wanted a meet right away. I looked at the clock and told him I'd meet him in an hour. After wake-up coffee, I took a cold shower and dressed.

As I rode to the airport I reflected that Manny's arrival was timely. I had a lot to tell him, and his coming eliminated my having to go to Guadalajara. So I was in an upbeat frame of mind.

But I hadn't counted on the labyrinthine workings of DEA.

# FOURTEEN

A T THE AIRPORT I got out of my taxi and started walking to the entrance. Then I noticed a Chevy sedan moving toward me. I was getting ready to retreat when I saw Manny's face under a beige Panama hat. The car stopped, and I got in beside him. He drove out of the airport, and I said, "You'll be glad to hear that last night I revoked Faustino Perez."

"Where?"

"On the yacht, *Bal Musette*. Manny, it's carrying a load of weapons to Guatemala." I told him about Comandante Enrique's barter deal with Cejas, guns for unrefined opium.

Manny whistled. I said, "So all you have to do is alert the Coast Guard when the yacht leaves PV. Now, do I fly Cejas' snow to Arizona?"

He glanced at me, and I saw that his cheeks were pale. "Afraid not. Did you transfer the five million *pesos* to Cejas?"

"I was holding back, waiting to see which way to go. So, I buy seven keys from him?"

He shook his head and pulled over to a deserted part of the road. "Not even an ounce," he said. "That's—"

"Why not? The buy's a confidence-builder. Last night Cejas sent a man to search my room. He was helping himself to the *pesos* when I found him."

"Yeah? What happened?"

"He contracted a fatal fistula."

"Meaning you killed him. Why?"

"I had the impression he was about to kill me." I stared at him. "What's the problem, *amigo?* Office work got you all soft and compassionate?"

131

"Maybe . . . I don't know. And I hate to tell you this, but as of now you're to drop everything."

"Drop . . . ? Why?"

"Orders, that's all I can tell you, because it's all I know."

My mouth was dry. "Look, I didn't ask to get into this—you came to me, remember? But now that I'm involved, I can't walk away and pretend nothing happened. The Gang of Three plus Pedraza is still in business, and I've handed you probable cause to search the *Bal Musette* en route to Guatemala. What the hell's the story?"

He took off his sunglasses, and I saw circles under his eyes. "I advanced you the five million *pesos* on my own authority, then advised headquarters. They didn't like that, and when they got your proposal to fly a load into Arizona, someone got so uptight that I've been ordered to cancel the operation and get rid of you."

I stared at him. "Makes no sense, Manny. If I didn't know Phil Corliss was in Miami, I'd say he was the headquarters prick who ordered cancellation."

"He is," Manny said quietly. "Give me back the five million, Jack, I'll pay you for your time, and that's it. Go back to Cozumel."

"And let the yacht deliver all that stuff to Guatemala, bring back a ton of gum opium?

"Apparently Corliss got DEA to ask the Department of State for concurrence. That put the whole thing on the table, and State said absolutely no. I figure the governments of Colombia and Mexico are protecting these bastards, and for 'diplomatic reasons' State doesn't want to mix in."

"Why not, for God's sake? Their narcotics are killing our people and financing guerrillas like Enrique."

Slowly he shook his head. "You know it, I know it, but Latin American politics are incomprehensible. For all I know, CIA is backing Comandante Enrique."

"Every dealer we arrest claims he's working for CIA."

"Listen, Jack, if it was up to me, you'd stay on the payroll until you liquidated the Mexican-Colombian-Guatemalan triangle. As it is, I've been ordered to repossess the *pesos* and pay you off." He swallowed. "How much?"

I grunted. "You couldn't come up with enough to satisfy my conscience. Forget the five million—as far as headquarters is concerned I bought the keys from Cejas and flushed them down the toilet. Hand me a thousand dollars for operational expenses and four thousand for two weeks' work, and tell Corliss I'm off the case."

He eyed me. "And you'll get off it?"

"As far as you're concerned. What I do on my own time is up to me."

For a while he thought it over, finally saying, "If that's your deal, I have to take it. But I'm not sure headquarters will buy it."

"You mean Corliss, the Perfect Circle."

"I try not to think about him."

"Yeah," I said, "that makes it easier. Suddenly Corliss, the Treasury reject, is making foreign policy. Manny, ever think how advantageous it is to be a bureaucrat, not a field hand—like you and me?"

"All the time," he said sourly, opened his briefcase, and counted out five thousand dollars. Handing the bills to me, he said, "I hope this takes you where you want to go, Jack. Don't contact me again—and for God's sake, be careful."

I folded the money into my trouser pocket. "All right, you have no further responsibility for me. But, if you ever see Empty Suit Phil, tell him I said he should wear a skin ring on his middle finger."

He said nothing, backed the car around, and drove back to the airport. Before I got out, he said, "Don't blame me, Jack."

"I don't."

"No hard feelings?"

"None," I said, and shook hands. "Who knows? You might even get back five million p's."

"That would help smooth things over," he said as I closed the car door.

Walking to the taxi stand, I reflected that I'd risked my life, revoked some deserving types, and still hadn't collected enough to pay the boatyard for my new engine and bottom work on *Corsair*. And DEA had backed away from an operation designed to eliminate a good portion of the cross-border drug flow from Mexico.

I got into a taxi and rode back to the hotel.

Time to see Cejas.


TAKING MY ROOM key, I noticed workmen outside on the patio replacing a broken concrete table. Part of the debris was stained dark brown. Nearby on his perch a crested macaw preened his feathers. The only witness.

A couple of heavy-set plainclothes types were strolling through the lobby followed by a pair of uniformed policemen. The hotel had to report the fallen body, but I didn't think the police would make much of it. Cejas owned the hotel, and the police chief was on his payroll. Scrape up the corpse and forget it.

133

From a lobby phone I dialed Cejas' penthouse, and after a while he answered. "Novak," I said. "Got a few moments?"

"*Sí.* Come up."

As FAR AS I could tell, he was alone. He mixed me a Bloody Mary and said, "Made up your mind? You gonna fly the load?"

"There's been a complication," I said, sitting down. "Last night a thief got into my room and stole my money."

"*Carajo!* A thief? You see him?"

I sipped the spicy drink and shook my head. "Slept through it, as did Inge. But when I looked this morning, it was gone."

He sat down across from me. "This morning they find a dead man down below. He must of fall from up high." He looked at me across the rim of his glass. "Maybe your room."

"Was the money with him?"

He shook his head. "No money."

"It could have been taken by an early riser."

"Maybe."

"Who's the dead man?"

"Nobody say."

"Well," I said, "I thought you might have an idea or two. You're the only one who knew I had five million *pesos* ready for you."

"*Señorita* Inge? She knew?"

"No. But your partners knew about our deal."

For a few moments he said nothing. Then, "You think they could sent a man to rip you off?"

"Someone did." I eyed him. "So that puts me out of business."

"Too bad," he said and drank deeply. "I got some bad news, too."

"Bad as mine?"

"Friend of mine got killed."

"Yeah? Who?"

"Perez. From the yacht. Some thief came aboard, take his gold and money, and shoot him dead."

"Last night? Maybe the same guy who stole my *pesos.*"

"Maybe. But I don't think so."

"Those girls of yours," I said, "probably have boyfriends who like to steal. So Perez is gone, eh? Like Humberto."

"And Pedrito." He finished his drink. "So now we talk about you. You need money, you fly the keys to Arizona. Okay?"

"I don't know," I said, "the way you've been losing personnel makes me think there's a leak in your operation. I wouldn't want to land in Arizona and find the Border Patrol pointing guns at me. I've only got one plane— and one life. Maybe I should just go back to Houston and find honest work."

He laughed shortly. "You like good living, eh? Work don't get it for you."

"It might—I never tried."

"You think Inge stay with you, without money?"

"Hard to say. I hadn't got around to asking her."

He grinned broadly. "But if you got money, she stay, right?"

"Guess so. Of course, she's contemplating a film career."

"Tomorrow the moviemakers go back to Guadalajara to finish the picture. Let her go with them while you fly the load."

"That would be a good time," I agreed, "but I need to know more about arrangements at the other end. Much more. Maps, a chart of the touchdown zone, recognition signals, where border radar is located. Without them I don't go." I got up. "The more I think about it, the less I like it, Fructo. You'd be better off with another pilot—and so would I." I stuck out my hand. "Thanks for the opportunity, but my heart's not in it."

He shrugged and took my hand in his paw. "Okay, any way you want it, *amigo*. We frens, eh?"

"Frens," I said. And left him sitting there with two empty glasses.

As I walked along the corridor, I thought about Sarita Rojas. Her suite wasn't far away, but she would be at the *barranca* finishing up location shooting. Cast and crew would regroup in Guadalajara—including Inge— but what about me? I'd told Manny I was going to work alone—the total singleton—but if DEA didn't care about Cejas, Pedraza, and the *Bal Musette,* why should I? There was enough money in my pocket to pay most of what I owed the shipyard, and I had to straighten out matters with my partner on Cozumel. The logical move was to go there. I'd turned down Cejas' proposal in a way that wouldn't offend him, so I was free to go where I chose.

But as I entered my suite I found myself thinking that DEA had passed up a unique opportunity to inflict major damage on its enemies. Cejas could easily find other ways of delivering four hundred keys across the border, but having me do the job was the equivalent of "making my bones" with his organization. Infiltrating it was where the big payoff lay, although unless DEA would back me, there could be no payoff.

I thought of Omar Parra and his thousands of acres of marijuana and poppies, his *haciendas,* airstrips and private army, the vast wealth the Parras had accumulated. Enough to control the government of Colombia, informed sources said, and be immune to DEA.

I was tired, and the bed looked inviting. A siesta would make up for lost sleep, so I stretched out and closed my eyes.

THE TELEPHONE RANG. As I opened my eyes I noticed the sun off the balcony, so a couple of hours had gone by. Groggily I answered, and heard Sarita's voice. "How are you, *querido?* I hoped I'd find you there."

"Feeling better," I told her, "much better." I sat up. "What's happening?"

"If you'll come up, I'll tell you. Gil went to Guadalajara, so there'll be no interruptions."

"Welcome news. I need some personal grooming, after which I'll be with you."

"You mean you've been sleeping all day?" She sounded outraged. "While I've been working?"

"No, I was up early and around, then got the feebles and turned in. Now I'm in prime condition."

"We'll see."

So I shaved and changed into clean clothing. I was walking toward the door when I remembered the *pesos.* I went to the suitcase and worked the broken locks enough to hold, then carried it to the elevator.

Sarita opened the door and glanced at the suitcase. "Moving in?"

I closed and locked the door, set the snub chain. "I need a favor."

Her arms circled my neck and she kissed me warmly. "Like what?"

"Keep this for me."

"Of course. What is it?"

"My personal bank." I kissed her and said, "Did you hear about the man who fell to his death on the patio?"

"Yes. Someone said he was a thief."

"Your place is more secure than mine, so I'd worry less if the money was here."

"I'll keep it with my jewelry."

I followed her to a narrow door in her bedroom wall. She unlocked it and I set the suitcase inside. She locked the door and turned to me. "Location shooting's finished—shall we celebrate?"

"By all means."

IN HER POOL we drank champagne and made love, and after a while, she said, "Last night a man was killed on the *Bal Musette.*"

136

"Crewman?"

"One of the owners—Perez. You must have met him."

"Lover's quarrel?"

"No one's saying. More likely an argument over drugs." She kissed the side of my face. "Jack, if you came here to buy cocaine, I wish you wouldn't. Those people would take your money and kill you as they'd step on a roach."

"I think you're right. I told Cejas I wasn't interested in buying."

She kissed me again. "I'm so glad. Tomorrow I'm leaving for Guadalajara to finish the picture—thank God. I want you to come."

"I plan to. Inge isn't quite ready to handle things on her own."

"I wonder if she realizes how lucky she is to have you as a . . . friend?"

"She deserves some breaks," I said, "and she's been a good companion, so it balances out. You've helped her, too."

"She's blonde and attractive, and if she spoke Spanish, she could do well in Mexican films. Of course, Hollywood is something else."

"In every way." I lifted her body, feather-light in the water, and turned her so that she faced me, loins around my hips.

"That's better," she whispered. "I was beginning to feel ignored." Her bottom undulated, and as our lips pressed, we began making love.

"STAY WITH ME tonight?" she invited.

"If you have no obligations."

"Gil's in Guadalajara, I told you. Even the yacht is gone."

"The *Bal Musette?* Where?"

"Colombia, I think. Does the name Parra mean anything to you?"

# FIFTEEN

I LEFT THE PENTHOUSE early and took the money bag down to my own suite. Inge was stirring, so I ordered breakfast. Over coffee she said, "My bus leaves at ten. Are you staying . . . or going?"

"I'll fly over. Not to Chapala, the airport."

"That's right. You can land on . . . land."

"It's what those little wheels are for."

Her fork toyed with the *huevos rancheros.* "You lied to me about that thief, Jack."

"You'd had enough to upset you. He was ready to kill me, don't forget."

"I haven't. It's . . . just that the body was being removed when I went through the lobby." She sighed. "I guess you're a really dangerous man."

"When my life is threatened."

She poured more coffee for us. "I suppose this is undiplomatic to ask, but will I be staying with you—or will you be staying with Miss Rojas?"

"Both," I said, "so don't worry about having a place to stay. Is the shooting to be in the city, or outside?"

"Zapopan, an old cathedral where the heroine takes sanctuary from Maximilian's soldiers. I'm one of the nuns who bustles around but says nothing. I'm afraid the costume will be hot and uncomfortable, but I won't have to wear a wig."

"That's a blessing—no pun intended."

She smiled. "You're too well-educated to be a villain—and you have a sense of humor, something criminals don't usually have."

I leaned across the table and kissed the tip of her sunburned nose. "As in the flicks, things aren't always what they seem. Pursue your career, and I'll pursue mine."

"Fair enough." She leaned back, smothering a yawn. "I could go back to bed right now and sleep for a week."

"Don't—the caravan leaves at ten, and the camels are restless."

"Why are they restless, *señor?*"

"Because they were promised water, but all they've been getting is *pulque.*"

"What on earth is that?"

"Fermented cactus juice—ruinous on the kidneys of man and beast alike. In Mexico they sell two kinds. One without flies, the other with."

"Uggh, I think Gerry tried it once." Her face sobered. "But he never tried it again."

And never will, I thought. This was the first mention of Gerry Fein since leaving Guadalajara. It would take her a long time to store those memories away. "Will you miss Puerto Vallarta?"

"How could I not? It's been . . . well, like paradise here. I'll always be grateful, Jack."

"Which reminds me, I owe you some salary." I peeled four hundred-dollar bills from Montijo's offering and handed them to her. She said, "Isn't that too much?"

"You may want to buy souvenirs in Guadalajara."

I went down to the luggage shop and bought replacements, one for her and a hard-side suitcase for my operational *pesos*. Inge finished packing and rang for a bellboy.

I said, "I'll have a room reserved at the Fiesta. See you there."

On tiptoes she kissed me and said, "Is Sarita flying with you?"

"No."

The bellboy arrived, I tipped him, and they left together.

I went down to the pool for a final swim, came back to the suite, and let the jacuzzi pummel my muscles enjoyably. Then I shaved, packed, and called for a bellboy.

At the cashier's cage I was told my bill had been taken care of by Mr. Cejas. I said I appreciated the courtesy, and reclaimed my ring from safekeeping. Then I had the bellboy follow me down the beach to where I'd anchored my plane. Overnight rain had washed salt-crusts from the hull, and the old Seabee looked ready for another excursion.

I gained altitude over the ocean before turning east and crossing the Sierra Madre. Over Juancatlán I picked up Guadalajara airport's radio beam, zeroed in on it, and touched down less than an hour after takeoff.

Before leaving the airport, I ordered general maintenance on the plane in case I needed to leave in a hurry. I paid in advance and took a taxi to the Fiesta Americana.

On the way in the driver told me the hotel had been the property of a recent president, who made a parting gift of it to his girlfriend as he left for affluent exile, just ahead of the gendarmes.

I believed the story—except the part about the pursuing police. They hadn't tried to prevent his fleeing, and hadn't tried to bring him back for trial. But in Magical Mexico anything could happen. If you gave it long enough. Even Moral Renovation.

My own time was limited. The *Bal Musette* was gone with its load of arms to be dropped off at a Guatemalan port on the way to Colombia. Returning with guerrilla opium, refined cocaine, and—Omar Parra?

On Cozumel, life had been a good deal simpler, I mused as I signed the register. Logic told me to go back and pick up things where I'd left them. The interlude with Sarita was drawing to an inevitable close, and all that postponed returning to Cozumel was Inge.

In the room, I unpacked clothing and distributed my *pesos*, MAC-10, and pistol between the bed mattress and bedspring. Hardly a novel stash, but I wasn't planning a long stay.

The telephone rang. Inge? I heard Sarita's voice saying, "I wanted to make sure you arrived safely."

"Thanks. Is the caravan in?"

"No—I flew in one of the General's jets."

"Where are you?"

"In the hotel. He wanted me to stay in his place, but I said I needed to be with the company. We're doing some scenes this afternoon. Besides, if I was locked up in his palace, I couldn't see you. But getting together will be risky."

"Still, I want to see you before I go back to Houston."

"Gil will be in Mexico City tonight."

"Then I'll be with you."

"I'm counting on it. *Adios, querido.*"

"*Adios.*"

I rode an atrium elevator down to the lobby and had lunch in the Chulavista. As I left the restaurant I saw the movie company checking in, so I collected Inge and took her up to the room.

"You were right," she said, "the air-conditioning *wasn't* working, and the bus windows wouldn't open." She patted flushed cheeks. "I have an hour to get ready for work." She began taking off her traveling clothes.

143

"We need to talk about your future."

"Yes. I . . . I've been expecting that." Naked, she strode into the bathroom.

While she was showering I called the maid and gave her a bundle of our clothing for laundry and cleaning. Inge emerged, toweling her short blonde hair, said, "That was a lifesaver," and got into shorts and a halter. She blew me a kiss and left.

There was nothing to keep me from a siesta, so I closed the blinds and stretched out atop my guns and treasure.

The room was dark when I woke. I opened the curtains and saw that evening had settled over the city. I had my guns and five million *pesos*, and no thoughts of how to use them against the enemy. I went down to the lobby bar and asked José to pour me a double Añejo. While filling my glass he said, "How did things go in Vallarta?"

"Your friend was killed by the Gang of Four." I sipped moodily.

"Too bad. Revenge warped his mind."

"Two of his killers disappeared."

"Ah. Disappeared?"

"A boating accident . . . they say."

"I understand."

"And I've been dis-employed."

"Why?"

"To avoid ruffling international relations."

He sighed. "That has happened before."

"So I'm leaving tomorrow." I drank and set down the glass. "I may have something for you to give Manny."

He gestured at the lobby. "The moviemakers are returning."

The actors were picking up their keys at the desk. I paid the bar check and went into the lobby. I saw Chandler Bates and Carla Santiago, but I wasn't looking for them. Taking a seat in a lobby chair, I scanned the arrivals for Inge, thinking she might enjoy a drink in the bar before changing. No Sarita, no Inge.

Carla caught sight of me and came over. She kissed my cheek and said, "Haven't seen you of late. How have you been keeping?"

"Pretty well. Seen Inge?"

She glanced around. "She should be here by now. She didn't ride with us, you know."

"Who did she ride with?"

Something flickered across her face. "I . . . I don't know. I saw her get into a limousine and drive off."

"Whose limousine?"

She looked around as though to make sure no one had seen us talking, said, "I'm sure she'll turn up," and walked hurriedly away.

I didn't like it, but perhaps Fernando Aguila had taken her to a bar to discuss future employment. But why not the hotel? I waited until the lobby cleared, waited another ten minutes, then went up to the room.

From the window I looked out over the glittering lights of the city. Below, couples were playing on the hotel's tennis courts. Where the hell was Inge?

After a while the telephone began ringing, and I picked it up, expecting to hear Sarita telling me the coast was clear. Instead, the voice was Cejas'. "You arrived safely? Good. Please join me for a drink. Presidential Suite."

"Sorry," I said, "I'm waiting for Inge. We have dinner plans."

"She not gonna be there, *Señor* Jack. Better come up an' talk about it." The line went dead.

The receiver was cold in my hand. Now I understood why Inge hadn't returned with the others.

Cejas had her.

What did he want from me?

THE PRESIDENTIAL SUITE had a high ceiling, pastel décor, a loft balcony, and a dining room. Fructo Cejas sat on a cream-colored sofa and stared at me. The old, forced cordiality was gone, and his face had settled into hard, cold lines that showed the brutality of the *cholo*. "Sit down," he said. "You wanna see Inge again? You gonna do a job for me."

# SIXTEEN

I EASED INTO A facing chair, the long coffee table between us.
"What kind of job?"
"Where's your plane?"
"At the airport."
"Good. You take off in the morning with the *coca* keys."
"Where's Inge?"
"I take good care of her. When you come back, you get her."
I swallowed. "First, I get to talk with her. By now she could be dead."
His lips curled into what passed as a smile. "She's valuable merchandise," he said. "If you don't do the job, we put her in porno films, maybe send her to Ecuador or Bolivia. Big demand there for blonde girls."
"What if I don't care that much about her?"
"Then you don' leave Guadalajara alive."
"I should have let Madero kill you."
"Ma—how you know his name?" He sat forward tensely.
"Pedrito told me." I'd made a slip of the tongue, and a fast recovery. "I need air charts, delivery location, signals, radar zones. Otherwise, I might as well *walk* into prison."
He picked up a large manila envelope and tossed it across the table. "All there," he told me. *"Entero.* Study it tonight, *amigo.* You gonna fly at dawn."
I picked up the envelope. On it was printed: *Fuerzas Aereas de la R.M.* And the government seal. From General Pedraza, no doubt. "No more than four hundred kilos," I told him. "When will you load?"
"At dawn. Don' worry about that." He dug down into his pocket and pulled out a roll of hundred dollar bills. "Two thousand for expenses,"

he said, and shoved the money across the table. "Don't feel so bad, Jack. You make delivery, come back, and you get the *señorita*. We want you to work for us, maybe take Padilla's place. First you gotta show what you can do. Get your hands dirty, like us."

"Have her at the plane tomorrow. I see her alive or I don't go."

He thought it over. "Okay, I wanna be frens, not enemies."

"This is a heavy strain on friendship," I said, and opened the envelope. "Where's that drink?"

He snapped his fingers, and one of the *artistas* peered over the balcony. "Añejo," I said. "With ice."

*"En seguida,"* she said, and presently I heard ice clink into a glass.

On the coffee table I spread out a chart of southern Arizona. Pink arcs showed border radar coverage. An X indicated the landing site east of Bisbee, off a bend of Route 90.

"Flying all day," I said, "I can't get there before dark. How am I supposed to land?"

"Lights on the ground. It says on the paper."

I picked up the instruction sheet typed in bad English. Car headlights would flash three times, four, then three. "How will you know I made delivery?"

"The *gringo* who gets it will telephone me."

"I'll stay at his side until he does. Am I supposed to collect payment?"

He shook his head. "Bank transfer in Panamá. Electronic."

"That's a help." I took the iced rum from his *puta* and sipped. After replacing the flight instructions in the envelope I got up again. "Have my girl at the plane," I told him and left the Presidential Suite.

Back in my room I spread out the navigational chart and looked for refueling stops. To fly the route I would have to refuel at Mazatlán, possibly Culiacán, Ciudad Obregon, and Hermosillo, where I'd refuel on the way back.

*If* I came back.

Cejas had the *cholo's* native shrewdness, but I'd managed to learn a few things in DEA. At wholesale, the load was worth about six million dollars, not a small sum even for Cejas. Why he wanted me to deliver it, he hadn't said, but I suspected there was heat along the border, and his own aircraft were known on the U.S. side. My Seabee could go in low and slow under the radar screen and land almost anywhere.

He'd sugarcoated the enterprise with talk about my replacing Humberto Padilla, but to gain their full trust I'd have to get my hands a lot dirtier— and bloodier—than they were. I wasn't interested in partnership, I wanted to get Inge out alive, and me with her. DEA couldn't have picked a worse moment to pull out, leaving the singleton to save himself.

The five million *pesos* weren't going to help me get her back. If I succeeded, it would be because of my guns and ingenuity. And I wasn't feeling particularly resourceful.

The telephone rang. Thinking it would be Cejas with a footnote to our conversation I picked up the receiver. "Novak."

"Jack—have you forgotten me?" Sarita.

"No," I lied, "not at all. Had dinner?"

"I was hoping you'd invite me."

"Good. All things considered I think you should dine here with me. Just the two of us."

"No Inge?"

"She's gone," I said. "C'mon down."


WE ORDERED DINNER from the room service waiter and I told him to bring a bottle of champagne before anything else.

Sarita strolled over to the table and picked up the Air Force envelope. "Looks like something *El General* carries around."

"It's a flight plan. For me."

"For you? Why is that?"

"Because the General's pals are forcing me to fly a load to Arizona."

Her face paled. "Forcing you? I . . . I don't understand. How can they make you do it if you don't want to?"

"Cejas has Inge and says he'll kill her if I don't. Or turn her into a whore."

Breath caught in her throat. "Are you *serious?*"

"Deadly. I'm to fly out at dawn. After I make delivery I'm supposed to come back and retrieve Inge."

"Does she mean that much to you?"

"It's because of me that she's captive—so I'm responsible."

The door buzzer rang, and in a few moments the waiter was pouring chilled champagne into tulip glasses. He said he would serve dinner in half an hour.

Lifting her glass, Sarita said, "It's very noble of you, Jack. You *will* come back?"

"I'll certainly try." Our glasses touched. We drank, then kissed. She said, "Is there anything I can do?"

"You can find out where Inge is being held, whether she's alive."

"How can I do that?"

"Tell Gil she's important to finishing the picture. Tell him you need to know when she's coming back to work. Something like that."

She swallowed, looked away. "He can be a hard, dangerous man, but I don't think he has any part of this kidnapping."

"Maybe not, but it's likely he knows." I gestured at the Air Force envelope. She closed her eyes tightly. "I'll *make* him tell me." Opening her eyes she said, "You mustn't try to take her by force. Do what they want you to do, and I'm sure Cejas will release her."

"It's also occurred to me," I said, "that once I turn over the *coca* in Arizona, I could be killed and buried in the desert. Cejas hasn't given me any guarantees at the other end. When I make delivery he'll have his money and Inge. Why not get rid of me?" I drained my glass and refilled it with bubbly. Sarita was falling behind.

"But you'll take precautions?" she asked.

"Against a couple of machine guns there wouldn't be much I could do." I took a deep breath. "Anyway, I wanted you to know why I'm leaving tomorrow. When will you see Gil again?"

"I don't know." Tilting her glass, she drank deeply. "I really don't ever want to see him, Jack."

An idea had been forming in the back of my mind. "Do you drive?"

"Of course. I keep a roadster in the hotel garage. Shall I drive you to the airport?"

"No. But they're bringing Inge to show me she's alive. Would you be willing to follow her car back from the airport?"

"I'll do it, of course. But how can I tell you?"

"I have to refuel at Mazatlán. I'll call you from there. Will you be here or in Zapopan?"

"I don't have to be at the cathedral until late afternoon—for the same light conditions as today. So I should be here until about three o'clock." She pressed my hand. "Anything else?"

"If you do that, I'll be forever grateful." I kissed her. We had more champagne and took our glasses to the sofa. She slanted over to lay her head against my chest. I kissed her forehead and stroked the smooth curves of her body.

"Maybe we should have postponed dinner," she murmured.

"I was thinking the same thing, but we ought to eat sometime."

"Do you think one bottle of champagne will see us through the night?"

"I don't think it will last through dinner." I was forcing myself into a better mood. Until tomorrow there was nothing I could do for Inge, and I would probably never be with Sarita again. Not like this. I nuzzled her hairline and said, "I'm going to miss you."

"I'll miss you more than I like to admit. Like the song says, 'I've grown accustomed to your face.' So, after the airport tomorrow I think I'll go to a church—to pray for you."

"I'll need all the edge I can get. An angel riding co-pilot would be even better."

"I want you to come back. Ever since we became lovers I've enjoyed living more than in a very long time. Are . . . are you married?"

"No. Are you?"

"You know I'm not. Does that mean you're interested?"

"Deeply," I admitted, and found myself wondering what Melody was doing just then. Sleeping, I hoped. Alone.

"Ever since you asked 'Where's it all to end?' I've been asking myself the same question. If there were no Gil, that would uncomplicate the situation. I don't know where it will end, Jack, but for the present I find myself very contented with you."

The buzzer sounded, and after a discreet interval the waiter trundled in the warming cart and set our table. On each linen napkin lay a fresh rosebud. Sarita picked hers up and smelled its fragrance. "I'm going to keep this," she said, and inserted the stem in her bosom. The waiter served us and said, "Anything else, *señor?*"

"Two more bottles of champagne," I told him. "In buckets. Well iced."

With a bow, he departed.

Neither of us had ordered a heavy meal. Sarita had shrimp cocktail and Dover sole. I ate a small salad and a juicy filet mignon, and by the time we'd finished the first bottle, two chilled replacements had arrived. The waiter wheeled out our cart/table and I set the snub chain on the door.

We sipped thick, syrupy coffee, but our minds were on other things. While I opened the second bottle of champagne, Sarita went into the bathroom. I heard the bidet running, and in a few minutes she came out, a towel around her body. "Your turn," she said, and took a champagne glass from me. "Try not to take forever." The back of her hand rubbed my cheek. "You'd better shave, too. Even with makeup, beard-burn is hard to conceal."

I kissed the tip of her nose and went off to the bathroom.

Shaved, lightly scented, and nearly naked, I went into the darkened bedroom. She had lighted a candle at the bedside, and the yellow-gold

151

glow gave her face the patina of an Oriental goddess carved from ancient ivory. I said so, and she laughed as she reached for me. "No one's ever paid me such an exotic compliment before—or did you mean I resembled an ancient goddess?"

"Enough," I said, and silenced her lips with mine.

THROUGH THE NIGHT we made love and dozed, made love and slept, bodies touching as though for reassurance that the other was still there.

Dawn was at six, so I left the bed at four-thirty and got dressed, slipping on the shoulder holster before pulling on a *guayabera*. Sarita had said she'd check Inge's clothing in the hotel baggage room, so I had my two bags to pack: one with clothing and the MAC-10, the other with five million *pesos*. I figured they might prove useful along the way.

At five I woke Sarita with a kiss. "I'll say good-bye now, *querida*. Don't forget Inge's stuff, and try to get to the airport before her car leaves."

Her hands framed my face as she drew it downward. We kissed lingeringly, and she whispered, "I love you."

"I love you," I told her, and in that moment I did.

Finally I left with my bags and rode one of the glass-sided elevators down the immense wall of the hotel's central atrium. As I paid my bill I looked around the silent lobby, probably for the last time.

A taxi took me to the airport, and at the Civil Aviation counter I checked coastal weather and filed a flight plan for Mazatlán, final destination, Hermosillo. I made sure that the clerk got a good look at my aircraft registration number: CN-1018.

The airstrip was gray when I walked out to my plane. For a few moments I looked around for arriving vehicles, then decided to get on with preparations. I undid the tie-downs, unlocked the cabin door, and got into the cabin. The nine-hundred-pound cargo was going to occupy most of the space, so I secured my scuba gear as far aft as possible, set my bags atop the twin air tanks, and turned to the instrumentation. Main tank and auxiliary filled. Ailerons, elevator, and rudder moved nicely. I started the engine and ran up enough revs to check the oil pressure, then cut the engine off.

Still no vehicles.

Under the seat I kept a .44 Star revolver. I got it out, checked the six loaded cylinders, and stashed it again. I transferred the air chart to my plotting board and figured the air distance to Mazatlán as 270 miles. Averaging 170 mph I should be there in an hour and a half. My range would allow me to overfly Mazatlán and refuel at Culiacán, but I had to make that call to Sarita as soon as I could.

I kicked the tires and walked around the plane. The wind was hauling, as it did at dawn, and I would be taking off to the west. Course to Mazatlán about 325°. Where the hell were they? Had they decided to cancel because Inge was dead? Where was Sarita? She'd had plenty of time to drive the distance.

I watched the wind sock swing around, and finally I heard the distant purr of an engine. Leaning against the plane, I stared into the grayness and folded my arms, so that I could reach the Beretta in a hurry.

The engine sound was closer, louder.

Along the access road came a large, white Mercedes limousine, followed by an army truck whose canvas sides were tied down.

The Mercedes led the truck through the gate in the perimeter fencing, pointed toward me, and stopped ten feet from the plane. A rear door opened and Fructo Cejas got out. He took a few steps toward the plane and halted. *Señor* Jack, the girl is here." He motioned, and I moved out from under the wing.

Going past him, I went to the open door and looked in. She was sitting beside a rough-looking type, and there was a gag in her mouth. Her wrists were bound behind her, and her eyes were bright with fear. "I'm sorry," I said. "It's all my fault, and I'll get you out of this."

She nodded her head vigorously, and I saw that she was wearing the same outfit she'd dressed in yesterday to act at Zapopan.

"Have they hurt you?" I asked.

She shook her head. Behind me Cejas said, "That's enough."

I turned to him. "If you harm her, I'll hurt you in ways you couldn't imagine." I brushed past him, but he caught my arm.

"You threaten me?"

I shook off his hand. "Your friends are disappearing, Fructo," I said and touched the underside of his chin. "While I'm gone, be very, very careful." I waved at Inge and walked to the plane where two soldiers had unloaded four canvas duffel bags from the truck. Opening the cabin door I showed them where to stow the load, then I strapped nylon webbing in place to keep the cargo from shifting.

As I got behind the controls, I looked beyond the fencing and saw a Mercedes roadster at the side of the airport road. I hoped Cejas wouldn't see Sarita behind the wheel.

Without looking at the limousine I started the engine, swiveled the

153

plane, and gave Cejas a blast of prop wind. Shielding his face he got into the limousine.

While the engine warmed I put on earphones and microphone; the radio was already on tower frequency. I requested takeoff instructions and was told to use the east–west runway.

As the plane rolled heavily to the flightline, I hoped the tires wouldn't blow during takeoff. Lightly loaded, the plane would leave water after a thirteen-second run. This heavy, and with runway friction, the plane would need double that to get airborne. I lowered flaps, richened the mix, and shoved the throttle ahead. The Seabee began to move.

As it overcame initial inertia the pace accelerated and the wings bit in, easing the load on the wheels. I followed the white line as the wings took more and more of the weight.

A hundred yards from the runway's end, the nose lifted and we were airborne. I brought up the wheels to decrease drag, gained altitude, and circled back over the field.

Cejas' limousine and the army truck were headed back toward Guadalajara. A quarter-mile behind them trailed the Mercedes roadster. I blew her a kiss, climbed to six thousand feet, and turned on course to Mazatlán.

# SEVENTEEN

WHILE THE PLANE was taking on fuel, I went into the weather room and used the pay phone to place a call to the Fiesta Americana. The operator said she'd call back, so I checked area weather and verified the next leg of my flight—to Culiacán. At the airport souvenir shop I bought a bone-handled fishing knife with a nine-inch blade and strung it on my belt in its leather sheath. By then the phone was ringing, so I answered it and told the hotel operator to connect me with Sarita's suite. After four rings she answered, and I said, "Where did the limousine take her?"

"Jack, I wouldn't have believed it, but I saw it happen. They took her to Gil's place, and I'm sick about it. Unless"—she hesitated—"he doesn't know."

"It's a charitable thought, honey, so maybe he won't let Inge be harmed."

"I'm sure he wouldn't . . . but he's so much under Cejas' control he might go along with anything."

"That's what I'm afraid of. Well, I'll be taking off shortly for Culiacán, and if all goes well, I should be back tomorrow night."

"Please be careful."

"What could happen? I'm a U.S. citizen traveling abroad."

"Don't joke. You'll call me?"

"Depend on it. And thanks for what you did."

At least I knew where Inge was being held. The trouble was, Pedraza's place was an armed fortress inhabited by men accustomed to kill at the slightest threat.

I paid for the avgas, checked the oil dipstick, and got into the plane.

Above, the sky was cloudless. CAVU conditions. I'd hoped for some cloud cover, but lacking it, I'd have to improvise.

As I taxied to the flight line I saw a twin-engine Cessna arrive. A load of sport fishermen got out, and a baggage-handler unloaded heavy rods and reels. My charter boat seldom got experienced sportsmen, so I supplied the fishing gear. Mine was good quality, but not premium equipment like theirs.

When the tower gave me clearance I took off into the ocean breeze and got quickly on course to Culiacán. I reset the radio transceiver on Culiacán's airport frequency and called in, giving the controller an ETA of forty-five minutes. Ample time for what I planned to do.

Turning slightly east I climbed over the *cordillera* and called the tower. "Having engine trouble," I said. "Losing altitude."

"What's your position?"

"North of Mazatlán. I'm turning west, heading for water."

"What's your altitude?"

"Six hundred feet. Oh, oh—engine's dead. I'm going to try reaching open water."

"Have you an emergency beacon?"

"No. You'll have to look for me."

No response from the tower, so I said, "Losing altitude fast." I waited five seconds. "This is Charlie Nan ten-eighteen going down. If I can clear the beach, I'll ditch, and—"

I clapped my hands to simulate crash impact, and switched off the radio. Then I banked southeast, picked up the Guadalajara tower beam, and went down to three thousand feet.

An hour and twenty minutes later I saw the silver sheen of Lake Chapala and touched down at the western end of the lake. Before taxiing to the anchor-buoy, I unsheathed my knife and stabbed the nearest duffel bag. Cautiously I tasted the white residue on the point, spat it out. Cocaine. Eight hundred and eighty pounds of it.

My impulse was to slit all the bags and jettison their contents into the lake, but the cargo was worth six million U.S., and I might need it for bargaining.

With that thought, I headed toward shore and found the buoy just off the fringe of water hyacinth.

The same *chamaco* rowed out to meet me and took my two bags into his boat. The time wasn't yet noon, and I didn't want to reach Guadalajara before nightfall, so I rode the bus to Ajijic and checked into the Posada in time for lunch.

Afterward I strolled along Avenida Colón where sidewalk vendors offered silver and turquoise jewelry, *sarapes,* and other tourist items. From one I bought a used Mexicana airline handbag and went back to my room. I wrapped my MAC-10 in a shirt and set it in my handbag, then got into swimming trunks and swam in the pool until I felt ready for a *siesta.*

As I lay in the cool, dark room I wondered if Cejas had heard about my crash. It might make the evening newspapers and radio broadcasts, and by tomorrow, at latest, Sarita would know. I felt badly about her coming sorrow, but that was unimportant compared to Inge's life.

I slept until six, dressed in dark clothing, and checked my *pesos* bag with the desk clerk. Happy hour was being celebrated in the bar, so I had a shot of Añejo before ordering dinner in the table section.

Looking back at the bar, I remembered Gerry Fein's argument and departure—the last time I'd seen him vertical. Since then I'd inherited his companion, converted her into bait, and now, because of me, Inge was a prisoner under threat of death—or worse. I didn't like the feeling, but I was going to try to normalize the situation.

Dinner was leisurely: I had time to kill. At eight-thirty I collected my handbag from my room and hired a taxi to drive me to Guadalajara airport.

There, I rented a two-door Audi whose engine sounded reliable, and drove two miles to where Pedraza's palazzo was set back from the road against the slope of a hill.

When I'd seen it before I hadn't been viewing his fortress as an assault target; now, with lighted watchtowers and guardposts, it looked far more formidable. There were four guard soldiers visible in front of the high wall topped with sawtooth wire. There should be an equal number of guards on each side. Plus an unknown number in the watchtowers and on roving patrol inside the vast compound.

No wonder Sarita didn't like staying there. But a man concerned for his life and possessions would accept the constant surveillance as a trade-off for personal security.

I drove slowly past the main gate. Unlike those of many other substantial homes, Pedraza's was not constructed of wrought-iron see-through grillwork. It was solid and faced with metal that looked thick enough to stop an antitank rocket.

I drove another mile toward the city and pulled to the roadside to do a little thinking.

If the Viet Cong wanted to take the place, they'd come with masses of yelling soldiers, mortar fire, grenades, and automatic weapons. They'd blow the gate with a Bangalore, swarm through the opening, and overwhelm surviving defenders.

But I was one man, not a VC battalion, and Inge had to survive. Unharmed.

I was faced with the fact that I'd arranged an elaborate deception to persuade Cejas that I was dead and no longer even a potential threat. He'd be more concerned over losing the four hundred kilos of cocaine than he would about my possible resurrection. Too, he had his partners, Alarcón and San Juan, to answer to for the loss of at least six million dollars. Perhaps that would occupy his mind and delay whatever plans he had for blonde Inge.

His scenario, I speculated, was to have had me deliver the keys and be killed at point of delivery. After which he was free to do as he liked with Inge, and I imagined that rape was the least part of his program. Rape and degradation were only the beginning. He'd keep her around with Lupita and the other whores before sending her to Quito or La Paz as a prostitute.

I turned on the radio and found a news broadcast, heard no mention of the Seabee's disappearance, and switched to another station. It was the tail-end of a sports broadcast covering the French international diving competition in Paris. The three-meter freestyle event had been won by Melody West, America's silver-medal champion in the recent Olympic games.

The news cheered me a little. At least Melody was succeeding at what she did best, while I'd completed only the first part of a rescue scheme that I'd failed to think through.

The announcer switched to south Mexico news and said that a light plane that had left Guadalajara earlier in the day had disappeared over the ocean north of Mazatlán. The plane's pilot was a North American, and because searchers had located no wreckage, hope remained that the amphibian was afloat and drifting with the Pacific currents. Search would continue for at least another day.

There it was.

Two fleeing bank robbers had been apprehended near Manzanillo following a midday robbery in Colima . . . I turned off the radio, hoping someone in Cejas' entourage had heard about the missing plane. For Fructo it should be disconcerting news.

And I wondered what Manny's reaction would be.

As I drove back toward Pedraza's guarded compound an official-looking limousine hurtled past and left me swallowing roadside dust as it disappeared ahead. When the dust cleared, I saw the Cadillac turn into the compound road. Lighting showed a government seal on the door panel, and fender flags proclaimed a three-star general.

Back from the capital, Pedraza had come home.

I slowed so that I could see the gate open and the car go through. Before guards pulled it shut, I glimpsed soldiers shoving from inside. That told me the inner compound also had guards. So there was a detachment of at least twenty armed men protecting Pedraza and his estate, in addition to armed hangers-on inside the mansion itself.

It was going to be a very tough nut to crack—unless I applied my intelligence to the problem.

Seeing the limousine pass through the gate had given me an idea, so I turned around and drove into Guadalajara.

I LEFT MY Audi on Avenida Vallarta, two blocks from the hotel, and walked to the entrance of the private garage, carrying my airline bag. An elderly man was snoozing inside the door. He wore an old khaki uniform, faded except where rating patches had been, and an Army cap with no badge. I tried to slip past him, but he woke and asked what my business was.

"Country Motors," I said in Spanish, "to check the timing on a Mercedes engine." I tapped the Mexicana bag and peered around. "I'm late, and *Señor* Cejas doesn't like delays."

*"Ya sé,"* he grumbled. I know.

"Is it gone?"

"No—over by the wall, beside the blue Marquis. Where all the movie people leave their cars."

As I began walking away, he said, "The *chofer,* Miguel, was polishing it a little while ago, so if the limousine is going out tonight, you'd better work fast."

"Thanks for telling me," I said, and passed him a thousand-peso note. "I'd be obliged if you wouldn't mention I go here so late."

He smiled. "I didn't see you, *señor mecánico.* You're not even here." He tilted back his chair and closed his eyes. Before I reached the white Mercedes he had begun to snore.

I walked around the long limousine, opened the driver's door, and felt under the seat. My fingers touched metal, and I brought out a sawed-off shotgun. After extracting the shell, I replaced the weapon and got into the rear compartment where Inge had sat that morning. Tucked down behind the armrest hinge was a Colt .380 pistol. I shoved it into my trouser pocket and kept on looking.

A panel beside the jump seat yielded a MAC-10 like mine. I put the magazine into my bag as a spare before replacing the empty weapon. As far as I could tell, I now had all the loaded guns. So I opened the bar panel and drank a slug of Black Label Scotch. It tasted like cold steel.

I left the Mercedes and got into the neighboring Marquis. Sitting on the rear floor I got out the .380 and withdrew the magazine. Full. I slapped it back into the grip, thumbed off the safety, and jacked a shell into the chamber.

What I planned on doing depended upon Miguel's return, and the old *sereno* had given me hope that he might. So, having no alternate ideas, I settled down to wait.

It was now around eleven o'clock. If the driver didn't appear with the ignition keys by two, the odds were that I wouldn't live until dawn. Because one way or another I was going to try to free Inge before she suffered more.

Half an hour went by. My legs were cramped so I shifted position. But for my siesta at the Posada I would have been too tired to stay awake.

I was easing back when I heard the *click-clack* of high heels on the concrete floor. Sarita taking out her roadster?

The footsteps neared.

Lupita heading for the limousine?

The footsteps ended about a yard from my feet.

The front door opened and someone got behind the wheel. I looked up and saw the back of a woman's head. The door didn't close, and the head disappeared. I got on my knees and the car creaked. The head popped upright and turned to look down.

Even in the poor light I could make out the face of Carla Santiago. Her gasp had a half-squeal like a punctured tire. "You're dead! Don't hurt me, I never did anything to you." Breath wheezed through her throat.

I showed her the pistol in my hand. "I don't want to hurt you, so behave."

"Wha . . . what are you doing here?" Her gaze flickered to the limousine. "Cejas—is that who you want?"

"Where is he?"

"In his suite—a party."

"Why did you come here?"

"I thought I left my purse in the car." He eyes narrowed. "We heard you died in a plane crash. Sarita nearly fainted at the news—left the set." She paused. "You two been getting it on?"

"Ask her," I suggested, "after a decent interval. Now, is the party going to stay in the Presidential Suite—or move on to La Langosta or another disco?"

"I don't know. If they do it won't be until later."

"Taking the Mercedes?"

"They usually do." She glanced nervously at the pistol.

"All right. Since I'm dead, I can get away with anything, right?"

She nodded.

"So there's nothing to prevent me from killing you—except my good will."

"I suppose so."

"And you want to keep on living."

Her lips formed a bitter smile. "I haven't much to look forward to, but, yes, since you ask me, I prefer to live."

"And you'll keep a bargain?"

She swallowed, and in a breathy voice said, "What do I have to do?"

"Two things. Make a phone call—and forget you saw me."

"Call who?"

"Fructo's driver, Miguel. He should be at the party."

"I noticed him, yes. What do I say?"

"Tell him you came down to look for your purse, and noticed a flat tire on the limousine."

"Is that all?"

"That's it."

She turned around and rested her forearms on the top of the seat. "You've got something against Miguel?"

"He sabotaged my plane, made it go down."

Her eyebrows lifted. "I believe you—but why would he do that?"

"I saw him put a bomb in Cejas' boat before it blew up. And I made the mistake of letting him know what I saw."

"Oh, God," she exhaled and closed her eyes. "I'm so tired of treachery and drugs and murders. It just goes on and on." Her eyes opened. "You're going to kill Miguel?"

"He owes me, Carla, owes me for my plane and what it carried. If he can pay, I'd rather have the money than his worthless life." I licked dry lips. "Understand?"

"I think so."

161

"There's a phone over on the wall. We'll go together—not that I don't trust you."

"I'll be talking in Spanish."

"That's all right, I had a year in high school. Nouns are no problem."

"Just the verbs." She managed a thin smile. "After I call him, I'm free to go?"

"Not quite. We'll wait here together—in case he enters shooting. So be a convincing actress."

"I always am."

We left the Marquis, and I listened carefully to what she had to say. When she hung up, I nodded, and said, "Just fine. Now we'll go back to your car and wait."

When she was behind the wheel I got into the rear seat. "If you try to warn Miguel, I'll kill him, and you'll be blamed for getting him here. Act accordingly."

"Don't worry about me—I'm with you, Novak."

"And if you live through this, not a word to Sarita—or anyone."

"I promise. Ah . . . this have anything to do with your girl, Inge?"

"Depends on Miguel," I said ambiguously, "now keep quiet." I began watching the service elevator door.

The garage was silent. Inside the car it was so quiet I could hear the pounding of my heart.

The elevator door opened and Miguel, the driver, stepped out.

# EIGHTEEN

TO CARLA I whispered, "Down, don't let him see you."

Her head vanished below window level. Miguel was the expert at hosing blood from garage floors. His face had a look of disgust. He looked first at the tires on the far side of the limousine and came around to squeeze between the two cars. When his back was to me, I jammed the pistol against his spine. "Don't move."

I got out of the Marquis. "Open the door," I told him, "and get behind the wheel." In Spanish. As he bent forward, I patted him down for a weapon, felt none.

Keeping my eyes on him, I spoke in English to Carla. "Don't show yourself until we're out of here. After that, my life is in your hands. And Inge's."

"Don't worry," she whispered, "I've been covering for people all my life. And to think you speak perfect Spanish."

"It was a hell of a sophomore year," I said, and got into the rear of the limousine. The tale I'd told her lacked a lot of elements, mostly truth, but Carla wasn't seeking truth, just motivation.

"Start the engine," I said, "and we'll drive out to the airport. Where you were this morning."

As he turned the ignition he leaned forward and came up with the sawed-off, pointing it at me with one hand. His ugly face leered across the backrest. "Drop it, *gringo,* or I'll blow your head off."

"Try it, asshole," I said, and heard the firing pin click on an empty chamber. Miguel stared at the weapon unbelievingly. I chopped my pistol barrel across the back of his hand and heard him yelp. I hoped I'd broken a few bones. "You've made your play, *chingado,* now we're going to get

163

organized. Drive out of here before I blow off your face. Try anything and you're dead."

He was sucking blood from his injured hand. "You're going to kill me."

"Maybe not." I retrieved the sawed-off and held up the shell in front of his face. "Only loaded guns work," I said, and fitted it into the chamber, locking the breech as the heavy car backed around. Miguel honked, and the *sereno* woke up and pressed the button that opened the garage door. We swung up and out onto the avenue. The old man had missed the opening act, he might as well sleep through the rest of the play.

Miguel didn't look around again. I was watching the route he took, though, in case he got rebellious. He followed Avenida Vallarta to the big Market Square building and swung right onto Independencia. At Agua Azul Park he turned left, and we were on Gonzalez Gallo, the airport road. "You're doing fine," I told him. "How's the hand?"

"It hurts."

"I can think of things more painful. Got an extra set of keys?"

"No."

I pushed the shotgun muzzle against his temple. "Try again, Miguelito."

He fumbled in his pocket and a key ring appeared. I took it from his hand and pocketed it. Savvy chauffeurs keep spares handy to avoid lockout embarrassment.

After we passed the cement plant I said, "Not quite all the way to the airport. You'll make a casual approach to Pedraza's place."

"They'll never let you in. They'll kill you."

"You'll die first," I told him, "because this gun has a hair trigger and my finger's on it. So it's in your lasting interest to persuade the guards that Cejas sent you with a special passenger. A man from Colombia to see the General."

"Inside the compound," I continued, "you'll park at the entrance and go up the steps ahead of me. Anyone asks what's going on you repeat the story, you don't know more."

"You want the blonde," he blurted.

"Surprise. Did you think I wanted to see Pedraza just to admire his ribbons?" I sat back feeling tired and suddenly old. "Yes, the blonde *señorita* is what it's all about. Does Cejas think I'm dead?"

"Everyone thinks your plane crashed."

"How little they know."

"You'll die soon."

"I'll take a crowd of *cabrones* with me. And I've got the *coca* where it will never be found. Any way you look at it, I come out ahead."

"They'll kill the girl, too."

"Better off dead than working the streets of Ayacucho or Mexico City—where your employers sent Javier Madero's wife." I pulled out the Black Label and swallowed a slug. The alcohol might slow my reaction time but I needed it for courage.

I wondered how much courage Miguel had needed to gouge out Javier's eyes.

As we drove through the night I thought of my dead wife, so young and beautiful. Over the years I'd tried to blot her face from my mind, but then I saw the track-marks on her arms, and that memory was even worse.

I drank again and put the bottle away.

Ahead, on the left, rose the fortress of General Pedraza, its cream stucco ramparts lighted with the brilliance of day. Staring at it, I decided I must be crazy to think I could pull it off. Alone.

As we neared the metal-shod gate, I opened the airlines bag and cocked the MAC-10. I didn't need to take it out; with the bag beside my thigh the trigger was within instant reach.

Ahead, the two guard soldiers perked up and peered at the oncoming Mercedes. One of them raised his hand and walked toward us, dragging the rifle butt on the ground. "Be persuasive," I told Miguel, "and act your usual surly self."

He muttered something as he slowed the car, stopped ten feet from the gate, and ran down the window. "I'm in a hurry," he told the guard, "don't fuck around."

The guard tried to peer inside. "Who's the passenger?"

"A friend of *Señor* Cejas, to see the General. Now, open the damn gate."

"I better notify *El General.*"

"Don't waste time," Miguel snarled, "we're late now." He gunned the engine impatiently. The guard hesitated, finally stepped back. He dragged his rifle all the way to the gate.

Propping it against the wall, he began opening the gate with his partner. It swung heavily outward, and as soon as it was wide enough Miguel laid rubber and shot through, narrowly missing a soldier.

He spun the wheel, and the car rounded a tiled drive to wide entrance steps. I said, "You're doing fine, I'm impressed. Now cut the engine and open my door. Then lead me into the house."

I followed Miguel into a large reception room in the center of which

165

grew a large palm tree. From huge ornamental pots, thick vines climbed the walls. Somewhere above, a cockatiel whistled and squawked. Standing just behind Miguel, I said, "Where's the girl?"

"Upstairs."

"Take me to her."

He hesitated, so I stuck a finger against his spine. "Move."

He led me into a semidarkened ballroom the size of a basketball court. Beyond it, through open doors, I could see glowing barbecue pits, and a long table heavy with food. Voices floated unintelligibly through the ballroom. I could glimpse a sliver of lighted pool. We hadn't been challenged because all hands were enjoying a late repast.

At the foot of the marble staircase sat a soldier, rifle between his knees. He looked unhappy and hungry. I wondered if he was planning to eat what the gentry left, and reflected that a few weeks' watching his betters cram and cavort could breed feelings of mutiny. As happened with Somoza's men.

The staircase curved up and around like a chambered nautilus. I kept to the carpet runner to avoid footstep noise. From the first landing I could see twin corridors, like those of a hotel, with rooms on either side. "Here?" I asked.

"Third floor," he grunted and kept going. "Don't kill me."

"You're doing fine," I told him. "Earning your life."

We reached the second landing, and Miguel was breathing heavily. "Which room?" I asked.

He said nothing. I moved aside and drew out my machine pistol. He would be thinking that this was his last chance to make a move. "Which room?" I repeated.

He spun around, ready to strike at where I'd been, and then he saw the gun. His jaw dropped, and he froze. I said, "Do I have to ask again?"

"Last one on the right," he said huskily.

"Where does the General sleep?"

"Fourth floor—above."

I looked up, and the corridor was dark and quiet. From there it was a long drop to the stone floor below where two women, holding glasses, lurched drunkenly toward the staircase.

"We'll go to the room now. Very quietly."

I marched him down the corridor to an ornately carved oak door. I tried the bronze handle, but the door was locked. I listened and heard a woman moan, cry out. "You first," I said, and stepped aside.

Like a rhinocerous he charged the door. The frame splintered and the door burst inward, sprawling Miguel on the carpeting beside the enormous bed.

On it were three naked figures. The one struggling in the middle was Inge. The men clutching her were Alarcón and Lucho San Juan.

THE DOOR'S SHATTERING made them gape at me. Alarcón rolled aside and reached for a revolver on the table. I shot him between the shoulders, and he fell off the bed. San Juan rose to his knees and crossed himself. His eyes were closed when I shot him through the heart.

Inge screamed and scrambled off the bed. "God," she gasped, "Oh, God, *Oh, my God!*"

"Pull on some clothes," I snapped. "Anything."

But she stood staring at San Juan's bloody corpse. I went to her and slapped her face. "Hysterics later, get dressed."

To one side stood Miguel looking at the night table revolver. I waved the MAC-10 to discourage rebellion, and his shoulders slumped. Inge was tearing at hangers in the closet. "Hurry up," I told her, "they'll have heard the shots below." I went around the bed and looked down at Alarcón. His hairy body lay on its back, throat blown away. To Miguel I said, "You'll help her down the stairs, and I'll be right behind."

Inge had pulled on a purple dress, and was trying to get into sandals. "You're decent enough," I said, "let's go." I shoved her against Miguel who put an arm around her shoulders and started out the doorway. I followed and we walked back along the corridor.

From below came buzzing voices. Two soldiers started up the stairs, rifles at port arms. They hadn't seen us yet, but they would.

"Keep going," I ordered Miguel. "Let's see how big your *cojones* really are."

By now I had the MAC-10 in the handbag. We reached the landing as the soldiers arrived. Below, people were staring up at us. The soldiers clutched their rifles and looked at us uncertainly. I said, "This is none of your business. Go back to your posts."

"But . . . the shots?" one of them blurted.

"There was a quarrel over the *rúbia.* Right, Miguel?"

*"Verdad,"* he said hoarsely.

"And you're taking us to Cejas."

He nodded, and we started down the last flight past the soldiers. I prayed they wouldn't shoot us down, but reasoned that they lacked orders.

We were halfway to the ground floor when I saw a man in uniform approaching the fringe of the crowd. His collar was open and there was a glass in his hand. He peered at us uncomprehendingly.

General Pedraza.

Nodding to him, I motioned him toward us. With a frown he parted the crowd and met us at the bottom of the steps. He said, "What are you doing here?"

"Collecting my reward. Didn't Cejas tell you?"

"I've been away." He looked up the staircase. "What about those shots?"

"Two men fought over the girl." I shrugged. "The old story."

His eyes narrowed. "I'm going up."

"You can't help them," I said, and raised the open bag so that he could glimpse the machine pistol. "But you can help me, General. It would be better for everyone if you went with us, then we wouldn't waste time on explanations. Unless, of course, you want the girl to tell everyone how she was held here against her will . . . and raped."

His face whitened. "That is not possible."

My hand dipped into the bag, touched the machine pistol. "We'll discuss it in the car," I said. "Tell folks to go back and enjoy themselves."

He swallowed, glanced again at my gun, and turned around. Raising his arms, he shooed the guests toward the party tables. Slowly, they began moving away. In Pedraza's palace, Pedraza's wish was law.

As Pedraza turned back to me, I put my left arm over his shoulders and said, "I don't want any more shooting, do you?"

He shook his head and moved toward the exit door.

With a sigh, Inge walked ahead of him, Miguel in front of me.

The four of us went down the steps, and Miguel opened both doors of the limousine. The night air was sultry, but that hadn't made my face perspire. I'd suspended breathing so long I couldn't remember my last breath. So I filled my lungs and spoke to Miguel. "You behind the wheel. General, you'll sit with us."

As Miguel got into the front seat, Pedraza stared at the rear door. "Easy," I said, "and no one gets hurt. Inge first, the General next." As they got in I closed the driver's door, then slid onto the seat beside Pedraza. Inge's teeth chattered with fear. She moved as far from Pedraza as she could, shaking uncontrollably. I closed the door. "Let's go, Miguel." I held the machine pistol between my knees, and said, "General, Oscar and Lucho are dead. I have four hundred kilos of cocaine, and I'm willing to deal."

The engine started and the limousine began to move. Pedraza said, "I . . . I don't understand. What's been happening?"

"Fructo will tell you—tomorrow. The *coca* is worth much more, but you can have it for six million dollars." I was talking to divert his mind from the reality of our escape. To Miguel I said, "Tell the General if I have the *coca.*"

After hesitating, Miguel said, *"Sí,* General, he has it, as he says." The car was nearing the gate. Pedraza said, "Where are we going?"

"To show you the *coca.* Tell the guards to let us out."

Beside him, Inge was whimpering, eyes closed, cheeks wet with tears. Rotten bastards, I thought, as the corporal of the guard came toward the limousine. Miguel braked and the corporal looked in.

The corporal stepped back, stiffened, and saluted. I nudged Pedraza. "Return his salute," I said, "don't forget your manners."

Pedraza's fingers touched his forehead, and the corporal barked out an order. The gate began to open. "Roll," I said, and Miguel drove out of the compound. "We'll go back to town," I told him, "so the *señorita* can dress properly. Then we'll get on with business." I tapped Pedraza's knee. "That satisfactory, General?"

He nodded slowly, and I realized that he was beginning to grasp the situation. Abruptly he said, "I don't have six million dollars for the *coca.*"

"But you can get it."

"Perhaps tomorrow."

"Your credit's good with me. But I insist you see the merchandise, so you'll realize how sweet a deal it is."

We were passing the big cement plant, heading north toward the city. Away from the road, on the hillside, stood a cluster of luxury homes. Some were dark, others showed a few lights. None could compare with Pedraza's dream house. He said, "You're working with Fructo Cejas?"

"I just became his only partner." I reached over and patted Inge's knee. "Feeling better?"

"A little. I'm not shaking so badly."

"You've gone through a lot. I'll try to make it up to you."

Her laugh was thin and bitter. "I wish I'd never met you."

I felt Pedraza move. His left hand was digging down behind the arm rest. "You won't find it," I told him, "so relax and get your mind on business." His arm stopped moving.

"That fellow Enrique," I said, "the *bandido* who calls himself 'Comandante.' What port does he use to pick up your weapons?"

Pedraza shrugged. "Ask Cejas."

"I'm asking you." I drew the MAC-10 into the light.

He stared at it for a few moments. "San José."

"How is the stuff moved from there?"

"Part way by vehicles. Mules into the hills."

"Ever go there?"

"No."

Ahead, a rim of city lights. Suddenly Pedraza blurted, "Who are you— FBI?"

"Nothing so glamorous," I said. "I'm in business for myself. Like you."

He didn't like the answer but said nothing. He stared through the window, and I wondered if he was expecting roadblocks ahead. By now one of the party-goers could have notified the highway police. Looking at him, I said, "I'm confident you'll help the police understand why Lucho and Oscar shot each other. On the other hand, it would go better if the police were never involved."

"They won't be."

"I hope that's a promise you intend to keep. Because if I see my name advertised, I'll be asking you for explanations."

Inge said, "Where are you taking me?"

"To the hotel. Go to the room and lock the door. Don't open it for anyone. After the General and I settle things I'll come back."

"Promise?"

I nodded.

While talking with her I hadn't noticed Pedraza's right hand sliding down toward his ankle. It came up with a shiny deringer, and the muzzle pointed at my heart. I tried to elbow it against the back of the seat, but he was strong and desperate. In the closed compartment the cartridge exploded deafeningly, and the bullet seared me with incandescent pain.

Inge screamed.

# NINETEEN

AS I FOUGHT Pedraza, hot blood coursed down my left side. I wasn't yet dead, so I clawed his eyes and face with my left hand and brought up the machine pistol with my right. He grabbed at the short barrel—too late.

The first burst took off the side of his face. Inge shrieked and huddled in the corner. That gave me space to fire a quick burst through Pedraza's chest. He collapsed forward, head on knees.

The driver was looking around, staring at us instead of the road. The wheels slid off into shoulder ruts, and the limousine plowed down into a narrow clearing. Miguel fought the wheel, then yelled just before we crashed into a tree.

Inge and I were slammed against the back of the front seat. I grabbed the MAC-10, and got up painfully to cover Miguel.

The engine was groaning in protest, the wheels spun, and the Mercedes shuddered. Headlights had been smashed, but I could see Miguel's body on the hood where it had been hurtled by impact. His head had broken through the windshield, and it was compressed like a squeezed pear.

I smelled gas. Ruptured fuel line.

*"Out,"* I told Inge. "Get away from here."

With a moan she opened the door and stumbled across the clearing. I grabbed the airline bag and crawled over Pedraza's body to the open door. Outside, the reek of gasoline was even stronger. Holding my left side, I lurched after Inge, who had taken refuge behind a stand of trees. I tripped, got up, and fell at her feet as the limousine exploded.

The concussion wave ripped across me, then a blast of heat. Inge cried out and dropped to her knees. Another blinding explosion, and the car

171

burned steadily. She turned me over and pulled up my *guayabera*. There was plenty of light, but I couldn't see the bullet wound; it was below and behind my left armpit. It didn't hurt as much as the rest of my bruised body, and if the bullet had struck my Beretta there would be no wound.

"How much damage?" I croaked.

Her breath sucked inward. "There's so much blood I can't tell."

I tore a piece from her skirt edge. "Mop until you can see."

Her hand trembled as she worked. Finally, she said, "It looks like a long, red mark. I can see bone."

"Shit!" I tore more of her skirt hem and told her to pad it against the wound. From her description I guessed the bullet had sideswiped my ribs. I sat up and told her to carry the airline bag. She helped me to my feet, and we walked behind trees while cars began to arrive. Every now and then flames would pop and subside into a steady crackling. People were leaving their cars and running toward the spectacle. I felt braver now that I knew Pedraza's bullet hadn't pierced my lung, and I gestured at the line of rubbernecking cars—about six—the last one empty.

"We'll move fast," I told her, "come out of the shadows."

Holding her hand, I guided her to the roadside. We kept low, behind the car, and I said, "Can you drive?"

"Not stick shift."

"Forget it." We separated, crept toward the front doors and got quickly in. The engine was idling. I jammed the shift into low, spun the wheel, and the little Ford pivoted around and fishtailed toward Guadalajara.

I double-clutched, floored the accelerator, and glanced in the rearview mirror. In the lengthening distance stood a couple, the man shaking his fist at me. Well, that was the cost of curiosity. No car followed.

Inge sat beside me, face expressionless—except for tightly set lips. I said, "Near the hotel we'll switch cars. Mine has a shift you can manage."

"Am I driving somewhere?"

"Yes, dear. Ajijic."

By THE TIME we reached the Cruz Verde clinic I'd been bleeding for more than an hour. But for the tight compress I'd have bled to death, but the field bandage had saved a lot of blood.

The doctor was asleep at his desk. I woke him, and when he saw my face, he frowned. "Emergency," I said. "On your feet."

Slowly he got up. "What happened?"

"Gored by a bull," I told him, and pulled off my bloodstained shirt.

172

Turning, he led me into what passed for an operating room, and I got onto the steel table. To Inge I said, "Unstrap my holster and keep the gun handy."

The doctor pulled on surgical gloves and adjusted the overhead light. He jerked away my compress, and I yelled as clots tore off with the bandage. I could feel bleeding resume.

The doctor said, "Looks like a bullet wound. I should notify the police. You got fifty thousand *pesos?*"

"All for you, sweetheart."

"Then I give you a first-class job. Stitches, clamps, bandage, antibiotics, and a shot for pain."

"Sounds like a bargain. And no police talk."

"All that talks is your money." He injected local anesthetic, swabbed out the wound, and began stitching with a large, curved needle. I could feel the needle puncturing, the sawing of the silk as he drew it through the flaps.

Inge sat in a wall chair, eyes closed. The adrenalin high that had kept her alert and active was draining away. The same would happen to me, but I wanted to be in the Posada by then.

Repairs took half an hour. I paid the doctor, and Inge drove me to the inn. The reception area was dark, so I took my room key from the rack and carried one of her bags. Despite the risk of being seen, she'd persuaded me to wait on Vallarta while she collected her two suitcases. All she had in the world.

In the room, I got out my first-aid bottle and drank deeply, then handed it to Inge. She tilted it and let a lot of liquor flow down her throat. I propped a chair under the doorknob and tried undressing, but my left arm was useless from anesthetic.

She helped me, then pulled off her torn, stained dress and went into the bathroom. Before the shower went on she called, "I feel filthy—contaminated. Those men . . . " Her voice quavered and broke off. I didn't know how to comfort her, so I lay back on the bed, and fatigue rushed over me in a torrent. Body aches submerged, and I slept.

WHEN I WOKE, it was morning. Inge was at the table eating sliced pineapple. She'd brought a plate for me.

I tried sitting up, but my left side was very tender, and the night's aches had returned. Inge brought over my plate and kissed my forehead. "I haven't thanked you for all you did. I know you promised to save me,

173

but when I saw all the guards at Pedraza's place I didn't think you possibly could. And those two men . . . " She looked away. "Animals."

"Worse. Hand me the rum, please."

I sprinkled some over the pineapple and chewed each slice of fruit with enjoyment. As the natural sugar entered my bloodstream, energy returned.

She said, "You risked your life for me."

"And endangered yours. The next thing is to get you settled somewhere safe. I live on Cozumel Island, and you're welcome to stay there until you decide what you want to do with your life. You don't have to decide right now."

Wistfully she said, "There was a time when I wanted to be your lady, but seeing you with Sarita ended that." She gazed at me. "How will she feel about you killing Pedraza?"

I finished the pineapple. "I don't know. He was her protector and he's dead." I levered my legs over the edge of the bed.

I stood in the shower stall while Inge gave me a sponge bath, keeping my bandage dry and avoiding the dark contusions. As she dried my body she said, "Were you really trying to sell cocaine to Pedraza?"

"That was just to distract his mind."

"Then there's no cocaine?"

"Oh, there is very much cocaine." I lathered my face and began to shave. "I'll tell you about it over breakfast."

UNDER TREES, AT a garden table, I told her what Cejas had wanted from me and why she'd been taken hostage. "Prisoner, really," I said, "because I was to be killed, and you were to be kept for their pleasure."

Shivering, she closed her eyes. Birds flickered through vines and branches, unseen doves were cooing. We had the place almost to ourselves and I was glad. Inge said, "If the offer's still open, I'd like to stay on Cozumel for a while."

I'd been thinking that I ought to go back, take care of the boat, and settle things with my partner, Rogelio, for better or for worse. On the other hand, I had unfinished business in Guadalajara, and Inge could carry the boatyard money to Ramón. "Okay," I said, "I have to linger a while and recuperate, so you'll fly on ahead and take care of a few things for me."

"I thought we'd be going together."

"I want you out of Jalisco. Take a commercial flight from Guadalajara, and leave my car at the airport."

174

"Remember, I don't speak Spanish, just English."

"Ramón does—he's my boat captain. His wife will get you settled, help you until I get there."

I picked a yellow hibiscus bloom and set it in her hair—then remembered with a pang the rosebud that Sarita had said she'd always keep.

Always?

"I was pretty groggy last night," I said. "Did the doc say when the stitches were to come out?"

"He told me a week. Jack, you were so damn *brave*. I can't thank you enough for what you did."

"We were lucky."

"You make your own luck."


I COLLECTED OUR badly used clothing and dumped it in the trash, along with my ornamental buckle. That ended the episode, psychologically, and I was ready to tie up remaining ends.

Because I didn't want a call traced back to the Posada, I walked slowly to the telegraph office and placed a call to Manny's consulate office. By a miracle, he was there and recognized my voice. "Boy, are you in a heap of trouble."

"Comes with the profession," I said. "I'm prepared to bribe you for some help."

"Help? I shouldn't even be talking to you. And what do you mean, 'bribe'?"

"How would you like to confiscate about half a ton of snow?"

"Where are you?"

"Remember the spot where I overnighted on my way to the Fiesta?"

"Sure."

"I'm still there. Room eight. I suggest you drive a pickup."

I paid for the call and limped back to the inn. Inge was in the bathroom washing a few things. And humming a tune.

An encouraging sign.

I made myself comfortable in a chair and drank the last two slugs of Añejo. When Inge reappeared I gave her a wad of *pesos* and told her to go to the town travel agency and buy a ticket to Cozumel, in any name but her own. And bring back a liter of Añejo. After she left I collected all my U.S. currency and put it into a hotel envelope. I wrote a note to Ramón about the money and told him to make Inge comfortable at my place. I didn't say when I was coming back, because I didn't know.

175

That depended on the next few days.

Stretching out on the bed, I prepared for my noonday siesta. My stitches were beginning to draw, so I knew that healing was underway. The rum eased my pain, and I slept until Manny knocked at my door.

WE SAT AROUND the table with Inge, to whom I'd introduced Manny by his first name. I said he was a consul and she didn't ask any questions.

To Manny I said, "How bad is the heat?"

"Flaming. What did you expect? You forced Pedraza from his place, and an hour later he and the driver are found carbonized. Everyone in Mexico wants your head."

"I'm counting on you to quiet things down." I unbuttoned my *guayabera* and showed him the padded bandage. "Twenty stitches and three clamps," I told him, "and you want me remorseful? The General damn near killed me. As for Miguel, he was a cruel *cholo* with bloody hands."

He thought it over. "Be that as it may, you're still a wanted man. Leave Jalisco as soon as you can. Whether Cozumel is safe for you is an open question. I think you're too hot to handle."

"But for four hundred keys you'll try?"

He grimaced. "Where's the *coca?*"

"Twenty minutes away."

"And my *pesos?*"

"Write them off against the keys. Only funny money, anyway."

He said, "You expect a lot for less than half a ton of coke, Jack."

"Gunfighting comes high. Bring the pickup?"

He nodded.

Inge said, "I'm glad I met you, Manny. So Jack isn't really an evil person?"

He smiled. "Jack just acts like one. Thanks for your help."

We went out to the street and got into the pickup cab. We bumped down to the lakeside and turned west. Manny said, "Y'know, this whole lake is going to be mud before long. They're running an aqueduct to Guadalajara, and that'll drain Lake Chapala."

"Progress," I remarked. "Easy on those potholes—my wound hurts like the devil."

"You ought to take it easy for a year or two—forget Cejas."

"Am I thinking about him?"

"You wiped out his three partners, plus Pedraza. You won't be satisfied until Cejas joins them."

"Maybe not even then," I said, thinking of Omar Parra.

"Well, you're strictly on your own."

"I'm used to it," I said. "There's the plane."

THE CHAMACO TOWED the Seabee to the beach and helped Manny transfer the heavy duffel bags to the pickup. They got their feet wet, but the boy was used to it, and Manny didn't seem to care. He snapped a tarpaulin over the duffel bags and paid the boy for his help. On the way back to Ajijic I said, "Inge's flight leaves in a little while. How about escorting her to the airport, seeing she gets on the plane?"

"Glad to."

"Keeping track of the *Bal Musette?*"

"Not particularly. Why?"

"It delivers those guerrilla arms to San José, brings back opium, remember?"

His jaw set. "Why should I when State doesn't want to know about it?"

"That's the Corliss attitude," I told him. "Do what you're told and don't be enterprising. Where's the *Bal Musette?*"

"Still at San José. I guess owners and crew are enjoying the nay-tive girls."

"Or waiting for Enrique to produce enough poppy juice to make the return trip worthwhile."

"I'd just as soon not talk about it. And please don't tell me what your interest is."

"Twenty tons of coke enter the U.S. each year from Mexico. That's a third of the total supply, *chico,* and interrupting the Enrique connection would cut off a lot of smack."

He said nothing, and we rode the rest of the way to the Posada in silence. Manny loaded Inge's bags into my rental car and I gave her the keys. For disguise she wore a large floppy hat and shades. I kissed her and said Ramón would meet her at the San Miguel airport. I watched them drive off and went to the telegraph office to call Ramón. He was happy to learn that boat money was on the way, and said he would gladly meet the *señorita* and introduce her to my house and dogs. I said I'd be home in a few days, and thanked his wife in advance. Then I went back to the inn.

Because of my bandage I couldn't swim, but I could drink at the garden bar, and I did so while the sun disappeared behind foliage, and evening filtered through the garden with soft, purple light.

I watched guests enjoying the pool and clustering around the open bar. The cheerful scene was a counterpoise to thoughts forming in my brain. I hadn't set out to eliminate the Gang of Four, but circumstances had allowed me to delete all but one man. Before the police found me, I resolved to finish the survivor.

Fructo Cejas.

# TWENTY

**B**Y STAYING AT the Posada, I was risking capture, but I was too worn out to go out and find another place for the night. Besides, I was hungry, and the Posada restaurant turned out a fairly good meal. Before going there I managed to strap on my shoulder holster, adjusting the pistol a little more frontward than I usually wore it, but I didn't want it banging the wound. Because I was planning an early departure, I repacked my suitcase and included the MAC-10, its carrier, and the spare magazine I'd taken from the Mercedes the night before. My money was still checked at the front desk. After dinner I'd reclaim it and pay the bill.

While I was examining the menu, a little Indian boy of eight or nine came up to me and asked if he could *brillar* my *zapatos*. I hadn't looked at them lately, and when I did I had to agree that they needed extensive work. The *maître* disapproved, but I ignored him, and when the *chamaco* finished, he got up, bowed, and flashed me an irresistible smile that showed teeth whiter than porcelain. I surveyed my shoes critically. First-rate job. Having no pocket change, I gave him a thousand-*peso* note—enough to keep his family in *tortillas* for a week. He practically wept, blurted, *"Mil gracias, señor,"* and scampered off with his sudden fortune.

Halfway through my *filete de lomo,* I noticed him peering at me from behind some shrubbery. I winked at him, he winked back and disappeared.

Then, while I was paying my bill, he sidled up beside me and gave me his happy face. I was afraid he was going to offer me his sister for the night—or forever—so I didn't say anything. The change I got from the cashier came to a few *pesos,* so I motioned him over and offered him the money. When he didn't reach for it, I said, "Take it, *niño."*

"What for? I didn't do nothing."

This was an unusual lad. I said, "Sometimes good things happen to good boys. Take it." He was making a big thing over what amounted to twenty cents American. I added a hundred *pesos.* "This better?"

"Too much. I take the other, *gracias."* Dexterously he removed the original sum and stepped back before bowing. Then he ran out of the door. I pocketed what he'd declined, and carried my money bag to my room, thinking that he was some rare shoeshine boy: courteous, frugal, and observant of the work ethic. The kind of boy I would want to have if I ever had a son of my own. Pamela had refused pregnancy because it would have interfered with her modeling career. Instead, her career— and life—had been wasted on heroin. The trade was incomparably worse.

I closed my door, propped a chair under the knob, and made myself stop thinking about my dead wife. How was Inge doing, her first night on Cozumel? The dogs would guard her as few humans could, and I suspected that she would take to Sheba and her puppies. Inge, I reflected, had a great capacity for love that had yet to be fulfilled.

By now, Melody would be in West Berlin, competing in the *Sportspalast,* and I wondered whether her life had become so filled with diving and travel that she never thought of me.

I opened the fresh bottle of Añejo and poured out a double shot. As I sipped it, my thoughts turned to Sarita Rojas.

Twenty-four hours ago her protector had been living it up in his mansion. Now he was dead, and she should have heard me mentioned as his killer. Her reaction was something I never expected to know, for it seemed unlikely we would ever meet again.

But if what she'd told me was true, then she was free of Pedraza's golden bonds, free to proceed with her life.

On occasions I'd seen Cejas gaze at her with a mixture of envy and admiration, so it seemed possible that he might make a play for her. But I thought she had too much sense to fall for it.

I touched the bottle label and considered a final drink.

No, I needed sleep, not brooding over lost loves, and I'd had enough of that for one night.

Breeze through open windows cooled the room, and I decided to rest for a few hours without undressing. So I lay back on the bed and closed my eyes. My wound throbbed, the stitches pulled when I moved, but when I lay motionless, the pain drifted away.

WHAT WOKE ME was a scratching sound at the window. Silently I reached for my pistol and stared through darkness.

Someone was coming through the window opening.

I saw the brief outline of a moving head and called, *"Alto!"*

The figure froze. As I sat up I heard a hissing whisper, *"Señor. Señor?"* Damned if the kid hadn't slipped in to rob me.

"Shhhhh," came his voice. "Don't shoot. I got to tell you something."

"It's too late for shoeshines," I told him. "Or too early. Go out the way you came, and I won't tell the police."

"The police—that's what I want to tell you."

"What about the police?"

There was no smile on his lips. His face was serious, eyes large as silver dollars. "The police are looking for a *gringo*—like you. They ask for the *posada* register."

"How do you know they're looking for this *gringo?*"

"Your name is Novak. *Señor,* I think you better go. Fast."

"I think you're right," I said, and got off the bed. "How come you don't help the police?"

"The police are worse thieves than anyone. They kick me and beat up my brother. They're *cabrones.*"

"Any ideas?"

"We go through the garden."

I removed the chair from the knob and unlocked the door. Before I picked up my bags I fumbled some bills from my pocket and handed them to him. He said, "You don't have to pay me, *señor.*"

"We'll argue later. Better you have it than the police."

Nodding, he went out of the door like a shadow. He looked carefully around and signaled all-clear, so I stepped out and closed the door. Following him, I jogged along the side of the garden, keeping in shadows. The pain in my left side was spectacular, but I kept going until he motioned me down. I peered around.

Moonlight glinted on the badges and pistols of two policemen who were creeping up on my room. "Wait," the boy whispered. "When they go in, we go on."

"Got it." Pain was shooting colored lasers through my head, but I saw one cop turn the door handle and tiptoe inside the dark room. Cautiously, his partner followed.

"Now!"

We ran past the pool and bar, and when we were on a cobbled street I heard the first whistle blowing. The boy urged me across the street toward an opening in a whitewashed wall. He must have seen pain on my face, because he came back and tried to help me with one of my bags. He tugged the money bag from my hand, and I let him drag it into the opening;

it was lighter than the one in my right hand that held clothing and the machine pistol.

Back at the inn, garden lights went on and more whistles sounded. Gingerly, the boy touched my left arm. "You're hurt?"

I nodded. "What's your name?"

"Carlos. You wait here, I bring my brother. He help you get away. He don't like police neither."

"I'll wait."

He winked at me, and melted into shadows.

As I sat there, my heart slowed and I began thinking that I had only myself to blame. Two weeks ago I'd signed the Posada register with my own name. Returning, I couldn't use another name—but then, I hadn't anticipated being hunted by the police.

Next time—if there *was* a next time—I'd take Manny's advice and use false ID, take the precautions agents did in Moscow.

My stitches felt as if they were tearing out. *Mierda!* At least the clinic doc would keep his mouth shut.

Where to go?

I wondered if there was a reward for my capture. Dead or alive. *That* would energize the countryside. *Gringos* would be hauled in and questioned, creating hysteria among Ajijic's arty set. The thought pleased me.

Ten minutes passed. Twelve, fourteen, while police beat the garden bushes, calling back and forth. The size of the force surprised me.

Finally, I heard a car cough and rumble down the street. As it neared I looked through the opening and saw an ancient Kaiser angling toward the curb. It was dented and battered, and the front fender and bumper were missing. So many different paint patches covered its body that I was reminded of a camouflage job. The antique stopped beside the wall opening. There was someone at the wheel, not Carlos. In another moment, his head popped up and he gave a short whistle, then motioned me in.

Stooping, I carried my bags to the old wreck, and Carlos hoisted them inside. As soon as I was in, the engine rattled and coughed, and the Kaiser chuffed down the street away from the lighted garden. With a pleased smile Carlos said, "This my brother, Roberto."

*"Encantado,"* I said and looked at the small figure gripping the steering wheel. "Where are we going?"

Without looking around, he said, "Where you want to go, *señor?*"

"Think we can make Guadalajara?"

"Maybe." At least he didn't object to the idea. Instead, he said, "You can pay for gasoline?"

"I can pay."

"Then we better get some."

I looked over his shoulder at the gas gauge. The needle was drifting just above the empty mark. "Soon," I said, and passed him some *pesos*.

We were driving east along the lakeside, and when the car reached Chapala village, Roberto steered into a dark Pemex station. In fact, the whole town was dark. I looked at the old gas pumps and shook my head. Carlos said, "Don't worry," as he got out of the car. He went to the nearest pump, picked up a flat stone at the base, and showed me a key. With it he unlocked the pump, flicked an interior lever, and gasoline surged into the overhead container. When it was full, Roberto eased the car ahead, and Carlos stuck the hose nozzle into the tank. The brothers made quite a team.

The Kaiser took a long drink, and I saw the gauge needle move full to the right. Carlos replaced the hose nozzle, turned off the pump, locked it, and replaced the key. That was one way to get gas in Mexico.

On the highway we chugged along at twenty-odd miles an hour. The speedometer wasn't functioning, so speed was only an estimate. What impressed me was that I'd been rescued by a small boy to whom I'd done a very small kindness, a boy who knew how to react to emergency and get things done. So far, Roberto had been silent. I leaned forward and said, "What's your name?"

"Roberto."

"I know that—your family name."

"Menocal."

"Your brother says you don't like policemen?"

His head turned and I saw the right side of his face. The dark eyebrow was interrupted by a thick scar. The cheekbone was indented. *"Mordelones,"* he said, using the contemptuous term for bribe-taking cops. "They want money to let you live."

He looked about fourteen, fifteen at the most. "How do you live?" I asked.

"Repair cars. I'm a good mechanic." He glanced back. "For a *gringo* you speak good Spanish. Carlos says you got hurt in your arm."

"Automobile," I said, "and we won't talk about it. If the cops stop us, say I forced you to drive me."

"Okay. Where you want to go in the city."

I hadn't thought that far ahead. "Maybe a hotel where they don't ask questions."

He chuckled. "No problem, *señor gringo.*"

The car coughed and sputtered up a winding grade. We barely made it over the top of the incline, then we were on the down side and I sighed with relief. Roberto had to be a good mechanic to keep that old engine going—on what sounded like four of six cylinders—but in Ajijic he probably wasn't appreciated.

Carlos had fallen asleep in the seat corner. Blessed, I thought, with an Indian's flexible temperament. I envied him.

On we drove through the night, eventually passing the airport, coming finally to Pedraza's palace. There were a few lights inside, but the high compound wall was no longer illuminated, and I could see no soldiers on duty. Roberto said, "You know that place?"

"Tell me about it."

"General Pedraza owned it, but he's dead. Two men killed each other there, fighting over a woman." He glanced at me briefly, then gazed steadily at the road. "I like girls but I wouldn't kill for one."

"Some men do crazy things." I wondered if anyone was guarding Pedraza's possessions. Maybe Cejas would take over the entire spread. And, although Sarita hadn't said so, I assumed there was a wife/widow in the background, with legal claims.

Soon I could see the glow of city lights. Below the road lay the shattered, burned-out wreckage of the Mercedes limousine. At least both men were dead before their bodies began to burn.

We passed through the sleeping village of Tlaquepaque, and Roberto steered through dark streets to a short, even darker, street off Rio Nilo. Over a doorway an illuminated sign advertising Corona beer gave the name of the hotel as El Triunfo.

The car stopped and Carlos woke up. Roberto said, "You pay ten thousand *pesos,* they don't ask questions. If you want, I go in."

I handed him the *pesos,* which seemed about right for the neighborhood. He took it and went into the open doorway. After a while he came out with a key. From the floor of the front seat he picked up a wide-brimmed straw hat and gave it to me. I put it on, and he and Carlos carried my bags into the hotel, past a disinterested clerk, and up a dark flight of stairs. Roberto opened the room door and turned on the overhead bulb.

Riches to rags, I thought as I looked around the cell-like room. There was a brown-stained wash basin, a wooden chair with chipped paint, and a narrow, swaybacked bed. It occurred to me that this was the sort of hotel police would routinely shake down when searching for fugitives, but I trusted the Menocal brothers' judgment. So far, it had been excellent.

Tomorrow I was going to dress Meskin-style and try to survive a few days more.

*"Servido, señor,"* Carlos said, and bowed. "May God protect you."

Roberto pulled down the window shade. "Anything else?" he asked.

"I want to give you something to take back to Ajijic." I opened my wallet and handed him fifty thousand *pesos,* another fifty thousand to Carlos. Altogether, about a hundred dollars.

Their eyes widened. *"Señor,"* Roberto exclaimed, "this is too much."

"My life is worth something," I said, noticing that both boys looked dazed. "Now you'd better start back. Next time I'm in Ajijic I'll know where to find a good shoeshine boy—and a good mechanic."

Carlos wiped a tear from his cheek. *"Cien mil gracias, señor.* I hope they don't catch you."

"Me, too," Roberto said. We shook hands and they filed out.

I locked the door and stuck the wobbly chair under the knob. I shoved the money bag under the bed and opened the other suitcase. From it I took my machine pistol and set it on the bed. Then I turned off the single bulb and, without undressing, lay back to resume my interrupted rest.

In José, the bartender, I had a potential asset—unless Manny had told him to stay clear of me. Sarita might help me gain access to Cejas, but I wasn't ready to place her in danger.

And there was Carla Santiago.

Whether the movie company disbanded would depend on whether Pedraza had financed production in advance—or whether he made periodic payments. If they were still shooting, Sarita and Carla would stay through the end. I had to see Sarita again, if only to hear what she had to say.

With my hand around the MAC-10 grip I fell asleep.

It was midday when I woke. I rinsed my face in tepid water and tapped my five-million *peso* lode to replenish my wallet.

I locked the suitcase and went down the staircase and out to the dingy street. Not far away was a clothing store where I bought a cheap *guayabera* and cheaper trousers, a sisal hat, and sunglasses. The proprietor stuffed my old clothing in a used shopping bag that I dumped near a bus stop.

The bus took me to the central railway station where I checked my money bag and got a receipt. From a pay phone I called the Fiesta Americana bar and asked for José. When he came on the line I said, "Recognize my voice?"

"Assuredly I do."

"I'm going to ask some questions. Is Carla Santiago at the hotel?"

"Yes."

"Sarita Rojas?"

"I think so."

"Are they going to continue making the movie?"

"So I hear."

"Is Cejas at the hotel?"

"He had drinks at the bar and left." His voice lowered. "They're looking for you. I don't think you ought to come here."

"Are you off at four?"

"Yes."

"Can you get me a waiter's uniform?"

"I . . . " He hesitated. "I'll try."

"Try to get my size, sort of medium-large, and meet me at the Revolution Theater. I'll be there at four-thirty. *Hasta luego.*"

The line went dead. I called Carla's room, but no answer.

For a few moments I jingled change in my hand as I considered calling Sarita. I wanted to, but risk was involved. To both of us. Chances were she and Carla were filming at the Zapopan basilica—why not find out?

I dialed the hotel again and asked for her suite. After four rings the phone was answered, and I heard the voice of Fructo Cejas.

# TWENTY-ONE

I CUPPED MY hand over the mouthpiece. *"Recepción,"* I said, nasally. *Puede comunicarme con la Señorita Rojas?"*

*"En este momento, no,"* he said curtly and hung up.

That didn't tell me if she was there, but I was far from pleased that Cejas was. Because my plans for Cejas didn't involve Sarita.

I left the station and went into a *farmacia* where I bought tape, gauze bandage, and a shaker of antibiotic powder. The pharmacist gave me directions to a novelty shop a few blocks away. There I bought a pair of nonrefracting glasses, a three-inch mustache, and a modest goatee, both matching the rather undistinguished color of my hair. The proprietor added a vial of spirit gum and wrapped everything together.

The time was two o'clock, and I was hungry.

At a working-class café I ate *tortillas* with *guacamole,* and a plate of refried beans, washing them down with two bottles of cold Tecate. The beer tasted considerably better than the meal.

Then, back to my cell at the El Triunfo, where I changed bandages and saw that my graze-wound was puckering around the clamps and stitches and seemed not to be draining. I shook antiseptic powder on it, while lying on my right side, and managed to apply a fresh bandage. The effort tired me, so I rested and dozed a while. At four o'clock I got off the bed, held mustache and goatee to my face, and looked at my reflection in the badly cracked mirror. The image was far from appealing, even less so when I added the stage spectacles. But I now had the appearance of another *tapatío* at whom no one was going to look twice. So I applied the disguise pieces with spirit gum and left for the Revolution Theater.

187

*        *        *

José ARRIVED FIFTEEN minutes late, carrying a bulky shopping bag. There weren't many people in the lobby, but he didn't recognize me until I approached. For a moment he peered at me, then handed over the bag. "I hope this fits you," he said, "it was the best I could do."

"Something is always better than nothing. Are you working tonight?"

"After eight."

"Stay loose—I may need you."

When he didn't react, I said, "Javier was tortured to death."

A spasm crossed his face. *"Buena suerte."*

More than good luck, I needed a miracle, I thought as I watched him walk away and vanish in the sidewalk crowd. Another honest Mexican, doing what he could to strike back at those who had brought tragedy into his life. For me, it was easy to empathize with José; I felt as though I'd written the guidebook on vengeance.

I took a taxi to two blocks from the Fiesta Americana and strolled around it, feeling secure in my disguise. There was still plenty of light so it was easy to locate the employee entrance. I lingered near the door, and the next time it opened I saw a security guard posted inside, checking ID.

That meant I was going to have to get in by another route, and an idea occurred to me. I took a turn around the side and looked down into the garage. The old *sereno* was there, a small radio on his lap. As I passed along I wondered if he had told anyone how I'd commandeered Cejas' limousine. Probably not, because his job would be at stake.

Chartered buses from the movie company arrived at the hotel entrance. Film work was proceeding, despite the backer's death. Inge could have her old job back—but for the existence of Cejas.

He was making it tough for everyone, and I wondered what he was thinking about all that happened. *Cholo* avarice would delight him over outliving his partners; now he was king of garbage mountain, and there was no one to share profits with. But street smarts would remind him that I was a threat to his reign, and if he hadn't yet posted a reward for my capture he probably would.

Carla's blue Marquis screeched up, braked, and honked at the garage entrance. Chandler Bates was behind the wheel, Carla beside him. To me they were harmless people with problems of their own, principally aging.

As I was turning away I saw Sarita arrive in her black roadster. She

188

turned it over to a valet and hurried into the hotel. I felt a lump swell in my throat, so I got into a taxi and rode back to the El Triunfo.

No glass had been supplied with the room, so I drank Añejo from the bottle and checked my MAC-10, deciding to carry it in the airline bag. I got into the waiter's uniform and found it a reasonable fit. Fortunately, the jacket was large enough to button around the shoulder holster and my Beretta. The dinner hour, when room service was busy, would be the optimum time to make an appearance, rather than late at night when a lone waiter in the corridor was likely to be conspicuous.

Carrying the waiter's jacket in my shopping bag, the airline bag in my other hand, I left my safe house toward eight o'clock and taxied to the Fiesta Americana. I entered the garage by the pedestrian door and found the *sereno* sleeping in his chair.

I went past him quietly and got into the service elevator. There I put on the waiter's jacket and rolled my coat into the shopping bag. I unzipped the airline bag to make the machine pistol available without delay and got out on the top floor, wedging the sliding door open with my foot.

Looking down toward the Presidential Suite, I saw a police guard sitting outside the door. Cejas had taken my warning to heart.

I got back into the elevator and left it on the floor below. Outside one door was a service tray with a champagne bucket and inverted empty bottle. I pushed the cork down into the neck, set the bottle in the bucket, and carried the tray to the elevator. I'd used the shopping bag as a door wedge, and decided to do so again. If I made it back, I'd need the jacket; if not, it was up for grabs.

As I stepped from the elevator I saw a room maid leaving one of the suites, a key ring hanging from her waist. I beckoned to her and when she was near, I said, "Anyone in Cejas' suite?"

"Why?"

"Because if there isn't, I can't leave this champagne."

"Where's your key?"

"Misplaced it—and don't want to tell the captain."

She nodded understandingly. "Let's find out. Come."

I followed her along the corridor to the suite door. The policeman glanced at us without interest. The maid unlocked the door and said, "Don't be so forgetful next time." She walked away.

The policeman got up from his chair. "You'd better ring the bell."

"They said not to." I peered at him through my glasses and listened for sounds within the suite. Silence. I began backing awkwardly into the foyer, grunted, and said, "Take this." I handed him the airline bag and used both hands to put down the service tray. When I straightened up I had the Beretta in my right hand. As the guard stared at it I held my left index finger to my lips. "Not a sound, or you're dead." Reaching over, I pulled out his heavy .45 revolver and motioned him into the foyer. "Close the door," I whispered, and when he turned to shut it, I hit the back of his head just below his cap. With a groan he pitched forward.

The fall didn't make much sound, but it was enough to rouse a body-guard from his chair. From the corner of my eye I saw him amble toward us, pistol in one hand. I knelt and began slapping the policeman's face. The bodyguard called, "What's going on?"

"He fainted. Give me a hand, will you?"

"Leave him there, I'll call a doctor." Turning, he started for a telephone.

"No," I said, getting to my feet and moving away. "Drop your gun."

He didn't. Instead, he whirled around and fired at where I'd been kneeling. As he realized his mistake, I fired the .45 revolver. Twice. Both bullets caught him in the chest and slammed him against the sofa. He slid down, looking stupidly at the blood on his shirt. His head lifted and the pistol fired, but it was only muscular contraction. His eyes glazed and his body shook as he died. I kicked his pistol away.

Four shots had been fired. If they weren't heard outside the suite, they were loud enough to waken anyone within.

I laid the .45 revolver near the policeman's hand, got out my machine pistol, and, in a crouch, eased carefully into the living room. All that was there was an empty glass and the crotch magazine the bodyguard had been reading. No one in the kitchen, so I went up to the loft floor and looked around.

Both bedroom doors open, and no one inside. Closets empty.

*Mierda!*

I could wait for Cejas to return, but he might not come alone. The policeman's empty chair would be noticed, and the shooting had probably been heard. Time to go.

I dropped the MAC-10 into its bag, picked up the champagne bucket, and opened the door. No one in the hall, so I toed the tray outside and into a corner. Carrying handbag and bucket I began walking toward the service elevator. Just then three men got out of a passenger elevator and hurried toward me. One civilian and two hotel security guards. As the civilian neared me, he called, "Did you hear shots?"

"No, *señor,* but I only just came."

One of the guards spotted the empty chair, and all three broke into a run. I headed away from them and saw that the service elevator door was closed. Recalling it would take too long, so I strode to the door of Sarita's suite and rang the bell.

Looking back, I saw the civilian opening Cejas' door. I rang the bell again. Urgently.

The door opened and I saw Sarita's face. "What is it?" she asked in Spanish.

"Room service." I held up the bucket and started in.

Frowning, she moved aside, and then I saw a man standing a few feet behind her. Staring at me, he said, "You made a mistake."

Fructo Cejas, with a gun in his hand.

"Pardon me," I said, and started to back out. "Sorry."

He took a step toward me. "Close the door, *mozo,* you look familiar."

Sarita was gazing at me, a troubled look on her face. Another moment and she'd recognize me. I turned around to close the door, bent over, and put down the champagne bucket. Cejas said, "What's in the bag?"

"I don't know—I was told to take it to a particular room."

"What's your name?"

"Salvador Gonzales, *a sus órdenes, señor.*"

"Put down the bag." The gun muzzle covered me.

"Because I'm a poor waiter you treat me like dirt." I tossed the bag at him and lunged after it.

Suspicion had made Cejas wary. He stepped back and swung the gun at my head. It glanced off the side of my face and hit my shoulder muscle. His knee struck my chest as I grappled with him, flailing for his gun. The barrel hit my head again, and half-stunned, I bore him over backward. The wound pain made my left arm next to useless as we rolled on the floor. I clawed his eyes, he yelled, and pounded the gun against my skull. Red lasers drilled my head, and I felt consciousness slipping away.

Cejas got on top of me and shoved the gun into my throat. "Where's my *coca?*" he snarled, and pushed harder.

Vision was fading. I croaked something and saw Sarita come up behind him, champagne bottle in hand. She swung it like a baseball bat, and it shattered against his skull, showering us with glass. Cejas fell forward, smothering my face, and I passed out.

Moments later I was breathing freely. Sarita was tugging Cejas' body from mine. "Thanks," I said weakly, and slowly got up.

"Jack," she said, "you *fool.* God, I'm glad you're alive, but coming here was crazy."

"I didn't know he was here," I told her. "I wanted to see *you.*"

She dropped Cejas' arms and came to mine. Sobbing, she said, "He was threatening me. I'm so glad you came."

I kissed her forehead and said, "I'm not in very good shape." Stepping back, I unbuttoned jacket and shirt, showed her my bandaged wound. "Pedraza shot me, I had to kill him."

She shuddered. "When I heard you had crashed I almost died."

"I couldn't tell you before. I had to save Inge."

"I know."

Picking up my MAC-10, I pointed it at Cejas, and knelt to feel his carotid artery. No pulse. I felt the left side of his skull. Soft as a cracked eggshell, and sticky. Getting up, I put away the machine pistol.

Tremulously, she said, "I killed him."

"He would have killed me. Don't think about it."

She was still staring at the body. "What will we do?"

"Get him out of here," I said, "after a drink."

"I need one, too." She walked quickly away and brought back a bottle of Añejo.

I drank deeply, and some of the lights in my head went out. I handed her the bottle and sat down.

She knelt on the floor beside me, head on my shoulder.

It was a strange scene, I reflected. The body of a dead man, broken glass strewing the floor. And two lovers consoling each other.

After a while I said, "Why was he threatening you?"

She shook her head. "Because Gil . . . Gilberto left his house to me. Cejas wanted it, said his money had bought it, and if I didn't sign the papers he'd kill me." She gestured at the table. On it lay a legal document. "Jack, what will we *do?*"

"Look in his pockets for the room key."

Reluctantly, she went through his pockets and pulled out a key. Handing it to me, she said, "The mustache and *bigote* aren't the real you. I thought I recognized you, but then you spoke in Spanish. You never told me you could speak Spanish."

"It wasn't time," I said, and told her what had happened in Cejas' suite a few minutes before. "My guess is the hotel won't want the killing widely known. Would you mind seeing what's happening? Cejas pounded the hell out of me." I gave her back the key. She went out, I had another pull at the bottle, and was feeling a little better by the time she came back.

"There were no guards outside, so I went in. The dead man is still there."

"And the policeman?"

She shook her head.

"Before there are cops all over the place, we'd better move him." I nodded at Cejas' corpse. "I'm still a little giddy, so we'll have to do it together. If anyone sees us, pretend Fructo is drunk."

She looked at the body, closed her eyes and shivered. "I'm not sure I can bear to touch him."

"Sure you can. You're the tough Meskin kid from Nogales."

At that, she smiled. "Right. I can do it."

I rested before kneeling beside the body. "Get his left arm over my right shoulder," I told her, "other arm over your shoulders, and we'll lift together."

The effort was monumental. Getting him upright was like wrestling a water bed, but we made it out the door and began working the slack body toward the end of the corridor. His toes dragged on the carpeting, and Sarita's breathing was labored. Every muscle in my body ached, especially my wound and my battered head. Effort pumped blood through it, escalating pain until I wanted to yell.

Doggedly, we kept going. Twice he almost slipped from our grasp, and jacking his body upright was extra effort I didn't need. Finally, we reached the suite door, and Sarita opened it.

We hauled him inside and dropped him on the foyer floor.

For a few moments we rested, then I said, "Onward and upward."

We each took a wrist and dragged him on his back through the main room to the stairs. I set my right shoulder in his belly and lifted him like a sack of sand. I staggered up the stairs, through a bedroom, and into the bath where I dropped him so that his head wedged against the toilet. I stuck his pistol into his belt and left him there. Then I went unsteadily down the stairs, gripping the railing most of the way.

We went back to her suite, unseen, and Sarita made ice compresses and applied them to my skull. After a while I began feeling better. Sarita said, "What now, *querido?*"

"I have to get out of here. The policeman I slugged will have described the waiter who did it."

"We'll go together."

I shook my head. "This isn't your project, honey."

"I killed Cejas."

"Saving me. Do yourself a favor and stay out of it."

"That's impossible, so don't even suggest it." She moved an ice pack tenderly. "I have a car, you know. We can go anywhere."

"All right—but what about the movie?"

"It's nearly complete. Let *me* worry about that. Is Inge safe?"

"Yes. San Juan and Alarcón were using her."

"I'm *so* sorry for her. Will she be . . . all right?"

"I think so. Hope."

"Are you well enough to fly your plane?"

"If you can drive me to Chapala."

"Then let's get out of here." She went away and came back with her beach bag and a wicker hamper. "Supplies," she told me, then adjusted my mustache and goatee. Stepping back, she smiled. "You have much to learn about makeup."

"It worked—almost." Taking her arm, I walked toward the door. Glass crunched under my feet. Looking down, I said, "What about *this?*"

"Don't be concerned—I'm famous for my rages."

I carried the wicker hamper as I followed her to the service elevator. She pressed the button, and I looked around.

On the wall was a fire alarm box. As the elevator doors opened I broke the alarm's glass, and bells started ringing. Along the corridor ceiling sprinklers began spraying water.

I stepped into the cage beside Sarita and punched the garage button. She said, "Why didn't you tell me you were going to do that? I had a terrible fright."

"Spur of the moment," I said. "Like this." I drew her to me and kissed her warm lips. She murmured something and pressed her body to mine.

From the corner of my eye I saw my shopping bag in the corner; someone had unwedged it and kicked it inside. As rapidly as I could I got out of the waiter's jacket and put on my street coat. I put the jacket into the shopping bag just as the door opened onto the garage.

We walked to her car, stowed the hamper and beach bag in the roadster's trunk, and then I got in beside her. Only then did she peel off my mustache and goatee. "Your beard tickled. This is better." She kissed me again.

Fire bells were sounding through the hotel. The *sereno* woke up and stared around. Sarita backed out, turned on headlights, and the street door opened. We bounced up and out onto the Avenida.

"I have a bag I'd like to pick up," I told her. "Clothing, shaving gear . . . a bottle. In a swell hotel on Rio Nilo."

As we cleared the first block she had to swerve toward the curb to avoid an oncoming fire engine. The *bomberos* clinging to it in their hats and oilskins looked happy at their work. They would be less happy when they discovered it was a false alarm.

When we pulled up in front of the Corona beer sign, Sarita looked around with distaste. "Reminds me of Nogales. Couldn't you do better than this?"

"Friends recommended it." I left the car and reclaimed my suitcase from my room, then joined her in the little Mercedes.

On the way to the lake I told her what had happened after I flew out of Mazatlán, how I'd come back to Chapala and taken refuge at the Posada Ajijic until roused by the shoeshine boy. I described the slow, uncertain trip to Guadalajara in Roberto's ancient vehicle. "And the rest you know."

"Not quite. How did you manage to take over Fructo's limousine?"

I explained how Carla had helped me lure Miguel to the garage—and told no one.

"That makes me think better of her," Sarita said. "If I ever see her again, we can be friends."

"Won't you be finishing the film together?"

"Actually, her part's finished—she was killed in the *barranca,* remember? She stays on because of Chandler. Without her I don't think he could get out of bed for a day's work."

"She helped me when I needed it, and that counts for a lot. By the way, where are we going?"

"Paradise Island. You'll be safe there, and I'll have you to myself. Without interruption."

"Can't think of a better idea."

As we drove slowly through Ajijic she said, "It's a shame you're a fugitive. Otherwise we could stop at the Posada. But under the circumstances I'll just have to wait."

I wasn't thinking too clearly. "For what?"

Her lips brushed the side of my face. "Guess."


IT WAS CLOSE to midnight when we reached the shore point where I'd left the Seabee. I could see moonlight on its wings, reflecting from the Plexiglas cowling.

The *chamaco* wasn't there, but someone else was. A man in uniform, sitting on the narrow beach, holding a rifle upright between his knees.

# TWENTY-TWO

*L A PINGA!"* SARITA exploded. "What bad luck! But let me handle this."

"You're out of your mind. The guy's armed and ready for business." I opened the airline bag and pulled out my machine pistol. "I'll take the *hijo.*"

Her hand pressed my wrists. "Please . . . if I don't get my way, there's time for that." She winked coquettishly. "I like to think I have *some* influence among my fans."

Had I felt better I would have argued more. Instead, I shrugged. "Go ahead, try. If he gives you any static, I'll blow him away."

"Such a violent man," she murmured, and left the roadster. There was a break in the low wall and steps down to the beach. She followed them, and I saw her walk sinuously toward the seated rifleman. Behind him she cupped her hands, leaned forward, and said, *"Boo!"* very loudly. He nearly fell over.

I heard her laugh as she gave him her hand and helped him to his feet. They were fifty feet away, but through the quiet night air I could hear almost every word they said.

Sarita: "It's nice of you to watch my plane. How much do I owe you?"

Guard: *"Your* plane, *señorita?* I was told it belongs to a *bandido.*"

Sarita: "You recognize me, perhaps? You know who I am?"

Guard: *"Sí, sí.* [Removing cap] *La Divina Sarita.*"

Sarita: "And you think I associate with *pistoleros* and *ladrones?* What an insulting thought. Surely the association of *serenos* should teach its members better manners."

Guard: *"Sereno? Señorita,* pardon me, but I am not a *sereno.* I am a policeman."

Sarita: "Oh, I am *so* sorry. I didn't notice your badge. You'll forgive me, won't you?"

Guard: "Of course. Here in the darkness it's a natural mistake. Think nothing of it."

Sarita: "We're friends, then . . . we understand one another?"

Guard: "Indeed, *señorita.* It's a privilege to be able to speak with you. I love your pictures. Juan Vélez, at your service."

Sarita: *"Encantada.* I have a fancy for a moonlight flight, so I brought my pilot. We are going to fly above the lake for a while [Looks upward] It's such a beautiful night." [Extends arms and thrusts chest forward]

Guard: *"Señorita,* what you wish is not possible. I have strict orders that no one takes this aircraft."

Sarita: "Even for a little while? Surely, you'd not deny me that—after coming all the way from Guadalajara?"

Guard: "Forgive me, *señorita,* but I have my orders from the captain."

Sarita: "Tell me where this captain is, and I will inform him that you are a very rude person, Juan Vélez. Do you believe for one moment that your captain would deny me an hour's flight in the beautiful moonlight?"

Guard: [Weakly] "No, but he would have to tell me so himself. And he is, lamentably, asleep."

Sarita: "Where?"

Guard: "In his home at San Juan Cosalá."

Sarita: "And you would make me drive there, all that distance, arouse him, and ask him to grant me what you could so easily do?"

Guard: [Firmly] "I know only that I have my orders and must obey them."

Sarita: "Very well. We will see if you will shoot Sarita Rojas. Did your captain order you to do that?"

Guard: "No, *señorita,* he did not."

I was getting impatient. My body ached. My muscles were stiff, and my head throbbed. I saw her turn and wave at me.

"Bring the bags," she called.

Stiffly, I got out of the little car, replaced my mustache and goatee, and opened the trunk. I heard the guard say, "What is your pilot doing?"

"What I told him to do—bring my baggage. I have a small place at Chula Vista and intend to stay there tonight."

"What of your vehicle, *señorita?"*

"You may guard it for me until the pilot returns."

Carrying our bags, I started down the beach steps. To the guard I said, "There's a *chalupa* over there. Have the kindness to help me into it."

The guard looked from Sarita to me, then at her imperious pose, and shrugged. He laid down his rifle. *"Qué sé yo?"* he said resignedly and helped me get the bags into the *chalupa.* I poled out to the plane and fitted our gear into the cabin where the heavy duffel bags had been. Then I poled back. Sarita stepped in, and I beckoned to the guard. "You, too. When we're in the plane, unfasten the buoy rope from the nose, and return the *chalupa."*

Hesitantly, he got in and took the pole from me.

At planeside, I steadied the little log canoe until Sarita was in her seat, then I climbed in, feeling fresh pain in my rib wound.

I handed the policeman ten thousand pesos, and he tipped his hat. *"Gracias, padrón, señorita. Buen vuelo."*

I closed the door and looked at the instrument panel. Over the cowling I saw the policeman untying the mooring line. Sarita gave me a smug glance. "See?"

"I see. And what I just saw was frightening. The power of a woman never ceases to amaze me."

"I've played that scene before."

"Obviously."

"It was in a movie I did three years ago. *La Hija del Duende."*

"I didn't see it," I said crossly, fitted on my headset, and turned the ignition lock.

The engine barked and grumbled, but it caught, and I ruddered the nose away from the beach. There was no appreciable wind, so I headed out into the lake, warming the engine as we accelerated. "Seat belt on?" I asked, and groped across her lap for it. Her loins trapped my hand. "Ummm. That's nice. Save some for later." She released my hand, and I transferred it to the controls. Flaps down, I shoved the throttle ahead.

Lacking waves to bounce the hull onto its step, the plane had a longer takeoff run than on the ocean. Presently we skipped into the air, and as I banked west Sarita said, "What a nice policeman—he just turned off my headlights. You should have done that, Jack."

"I was busy thinking how I was going to kill him. How are you going to explain all this when you go back?"

"I'll think of something. Isn't it beautiful tonight?"

"Gorgeous," I said, "not to mention dangerous."

"I think you've given me a taste for danger."

"You handle it well," I said, remembering how Melody had responded to lethal danger. In spirit they were two of a kind.

I tuned in the Puerto Vallarta tower, got out my plotting board, and figured a course to Isla Paraiso that would avoid PV airport radar and still get us to the little island before running out of gas.

With clear moonlight we had a good chance of finding it in the dark ocean, but if cloud cover intervened, we were lost, in more ways than one.

Beside me she said, "Remember . . . I was the one who didn't want to get deeply involved? Now I've killed for you—how deeply involved is that?"

"All the way. Ain't no further."

She sighed. "Are you *ever* going to tell me about yourself . . . who you really are?"

"You've earned it. When we're safely down."

"I hate waiting—for anything. But tell me this to satisfy my curiosity. Did you come or were you sent to Guadalajara—to do what you did? Kill the Gang of Four—and Gil?"

"I was on a fact-finding mission, as they say. It expanded."

"Expanded?"

"Became complicated. Let me tell you in my own way . . . when we're on the beach."

Over the *cordillera* I took a visual fix on PV, flew as low as I could, and dropped down over the Pacific side. All up and down the coast, breaking waves were phosphorescent in the moonlight.

"We'll need both sets of eyes now," I told her, and turned northwest toward where I remembered the little island to be.

The main tank was low, so I switched on the auxiliary, trimmed tabs to compensate for the warmer ocean air, and steadied at four thousand feet. The old pusher engine hummed like a happy bride.

Another ten minutes and I pointed over across the nose. "Should see it soon, honey—if it's still there."

"It is, and we'll find it." She looked at me. "We've come too far not to."

"I can't use all the gas tonight. I have to leave enough to fly in from the island for refueling."

I was the first to see the ring of phosphorescent waves around her island. "There it is," I said. "Now to get through the reefs."

"I have full confidence in you, my captain. Besides, this is a charmed flight to a magic island."

200

I smiled at her youthful outlook and eased the throttle to lose altitude. The island came up sooner than I'd expected, and I circled twice, spotting the reef channel by wave formation. Unless there was a lot of current, we should make it through without getting holed.

I turned back and made a long run, keeping the channel in sight, lowered flaps and reduced airspeed, and suddenly we were on the water, seafoam splashing over the windows. I was glad I'd made allowance for current, and ruddered the Seabee through the channel in a straight shot. A wave picked us up and bumped the nose on the sand, I gunned the engine, and the next wave deposited us on the gently slanting beach. I got out and carried the anchor forward, sank the hook in the sand, and turned back for Sarita.

She was already hauling out the beach bag and hamper. "Where do you want to sleep?" she called.

"Where we first made love."

"Over there, then. I hope I don't have to step on another sea urchin to get your attention."

"Hardly. But I'm kind of beat up and battered."

"You'll do," she called. "You'll be surprised how well you'll do."

Then she was out of her clothing and pirouetting across the moonstruck sands, innocent and free, the heroine of a fairy tale, and my throat swelled as I thought that I had never seen such grace and beauty beyond my boyhood dreams.

Slowly she spun toward me, and I took her silvered body in my arms and kissed her lips and throat, the softness of her breasts, and soon we were together on her beach towel, remembering the first time, and knowing that now, after danger and death, with bright stars and moon above, there would never again be anything to match it in our lives.


BEFORE DAWN THE breeze turned cool, and we warmed each other with our bodies. Hers must have drawn pain from mine, because I was comfortable with her arms around me, her legs twined with mine. And all that I had gone through and done seemed dim and far away, a tale told by a drunken fool when I was only partly listening to what I knew were lies.


SHE WAS UP first, cleansing herself in the low surf like a naiad unaware, and I walked down to join her.

In deeper water I held her body in my arms, letting wavelets lick over it, and felt my bandages come loose. Saltwater stung, but it was sun-washed and pure, the healing lotion of ancient man. The stinging dwindled as she clasped my body with her thighs and made me whole again.

She had crammed food into her picnic hamper—rolls, cans of fruit, blanched asparagus and tomatoes, a spicy *chorizo,* and a liter of water. Plus two bottles of Dom Perignon, one of tequila, and a bottle of Añejo. In my plane was a gallon of drinking water and emergency rations, so we could stave off thirst and hunger for several days.

After breakfast I said, "I'm going to look for a place to conceal the plane from passing aircraft."

"What are we looking for?"

"A tree or two that overhang the beach. Better put on shoes, the sand will wear the hell out of your feet."

Holding hands, we walked north along the water's edge. Fiddler crabs scuttled away, sand-shrimp buried themselves. In the shallows, a small, speckled ray hunted for fry. I scanned the offshore water for shark dorsals and saw none—but that didn't mean they weren't there.

High above, a plane laid a chalk trail across the light blue sky. From Acapulco, probably, and heading for Baja. He was too high to spot my Seabee, but other planes flew lower, and could.

We rounded the north curve of the island and within a hundred yards came to a small inlet overhung by palm and seagrape trees.

While Sarita waited in the shade, I jogged back to the plane, put our belongings in it, and taxied over calm water. Before turning into the beach, I put down the wheels and got enough momentum so that the plane rolled right up the sand and into the shade of the trees.

We were safe now, secure. Paradise Island was ours alone.

We shared a bottle of Dom, and I remembered how she'd smashed Cejas' skull with a similar one. That was last night, but already it seemed a year away, so quickly was I losing track of time.

We'd made the island on auxiliary fuel, so I checked the tank level and figured I could fly about sixty miles on the remainder.

Alone.

I couldn't refuel at Mazatlán or Puerto Vallarta, so I'd have to cruise the coast, looking for a place that might have high-test gasoline. Maybe a farm that kept a crop-dusting biplane, or some out-of-the-way marina with a racing boat.

As we sat in the shade beside the plane, I said, "Sooner or later we'll have to leave here. Have you given any thought to where you want to go?"

"I just want to be with you." She kissed the side of my face. "Do we have to talk about the future? The future is a reel of film waiting to be exposed. Let's talk about the past—yours."

So I told her about my childhood, the Naval Academy, Vietnam, the death of my wife, my time with DEA, and my refuge on Cozumel. "I sent Inge there," I told her, "to be cared for by friends. She still has a chance to make something of her life."

"With your help I'm sure she will. I'll sell Pedraza's palace as soon as I can find a buyer. Use the money to finish the film. I owe that to the other players, to Carla and Chandler."

"That will certainly cheer them up," I said, "but finding a buyer isn't going to be easy. There's not that much drug money around any more."

"There will be. Other men in that organization will keep it going. You cut off the head, but the body is still alive."

"I'm afraid you're right." I thought of Omar Parra and Enrique's opium poppies, but I couldn't do it all by myself. It was too big a job for a singleton. I was beaten up and tired, and if the governments involved didn't care, why should I? Besides, I had major personal problems—such as being wanted in connection with Pedraza's and Miguel's deaths, and possibly those of Lucho San Juan and Oscar Alarcón. The police guard could tie me to the two bodies in the Presidential Suite, but I was home free on Pérez, Padilla, and Pedrito. Socialist Mexico had no death penalty, but a Mexican prison could be even worse.

The time seemed opportune to repatriate myself to the U.S.A. and stall off extradition.

Sarita must have been reading my thoughts, because she said, "You're in danger as long as you're in Mexico. Where will you go, Jack?"

"Haven't decided. Your island is my sanctuary, so let's enjoy it while we can."

We swam for a while, soaked up some rays, and when the sun was overhead, shared a light lunch in cool shadows by the plane. Then, siesta time, and as we lay side by side, I said, "That roadster you abandoned is worth a lot of money—doesn't it worry you?"

"Why should it? If it's stolen, I'll collect insurance. It's not a problem."

I was the one with the heavy problems, but from the island I could do nothing about them. So I stopped thinking about arrest and prison and fell asleep beside my woman.

SARITA'S SMALL RADIO wouldn't bring in Guadalajara stations, but Puerto Vallarta carried across the water. When night fell we ate chunks of fresh coconut and listened to music and news. The announcer said that a policeman guarding the suite of wealthy Jalisco investor Fructo Cejas was suspected of killing Cejas and his bodyguard. However, there seemed to be no motive for the killings, and the evidence was insufficient to bring charges against the man. Members of a motion picture company speculated that the disappearance of film star Sarita Rojas was attributable to overwork coupled with the death of General Gilberto Pedraza, whose companion the well-known actress had been.

After a story about the loss of a shrimp trawler out of Mazatlán, the music program resumed. Lying back, Sarita said, "At least your name wasn't mentioned."

"Which doesn't mean they're not looking for me."

"True," she sighed. "I suppose my name will be linked to Pedraza's for the rest of my life."

"Not if you change it."

"To what, for instance?"

"Novak, for instance."

She drew my face to hers. "Are you serious?"

"The first time I saw you I wanted you. I'd be out of my mind to let you get away." I kissed her, held her close, heart pounding. "Right now I can't predict much of a future."

"Whatever it is I want to share it with you, be wherever you are, wherever you go."

Throat thick, I swallowed. "It's a deal?"

"I was afraid you wouldn't ask. Yes, darling, it's a deal."

"Then we'll get to the States."

"Yes, but if you're arrested in Mexico I have influential friends who can help."

"You're the only friend I'll ever need."

We kissed. The kiss lengthened, the tip of her tongue outlined my lips, and soon we were making love.


EARLY IN THE morning we shared a can of fruit laced with Añejo, hot rolls, and roasted *chorizo*. I squelched the fire and said I was going to fly off for fuel.

"I'll go with you."

I shook my head. "I have to get maximum miles out of every gallon. Light as you are, your weight would cut my range."

She frowned. "How long will you be gone?"

"Hard to say. But if I'm not back by noon, start sending up smoke signals."

"Don't joke about it. Can't you take out your scuba gear?"

"I'm going to. Even then—"

"I don't feel good about this. I know I should go with you. If something goes wrong, we should be together."

"Then I'd never forgive myself. Look, I'll find gas somewhere. That's a promise. And then we can fly wherever we like. Together. Meanwhile, in case *yanquis* or other reprehensible types invade your island, I want you to have this." I produced my Beretta and made her fire it at the empty fruit can. Holding it, she said, "This makes me feel even worse."

"Makes me feel better that you can use a pistol." I hauled scuba tanks, flippers, and masks from the plane and put in the machine pistol.

"What's that for?" she asked.

"In case I come across bounty hunters. Now, help me turn the plane and head it into the water."

When foam covered the wheels, I took Sarita in my arms and held her for a long time. She touched my face and said, "You've become my life. Come back quickly."

"I will, *querida*. Then we'll leave together."

We kissed, then, and I got behind the controls.

The engine started, I steered carefully through the shallows, and when I could see blue water I turned into the wind. For a moment I saw her standing knee-deep in the water, waving the colored kerchief from around her hair. I waved back, blew her a kiss, and shoved the throttle ahead.

Airborne, I flew southeast, toward Mita Point, the big hook of land at the northern tip of Banderas Bay. My thought was to stay under PV's airport radar until I reached the coast, then follow it at a thousand feet toward Mazatlán. If I didn't find a place to refuel, I'd land on a beach, and somehow make my way back to the island for Sarita. Hire or steal another plane at Mazatlán's airport. Why not? Aircraft theft was trivial compared to other charges against me.

I glanced at the MAC-10 on the other seat and decided I had nothing to worry about.

The coastline dipped in toward Tepic, rounded out smoothly at Los Corchos where a river flowed into the sea. There were small fishing boats but no gas drums or pumps that might have 100-octane gas. I examined the chart and turned slightly inland, looking for duster planes. The new course took me over a large, irregular lagoon, identified as Laguna de Agua Brava. Nothing I could see below. Novillero was the next coastal town, and it was much like Los Corchos from the air. Rickety wooden piers, fishing boats, and no visible supply of gasoline. The next village was Teacapan, just fifty miles from Mazatlán. I was nearing the end of my flying range, the fuel needle jiggling at empty, and I began to think of places to come down. The Laguna de Agua Brava extended inland, its marshes ending close to a road. Rosamorada was the nearest village on the road, with Tecuala, a larger town, a few miles to the north.

Banking, I turned around and flew toward the far end of the lagoon. It was surrounded by marshes and tule grass, but the middle of the lagoon showed deeper water. As I lost altitude, I saw channel markers with green and red reflectors to guide boats' passage after dark. Deep enough for boats, deep enough for my lightened Seabee. I lowered flaps and prepared to land as the engine sputtered.

It caught again, long enough for me to bring the nose up, then died. The controls went mushy, and the eerie silence was broken only by wind whistling through the struts.

My short glide ended with a harder than usual water impact, and momentum kept the plane moving toward the end of the lagoon.

As I peered ahead I saw something I'd missed from the air: a long, black boat tied up alongside a wooden pier. Above it camouflage netting was draped from poles, and as I coasted nearer I began to feel better.

The boat wasn't a Cigarette, it was a smaller Saber, like Melody's, and its engines took high-octane gas.

A man got out of the boat, came down the pier, and stared at my plane, then motioned me away.

I opened the window panel. "Out of gas," I called. "Let me buy some of yours."

Shaking his head, he called, *"Fuera!"* Get out of here. And jerked a pistol from his belt.

The setup spelled drug-running, so I had no scruples about producing the machine pistol and firing a burst under his feet.

He got serious then, and I told him to put away the gun and tie the plane to the pier. He was surly about it, but did so, and when I climbed up the short ladder I said, "Listen carefully, *amigo.* What you and the boat do is your business. I'm out of gas, so I'm going to buy some of yours. Help me out or I'll kill you and take your fucking boat."

"How much you need?"

"Two drums—a hundred gallons."

He wiped sweat from his forehead. I said, "Let's go," and prodded him to the foot of the pier.

Set away from the boat, and also under camo netting, were a dozen drums of 100-octane gas. One was mounted on rollers, a hand pump on its top. "I'm in a hurry," I told him, "start pushing."

He rolled it to where the plane was tied and held the nozzle in the main tank while I pumped gas through the hose. When the drum was empty we took it back and transferred the pump to a full drum. That one topped the main tank and filled the auxiliary.

The man stood looking at me, thinking I was going to kill him anyway, but I handed him twenty thousand pesos and said, "I'm not a thief, just a pilot in trouble." I took his pistol and dropped it in the water. *"Carajo!"* he said, *"coño,"* and looked away.

I untied the nose line, got behind the controls, pumped gas into the carb.

On the third try the engine caught, prop blades bit, and I ruddered into the channel. There was a crosswind but no directional choice, so I accelerated down the marked channel and lifted off over the marshes to the ocean.

From there I set course for the island and saw it thirty minutes later. In all, I'd been gone about two hours.

I buzzed the west side beach, zoomed up in a power pull, and banked to come around the eastern side, expecting to see Sarita appear as I cut power.

Looking down, I saw her lying on the sand, face down. The attitude of her body was awkward, and I decided she was playing possum—to punish me for leaving her alone.

But when I nosed onto the beach and still she hadn't risen to greet me, my stomach went cold.

I jumped out and ran to where she lay, seeing the pistol near her outflung arm. Her right leg was hugely swollen, and when I turned her over I saw that she had bitten through her tongue.

Her body was still limp, the sun's heat had kept rigo from setting in. My body was ice.

Two yards away, half-covered with sand, lay the twisted body of a brightly banded snake. A bullet had nearly severed its venomous head. *Coralillo.*

Kneeling, I began to weep. My fingers closed her staring eyes. A shadow passed across us. Another.

I looked up and saw buzzards circling.

Waiting.

# IV

# TWENTY-THREE

**I** DON'T KNOW how long I knelt there, cradling her body in my arms. I kissed her face and cheeks until they were wet with my tears. I gasped her name between convulsive sobs, as though repetition could call her back to life.

My mind blacked out.

I was on my feet, firing at the dead coral snake, firing until the pistol emptied. I left the snake on the beach for the gathering buzzards to tear apart, and threw the Beretta as far as I could into the jungle.

I turned to the sky and screamed despairingly. Never in my life had I felt so utterly alone, so empty and abandoned.

My fault, I told myself, as I lifted her in my arms. If I'd been with her, she wouldn't have walked the beach alone. Or died alone.

The thought of her dying agonies destroyed me.

As in a sleepwalking nightmare, I got her body into the plane and onto the deck behind my seat. Out of habit, I hauled gear aboard and spat my hatred on the baking sand. The island she loved had killed her. Tears filmed my eyes. We had planned a future together. Now there was nothing. I didn't care whether I lived or died.

As I flew east toward the coastline, my mind cleared enough to find the course to Guadalajara.

Below, the water looked clear and pure and inviting. I thought of shoving the stick forward and plummeting into it, and all that restrained me was respect for her remains. I wanted a public funeral for her, with thousands of sorrowing fans paying tribute at her bier. She deserved that— and a great deal more.

Above the mountain range I cursed myself again for not taking her with me. But even if I'd stayed with her, and she'd been struck by the snake, I had no antidote for *coralillo* venom in the plane, only for rattlesnake poison. And I'd have seen my beautiful love scream and twist and die.

Still, if she had flown with me . . .

She was with me now, I thought bitterly, our final flight together.

Tears blinded me, and I couldn't see the compass heading. The tanks were full, but if they were empty I couldn't have cared. I realized that I was indifferent to living. Whatever happened to me was unimportant. The MAC-10 lay on the seat she'd occupied. I thought of pressing its muzzle to my head and pulling the trigger.

Only, that wouldn't bring her back.

Nothing could.

I flew like an automaton, came into the Guadalajara airport without contacting the tower for landing clearance. The controller would think my radio was out.

As I taxied toward a civil aviation building, I tried to think what I should do. I was finished, but I wanted Sarita to be treated with kindness and sensitivity.

I left the plane and entered the building, found a pay phone, and called the Fiesta Americana.

Chandler Bates answered, and I asked for Carla without giving my name. When she spoke, I said, "Novak. I'm at the airport. Sarita's dead—coral snake. Her body's in my plane. Please take care of her."

I hung up before Carla could say anything, and then I walked back to the plane, opened the cabin door, and stared at her lovely face, so tranquil in death—as though she were sleeping. I wanted to wake her, tell her we'd arrived safely, but all I did was touch her hand and kiss her lips a final time.

Then I closed the door and walked like a zombie to the office of the airport police.

THEY ARRESTED ME, of course, and drove me in handcuffs and leg-irons to a central building where I was photographed and printed and thrown into a holding cell. They didn't book me, as I'd expected, or read me my rights. Under Mexico's Napoleonic Code you're guilty until you can prove yourself innocent, so legal formalities were of no consequence.

I lay in the barred cage while policemen and detectives looked in on me as they filed past. I recognized Cejas' suite guard, the one I'd cold-cocked and whose service revolver I'd used. He stared at me for a long time before shaking his head. So, my false beard, mustache, and glasses had been useful. Not that I cared. All that was important was minimizing Sarita's involvement with me.

I asked for water, and after an hour a metal cup was passed through the bars. The water smelled stale, and pieces of sediment floated through it. I wet my lips and tongue and tossed the cup on the floor.

The jailer didn't like that. He came into the cell and beat my back and shoulders with his nightstick. It didn't take much courage on his part because I was manacled hand and foot. But after I stopped howling, I bucked his body against the bars and kneed him in the crotch. His eyes rolled wildly, he snapped forward, and my knee caught the point of his chin. He dropped to the cell's filthy floor.

Another guard came running, and I snarled, "Until I'm convicted, you'll treat me as a human being." I kicked the fallen nightstick into the corridor. "Next one who tries to beat me is going to be killed."

His face paled, and he swallowed. Then, covering me with his revolver, he dragged the jailer's body from my cell and locked the door again. I sat down and rubbed my bruised back against the wall.

Long after dark they hauled me upright and shoved me out to a car. I figured they'd finally found a judge to hear the charges, but that wasn't to be. They blindfolded me, drove for a long time, and kicked me down a flight of stairs. From the musty odor I knew I was underground, in some kind of cellar.

When they jerked off the blindfold, I was standing on a dirt floor, a metal stanchion in the center. They handcuffed my arms around it and beat me, using sand-filled stockings and leather saps. The men had coppery faces, mustaches, and uniforms. I was in the hands of the law.

When one jabbed my belly with a nightstick I vomited on his uniform. He clubbed my head and I passed out.

That was better than standing and taking their savagery.

I woke in a dark room, eight by eight. No windows, a metal-shod door with a Judas window-slot. No furniture, not even a moldy mattress. Corner stench told me where the latrine was, so I used it, trying not to wet my trousers and wishing there was enough light to tell if I was passing blood.

As I moved painfully about, cockroaches crunched under my feet. The famous Mexican *cucaracha. Norteamericanos* thought the familiar song was about a roach, when it praised female pudenda.

I didn't let thoughts of escape enter my mind. I didn't want to escape; I wanted them to kill me—as soon as possible. I sat down against the wall and felt roaches run over my legs. Some got tangled in my hair, but I didn't try brushing them away, there'd only be others.

I couldn't do anything about the pain suffusing my body, but thirst was an immediate problem. I kicked the door and yelled for water until the door opened and a bucket was shoved in. The water didn't smell much better than the cup's, but I knelt and shoved my face down and drank like a camel, not knowing when I'd have another chance. And the water rinsed the sweat from my face.

As I'd learned in Vietnam E&E briefings, darkness and isolation beget disorientation. Sense of time fails, and the biological clock turns off. This was my first experience of prolonged isolation, and I had to agree with the briefing. A sense of hunger suggested morning, but sensory deprivation could have tricked my stomach, too. But I was beyond caring.

Having softened me up, they hauled me out again and shined a strong light in my light-sensitive eyes. A man I couldn't see said he was from the *Procuraduría del Estado*—state prosecutor's office—and had a statement for me to sign.

"What does it say?"

"You can read it after you sign."

"Has the American consulate been told of my arrest?"

Silence.

I said, "Until I've seen a consul, I'm not signing anything."

"You're a *gringo* killer, an outlaw. The consulate wants nothing to do with you."

"Let a consul tell me."

"I recommend that you sign this. Now." Several typed sheets appeared in the light.

I told them what they could do with it. The papers vanished, and the *procurador* muttered, "He's not ready, yet. Careful with his face." Steps walked away.

They handcuffed me around the stanchion and worked me over from neck to ankle, then back again. When I passed out, they sloshed water on my body and hauled me to my knees. One of them stuck a revolver barrel in my mouth and threatened to pull the trigger.

With the metal between my teeth, I managed to gasp, *"Do it. Kill me now!"*

The revolver jerked out and beating resumed. Another round, and I slumped unconscious.

I woke in my dungeon having no idea how long I'd been there. I lay

214

face down and prayed for death. Perhaps I could immerse my head in the bucket and drown.

I tried, but my head displaced too much water to cover my nose and mouth.

I sat against the wall, water running from my hair, down over my body. The prosecutor had warned them not to mark my face, I remembered. That implied that eventually I was going to be produced in court—preferably with a signed confession.

It occurred to me that behind the scenes there was a conspiracy to bury me in prison before I could tell what I knew. Or in some potter's field, like Gerry Fein.

My death wish involved expiation for Sarita's dying, not because I'd killed Mexican hoods. I felt no guilt for that, was never going to. So I wasn't going to have these creeps determine my fate. Besides, I'd done more to stamp out high-level crime than the Federal police force had in the previous five years.

I was losing count of the persuasion sessions at the stanchion. After the next two or three, the *procurador* returned with the same demand. "Fuck yourself," I told him. "Bring a consul, and we'll talk."

"I want to show the consul your signed confession."

"That's what I figured," I told him. "Forget it."

He hesitated. "We can write your signature for you."

"Go ahead. And I'll say I'm illiterate like your *cabrones* here. *Analfabeta.* Can't write."

He thought it over until I heard his chair scrape on the dirt floor. "He's not ready yet. Don't call me back until he's ready."

Apparently they were getting worried about killing me before I signed, so a pan of food was brought me. Cold refried beans. Eating in the dark, I suspected that the soft meat I chewed was maggots. Still, what I ingested was life supporting, and rage over what they were trying to make me do detoured my thoughts from dying.

Either the next round of beatings was less brutal or I was becoming accustomed to pain. I estimated the length of my incarceration from the number of times I'd had to urinate. About three days, so far, but kidney damage could easily have thrown off the intervals.

They fed me once a day: *tortillas* and water, *frijoles* and water, *refritos* and water. Bad as the water was, it was tastier than the food, which I figured to be scrapings from the guards' plates.

The beatings came whenever the guards were rested from the previous session. Urinating was increasingly painful, and my whole body was swollen. But not above the chin.

If that was their—and the prosecutor's—game, I declined to be a passive party to it. So I banged my forehead against the wall until it was bruised and swollen, scraped my chin and cheeks against the concrete blocks until blood ran down my neck.

Satisfied with my revolt, I slept for what must have been several hours, and the next time they dragged me out and shined a light on my face, there was consternation.

A billy club slammed across my stomach, and I snapped over to keep from yelling.

*"Chingado,"* the invisible guard shouted, "you have no right to mark yourself. You make fools of us."

"It wasn't hard," I said huskily, trying to keep from vomiting. "Now, tell the *procurador* I'm ready to talk."

They sapped my spine and kidneys anyway, and the backs of my thighs and calves, but nerve endings sent only dull signals, not the excrutiating pain I'd first known. After that I was shoved back into the dungeon, and the door slammed shut.

Roaches crawled over me, pricking my flesh with their feelers, scraping it with their rough legs. My heartbeat was irregular, my body unwilling to move. I was nearly finished, I thought, and went unconscious for a time.

The creaking door made me open my eyes. Two men half-carried, half-dragged me from my isolation cell. There was a dim light in the torture chamber, but my swollen eyes refused to define the figures beyond the cast-iron stanchion.

They moved. One figure was in a light-colored suit. Words came from his mouth. "We have decided to grant your request, *señor*. From here, you will be taken to the State Hall of Justice."

"Is it as bad as this?" I croaked. "Then leave me here."

*"Silence while I speak!"*

"Say your piece." I was too faded to stand without leaning on a guard. I closed my eyes and listened.

"At the Hall of Justice you will be permitted to see a representative of the *yanqui* consulate-general in Guadalajara. As was your wish."

I recognized the voice as the *procurador's*. "When I was brought here . . . now I don't care."

The response confused him. He must have expected me to break down with sobs of gratitude. After a pause, he said, "Nevertheless, it will be done. And you will explain your bruises as the result of an accidental fall."

"Was that how it happened? What else am I to tell the consular representative?"

"That you have, of course, been well-treated—as is the policy of the government of the Republic of Mexico."

"I've been wondering what the policy was. Well, I'll be glad to describe it." I opened my eyes and stared at my swollen, filthy hands. Nails broken, bits of dried food, crusted blood. He hadn't said anything about the confession I was supposed to sign, but there'd be time for that.

"Let's go," I said.

"First, you will shower and make yourself presentable."

"I go as is. I won't be your accomplice."

*Whack.* Across my spine a nightstick struck. Incandescent lights exploded in my brain, and my knees buckled.

They dragged me upstairs and into a large, tiled shower where they took off handcuffs, leg-irons, and clothing. Two guards held me naked under a strong spray. I gulped clean water and tried to keep upright on the slippery tile. Wrists and ankles were raw from chafing, the red circles stung. I couldn't use a towel very well, so I blotted what I could, and they handed me a khaki uniform to put on. To do it, I had to sit on a bench, but the clothing smelled clean and improved my spirits.

As I stepped into my dirt-scraped shoes I was glad there was no mirror. What I could see of my welted, bruised body was quite enough; the backside was probably worse. Handcuffs were snapped on, but not the leg-irons. Probably overlooked.

In the car they blindfolded me, and after a few minutes I heard the approaching sounds of traffic. When the blindfold came off, sunlight rasped my eyes, and I saw the Hall of Justice building ahead.

We went in through a side entrance, up stairs, and through a heavy door that had to be unlocked. Guards guided me into a visibility cage, three sides of which were bars. Against the buff-painted wall was a basin and a toilet without its porcelain horse-collar. The barred door clanged shut.

There was a small table and two chairs. I sat in one, rested elbows on the table, and waited.

After a while metal hinges squeaked, and I opened my eyes. A guard was opening the door to let a man in.

He was about twenty-five, and his blond hair was thinning above a high, pink forehead. He wore rimless lenses, an unsuccessful mustache, and a dark suit. One hand held a russet leather portfolio embossed with the Aztec calendar.

He set it on the table and drew up the other chair. "I'm Thane Jordan from the consulate." He peered myopically at my scabbed and swollen face. "Are you Juan Novak?"

# TWENTY-FOUR

**W**HAT'S LEFT OF him," I said, "and my given name is John."

He dug a photocopy from the leather case and glanced at it. "That's odd. They have you as Juan Novak, Mexican citizen."

"Check my passport renewal form."

"I did. And you don't look much like the photograph."

"I'm the worse for wear," I told him. "What took you so long?"

Stiffly, he said, "A question of not knowing."

"When did you find out?"

"The consulate learned yesterday."

I grunted. "That's interesting, because for the past four or five days I've been held in a lightless dungeon and beaten every few hours. So I'm surprised the *procurador* informed the consulate."

Jordan bent forward. "He didn't. The information came in a tip." His milky-blue eyes scanned my face. "I guess they treated you pretty badly."

"You should see the rest of my body. Children would run off screaming, women faint."

"That's too bad, but of course there's a long list of crimes against you, including murder."

"You believe that?"

He shrugged. "Whether I do is not important. It's what the Mexican authorities believe. You're in their system of justice. Our government can't intervene."

"Some system," I said bitterly. "I haven't been charged officially, but they prepared a confession for me to sign."

"Is that so?" His scanty eyebrows lifted as he scribbled a note. "That's why you were maltreated?"

"That's a nice word for it. Sounds like dunce cap, face in the corner,

219

and no chocolate cookies. A *procurador* told his gorillas to soften me up and force me to sign."

"But you didn't."

I shook my head.

He lifted a long document in Spanish. "According to this, you kidnapped Sarita Rojas and may be responsible for her death. You killed General Pedraza and Miguel Speranza. Before that, you kidnapped a woman named Julieta Montes, raped and killed her—"

"Where was that?"

"Guanajuato . . . last month."

"Last month I was in Miami."

"Near Villa Obregón you murdered a driver and stole his truck. In Durango you killed two men and stole their drugs, shooting a policeman who tried to stop you. In Aguascalientes you robbed a bank and shot a woman teller." He looked up. "Shall I go on?"

"Evidently I've been pretty busy. Hardly time to eat between crimes."

He handed me the document. "Is this what they wanted you to sign?"

"I haven't read it. The process is called wiping the books. I'm charged with every unsolved or inconvenient crime they could come up with on short notice. Is the consulate prepared to see that I get a fair trial?"

"That's beyond the scope of the consulate's duties."

"I thought the consulate was supposed to protect American citizens."

"That's heavy stuff, Mr. Novak. Have you got a lawyer?"

"Don't be ridiculous. This is the first time I've seen daylight in four days."

"Can you pay for a lawyer?"

"They took my billfold when they fingerprinted me. Can you get it back?"

"I'll try." He got up and called the guard. The door was unlocked, and Vice Consul Jordan disappeared down the walk.

I was cramped and stiff from sitting upright, so I lay down on the floor to rest. After maybe half an hour Jordan came back. I pried myself off the floor and eased into a chair. He laid my billfold on the table. "Not much there," he said, "and no money at all."

"Surprise." I went through the billfold and felt the storage-claim ticket. "Do you know Manuel Montijo?"

"I've met him—new man at the consulate."

I palmed the ticket to him. "I'd appreciate it if you'd give him this."

He looked at it doubtfully. "No message?"

"He'll understand. Just deliver it personally."

"Okay." He began shuffling papers back into his leather folder. "In two years here I've never been involved in a case like yours, Mr. Novak. Why do you suppose you haven't been formally charged?"

"Because highly placed *politicos* don't want me on the witness stand. They want me to confess and go to jail—where I can be conveniently murdered."

"Who are the 'highly placed' people?"

"You're better off not knowing."

He stood up, and I said, "Can you tell me anything about Sarita Rojas?"

"Yesterday, in the capital, she was given the equivalent of a state funeral. Streets jammed with mourners, orations by the president and cabinet members, the head of the cinema union . . . a very big show. I understand she's to be buried in Nogales, probably today."

My eyes filmed over. I wiped tears on my sleeve. I should be there, I thought. Maybe someday . . . "If you could, you might try to see me in three or four days. Check if I'm still alive."

"I'll try. Unfortunately, you can be held indefinitely, while they look for evidence."

"That's going to be a big problem for them, because there isn't any. Not that it can't be fabricated."

He sighed. "Wish I could do more for you, Mr. Novak, but this is out of my league."

"You probably saved my life," I told him. "Can't ask for much more."

We shook hands, the guard unlocked my cage, and Vice Consul Jordan trotted off. I lay down on the floor again.

Later I was taken to a cell in the same building. It had a barred window, basin, toilet, and a metal cot with mattress. I lay on it and slept until nightfall, when I was given a bowl of rabbit stew and a metal cup of potable water.

That night, no beatings. They left me alone until mid-morning when they took me out and back to the holding cage. Before the guard left I said, "What's this about?"

"Your lawyer is coming."

"What lawyer?"

"Why, *Licenciado* Galindez, the best criminal lawyer in all Jalisco. To pay him you need much money," he said enviously.

Heels strode down the walk, and a portly man heaved into view. He was neatly dressed and perspiring. The guard let him into my cell.

*"Buenos días,* Mr. Novak. I am *Licenciado* Moisés Galindez, retained to prepare your defense." He gave me a damp, plump hand, and sat down.

"Who retained you?"

"Doubtless some friend of yours. He asked to remain nameless."

Manny had acted promptly. Galindez said, "First, what are your immediate needs?"

"Soap."

"Of course. Is that all?"

"I haven't much experience of Mexican jails, but I understand if you can afford it, better food can be provided."

"That is the custom."

"Can I pay?"

"I will pay for you." He made two quick notes and gazed at me. "You realize that your case has political connotations."

I nodded. "They'd rather kill me than have me stand trial."

"So I understand. The problem to be resolved is how to satisfy both sides." He dug into a vest pocket and brought out a toothpick with which he began to probe his lower teeth. Before mining the upper row, he said, "I've had little time to familiarize myself with the circumstances, or to contact higher authorities, but I've been thinking, generally, of a formula something like this. You confess to a number of charges. In return you will be given safe-conduct to the frontier. No prison for you, no publicity."

"And no trial."

"No trial," he agreed.

I breathed deeply. "Very convenient," I said, "for those who don't want to be named as having been corrupted by the dead *narcotraficantes*."

His eyes brightened. "You know something about that?"

"A great deal. For a time, I was in the confidence of the Gang of Four. As well as General Pedraza. He, by the way, stole arms from the Mexican government and traded them to a Guatemalan rebel in return for gum opium. A certain police chief is corruptly involved, as well as the deputy governor of Jalisco."

"Who wants to be President of Mexico," Galindez said musingly. "Of course, you can prove none of what you say."

"I can tell it from the witness stand. Then there would have to be investigations, with subsequent damage to political careers."

"Undoubtedly." He sighed. "Small wonder they want either your confession—or your death."

"I won't accept banishment in return for a false confession that will dog me the rest of my life."

He cleared his throat. "You don't give me much to work with, *Señor* Novak."

"I think I've given you a good deal to work with. Also, it happens that I like Mexico. I like living here. I have a home and business on Cozumel. In the States I have nothing."

"Many men would prefer to be alive and naked in America than dead in a Mexican grave."

"Not me."

He shrugged. "It may come to that, you know. Frankly, your demand for total freedom seems unrealistic under the circumstances. I can act as a broker to resolve differing points of view, but how successful the outcome will be, I cannot predict. If no resolution is possible, then I must warn you that you will probably be disposed of, to end the matter."

"I've known that all along." Standing, I stripped off my shirt and showed him my torso, back and front. "They tried to persuade me."

His eyes widened, and he gave an involuntary start. "You must be seen by a doctor, at once."

"A private one, of your choosing. I don't want the Borgia treatment."

"You mean . . . poison."

I buttoned my shirt. "Right now," I said, "the conspirators are in a quandary. If the consulate hadn't asked about me, I'm pretty sure I'd be buried in an unmarked grave, and we wouldn't be sitting here talking about the future."

"Doubtless you are right." He blotted perspiration from face and forehead. "Will you tell me the facts surrounding the death of Sarita Rojas?"

I related them to him and said, "I could have flown to the States and stayed free. Instead, I brought her body here."

"Knowing you would be arrested." He thought it over. "Why?"

"I loved her," I said. "When she died I didn't care about living."

"But you feel differently now?"

"The beatings changed my outlook."

His fingers laced, and he leaned forward. "I cannot promise you that there will be no repetition of abuse, but I will do what I can to prevent it. Do you know the name of the *procurador* responsible?"

"No, but I'd recognize his face and voice."

He stood up. "I have much to do. A mutually satisfactory arrangement is going to take time to bring about. In the meantime, I will try to see that you are kept in decent conditions, with adequate nourishment. And I will send a doctor who will report to me."

"If you can't come daily, send someone from your office to check on me."

"I will do so." He paused. "I suspect that this matter will have to be taken to the highest levels of our government."

"Your government."

THAT AFTERNOON A doctor examined me, bandaged open sores, and

223

removed stitches from the old wound. He gave me antibiotic capsules, and the following day he said that the blood in my urine was diminishing. My food was coming from a nearby restaurant, and I'd been given a sheet and pillow for my cot. Treatment had definitely improved, but I knew that conditions could change abruptly.

On the fourth day after my lawyer's initial visit, as his law clerk was leaving my cage, the guard told me to wait there. I had another visitor.

I didn't expect Manny to come, so I was curious about who it might be. Inge, I wondered, but Cozumel was far away, and my arrest, so far, had not been made public.

Spike heels clicked down the walk, and I saw the strained face of Carla Santiago. "Don't get up," she said, "I'm not coming in. I have just this to say." Her fingers gripped the bars as she faced me. "I don't know who you are or why you came, but I know that before you there were parties and good times and a picture to be made. We were all working, and I was happy. But you changed our world with death and destruction, and now there's nothing left. Nothing at all. I'm sorry I ever helped you, and I'll hate you to my dying day."

"I've lost, too," I said quietly, but she burst into tears and hurried away.

LATE THAT NIGHT I was visited by Manny Montijo.

# TWENTY-FIVE

**M**ANNY HAD ARRANGED for a private visiting room where we wouldn't be overheard and he couldn't be seen by other prisoners.

Unlike Vice Consul Jordan, Manny came in a *guayabera* and Sonora boots, but he was visibly uneasy about being there.

After an *abrazo,* I said, *"Hermano,* I truly didn't expect you to come. Must be important."

"It is. As soon as I learned you'd been taken off for 'special treatment' I sent Thane Jordan to ask questions. His persistence paid off."

"Then he's a better man than I thought. How did you get word?"

"A confidential police informant. He was out there with you. That was luck, and you're luckier that Phil Corliss is in Thailand."

"Why am I lucky?"

"Because if Phil was around, he'd have spoiled the deal."

"What deal is that?"

He sat back and lighted a Veracruz cigar that looked and smelled like tarred rope. "Galindez is a good man, but there was a deadlock he couldn't break. Certain governmental figures finally agreed to let you stay in Mexico—but only if you signed a confession to all those crimes."

"Which could always be held over me."

"Right. You'd told Galindez you wouldn't falsely confess, and under the circumstances I can't blame you. You're a hard-nosed, principled bastard."

"So they say."

"I'm . . . sorry about Sarita, Jack. I guess she meant a great deal to you."

225

"She did," I said tightly. "Keep talking."

"Okay. When Galindez told me he'd come up empty-handed, I decided to boot the thing to Washington, see if they could bring influence to bear."

"Why?"

"The four hundred keys you handed me are one reason—and they helped. Mainly, though, I had an obligation to you because I'd brought you here, and headquarters cut you off."

"You don't mean to tell me remorse was a factor?"

He blew dark smoke toward the wall. "It was convenience," he said. "Unknown to you, but not to me, Omar Parra was arrested in Los Angeles last week, trying to set up a major outlet for his drugs. He's in jail there, but he's retained a very big civil rights lawyer to at least get him out on bond. Omar can post two, three million dollars and never miss it, right?"

"After which he'd blow town and surface in Colombia."

"Exactly. Besides which, the Department of Justice isn't sure of a conviction." He exhaled more foul-smelling smoke. Coughing hurt my ribs. "Sorry," he said, and ground out the cigar on the floor. "Meanwhile, the Colombian government has been protesting the arrest, claiming Omar had some sort of diplomatic immunity—commercial delegate, whatever. State has numerous irons in the fire with Colombia, and Omar's arrest became an embarrassment, what with the ambassador phoning the secretary of state every few hours, demanding his release. I flew up there and proposed the following. The government of Colombia asks the Mexican government to release you and expunge the charges against you. If the Mexican government agrees, Justice lets Parra go."

I looked at the bare wall. "Amounting to a wash."

"It amounts to your freedom."

"And Omar's."

"And saves three governments continuing embarrassment."

I thought it over. I didn't like Parra getting off, but if he bonded out, he'd be gone anyway. I said, "That's stratospheric summitry, Manny. Suppose it goes through, can I stay on Cozumel?"

"As though nothing ever happened."

"Except that it saves the *cojones* of a bunch of corrupt animals."

"You nailed five of their patrons," he remarked, "which isn't bad for a couple weeks' work."

"Still, the overall picture isn't going to change. *Según el refrán—'como Mejico, no hay igual.'*"

"You don't have to be so cynical about Mexico."

"You don't have to be protective, either." I squinted at him. "But for you, the *cholos* would be stomping down my grave."

226

"Maybe. But you won't be displeased to learn that the *Bal Musette* was stopped off Guatemala and a load of gum opium found in the hold. Calixto and Alonso are getting acquainted with Guatemalan jails, and the yacht is being auctioned."

I got up and limped across the room. "When will you know if the three governments agree to the trade?"

"I was called to the consulate for a priority message. The exchange is set. You'll be free in a couple of days."

I'd supposed that was what he'd been working up to, but hearing it made me slump into a chair and cover my face. After a while, I said, "It's hard to tell you how grateful I am."

"Goes both ways. You risked your neck for DEA, they went to bat for you."

"*You* did it," I said, and wiped damp eyes. "Now all I have to do is stay alive."

"You're under cabinet protection now. I think the risk is minimal." He began lighting another cigar, remembered, and tossed the match away. "I've got some money of yours."

"Mine?"

"The 'buy' *pesos* I picked up at the baggage room. I used half a million to pay Galindez, the rest is yours."

"How do you figure?"

"They're off our books, Jack. To get them on inventory again would mean endless memoranda, explanations, and aggravation. It's better for everyone if you just take them—compensation for what you've been through."

"That certainly sweetens the arrangement," I said, "again, thanks to you."

"Hell, you're doing me a favor. Money's at the consulate, so pick it up before you leave town." He yawned, stretched, and got up. "If you're not free shortly, I'll have Galindez find out why."

I felt like hugging him, but all we did was shake hands.

After he left I was taken back to my cell and had a good sleep for the first night in a long time.


IT WAS ANOTHER three days before they let me out. Even then, it was a lot faster than I expected, knowing something of intergovernmental speed.

A police car took me to the airport, where I had a hangar mechanic go over the plane with me—very carefully. I even had the gasoline drained and replaced with filtered avgas from the transient pump. When I took off I knew there were no bombs aboard and the Lycoming wasn't likely to conk out on the way back to Cozumel.

CAVU flying conditions got me to Tampico without incident, and after refueling, I set course for Cozumel, spotting the island in late afternoon. There were the usual cruise ships in port, and offshore, among the charter fishing boats, I spotted my *Corsair* with a party aboard and Ramón at the helm. I flew low over it to let him know I was back, then banked and settled into a long glide that ended off my pier.

César and Sheba greeted me as I tied up the Seabee, leaping and licking my face and hands, tugging at my trouser leg to hurry me to the house.

The puppies were frolicking in a playpen that hadn't been there before, and I realized that Inge was probably responsible.

Where was she?

I called inside, but no answer.

Stale food in the refrigerator and a note on the kitchen table, dated three days ago.

> Dear Jack:
>
> Not hearing anything from you I've been feeling sort of abandoned. I hope you're okay, but I've been going nuts here all alone, wondering what's happening in the outside world. Besides, you lead a violent, scary life, and I don't ever want to be kidnapped again. Though I'm grateful for what you did to rescue me.
>
> Last week at Morgan's, I met the purser of a cruise ship—never mind which one. He told me the girl who runs one of the boutiques on board had an emergency appendectomy and he needed someone to take over. That was the best offer I had since yours, which turned out much different than I expected, so I'm leaving today, and I guess I'll never see you again.
>
> It's probably for the best, because you never realized I was falling for you. I'll get over it aboard ship.
>
> I'm sorry about Sarita and wish things had turned out different—for all of us. My last regret is that we never made it together—you didn't know what you were missing. Now, you never will.
>
> Love,
> Inge

She'd added six kiss-marks across the bottom of the page.

I thought about what she'd written and agreed it was probably all for the best. I pulled a Tecate from the fridge and drank it while I fed my dogs. The puppies were going to make great companions in a lonely house.

I thought of the Menocal brothers, Carlos and Roberto, who had helped me so much. After I pulled myself together I might invite them to stay with me. Roberto could maintain *Corsair* and work in the boatyard, while Carlos attended school.

They might not want to come, or things might not work out, but I wanted to ask them anyway.

Tomorrow I was going to brace my business partner and get things straightened out. I had enough *pesos* to buy Rogelio's share, if that's what we decided; or if he made an offer, I'd have an accountant examine the books. With care.

The gate bell rang, the dogs began howling, and I let them accompany me outside. A jeep was there and a postman waving a letter at me through the gate bars. "Registered Delivery," he called, "sign here."

I did so, then saw Melody's familiar handwriting on the envelope, postmarked Miami, yesterday.

Lover—

I've been phoning for days, but hanging up when that female answers. Get her out of there, because I'm flying to you tomorrow evening on AeroMexico.

I suppose you've been off on some silly fishing excursion with your broad, but that's over now. If you're too pigheaded to give a little, it's up to me, I guess, because I love you dearly and am truly yours. Forever. The point is, I'm eager to work things out, and we *will.*

Be sure to meet my plane, dear. I don't want to come to the house and find you *in flagrante.*

Your Melody

I looked at my watch. The evening flight would arrive in an hour and a half. I straightened the house, tossed out the old refrigerated food, and tried making myself presentable. The rib scar was puckered, but pink and healthy, and my urine was clear of blood.

I poured Añejo over ice and drank on the patio. Seeing the plane bobbing silently off my pier reminded me of my last flight with Sarita.

But I didn't want to remember that. I wanted to remember her pirouetting across the sands like a water nymph freed from a magic spell. The warmth of her body and lips, the sound of her voice, and her fingers on my cheek.

All those things were golden threads in the tapestry of my mind, and they belonged to just the two of us. Forever.

In a month or two, perhaps, I would go to Nogales, kneel at her grave, and leave a red rosebud like the one she'd saved that night. Then I'd leave her at peace and try to get on with a future she would only share in memory.

As I sat there, pier shadows lengthened across the water, and finally the evening plane passed overhead.

I got into my jeep and drove toward the airport to meet my girl.